Sarah's Son

Jerry Eicher

Book List of Published Novel Titles

A Time To Live
Sarah
Sarah's Son
Hannah's Dream

Sarah's Son

Fiction/Contemporary

Published by Horizon Books
768 Hardtimes Rd.
Farmville VA 23901

www.readingwithhorizon.com

Editor – Jon Marken

Cover design by www.KareenRoss.com

ISBN 978-0-9787987-2-7

DEDICATION

In dedication to the goodness of God,
and the faith that walks towards it.

CHAPTER ONE

"*Ess macht vay*" (it hurts). James, having been home from school for only an hour, held up his hand for his mother to see the cut higher on his arm, dirt falling down from his fingers and clinging to his elbow.

"Where have you been playing?" Sarah squinted in the still bright afternoon sun. "In the barn? Did you cut it with your knife? You know you could get infection in this cut."

James with his seven-year-old mind knew little about infections. He shrugged his shoulders. "I don't know. I was just playing in the barn like usual with Nelson. It didn't happen today anyway. It's been hurting for a while already." He turned his face upwards, his eyes searching hers for an answer, the child knowing this problem was beyond his control and must be placed in her hands.

She took his arm in her hand, her touch comforting him, and turned it until the wound was fully visible. "Ya, it doesn't look good." She paused as if thinking, then decided that what she was seeing was really normal after all. "I'll put a bandage on it. Okay? That should do it."

He nodded his head, accepting her verdict, already in his mind moving on to other things more important to him than a cut on his arm.

He followed his mother inside as she went to get the bandage from the vanity in the bathroom. On the way, Sarah could not keep the troubling thoughts from her mind. Was there something more seriously wrong with him? Something about what she had just seen, the cut's not quite normal look, bothered her. Getting the bandage from the vanity above the sink, she pulled off the tabs, placing it gently over the red cut. "You feeling okay otherwise?" she asked, checking his face carefully.

He shrugged again. "I don't know, maybe not. I get tired easily at school when we play softball. I can't keep up with Caleb anymore when we run into the school house after lunch. Used to be I could." He glanced at the floor, embarrassed in his confession.

Concern flickered in her eyes, but she said nothing, uncertain if this meant anything, unwilling to have her concern passed on to him. "You run and play," she told him, brushing his head with her hand, her eyes on his arm.

Standing there in the front yard, she watched him run across the yard, hurrying to join his brother again, each foot barely touching the ground before going airborne again.

"God has been good to us," she said aloud when James was out of earshot. *He really has. We have had so little go wrong in these last years. His mercies do indeed endure forever, as Bishop Amos says so often in his sermons. Yet He is the God who let Job suffer, terribly suffer. Will there be a time when he will allow us to suffer like that too?*

She felt little chills run down her back at the thought, conflicting emotions running through her about what God might and might not allow to come their way. Looking heavenward, she allowed her eyes to follow a cloud, long, wispy, and string-like, hurrying across the sky.

He will never leave us nor forsake us. Wasn't that a verse from somewhere, quoted on Sunday morning by many of their ministers? She was certain it was, and letting the comfort of the thought run through her mind, she felt a settling inside her. A way would be made for them to walk though whatever God had in store. In the meantime there was no reason to worry and cause things to happen that were not happening.

Melvin, having finished work in the fields for the day, was driving the double team up towards the barn to unhitch the horses and settle them in for the night. The hay cutter was behind him, left on the end of the field nearest to the house where he had finished with the last row of cut grass.

He thought of Sarah as he hung on to the thick reins of the two horses, half being pulled along by their haste to get in for the day. Only moments before they had acted too tired to make another round in the hay field, but now the thought of good food gave them plenty of pep to get up the dirt lane to the barn.

Life had placed him here, Amish and married to Sarah some eight years now, for which he was totally grateful to God. The thought of his life with her and of the years yet to come sent warm feelings around his heart. She was a dream come true for him, in more ways then one.

After pulling the harnesses off the horses and seeing

they had hay and feed, he walked to the front porch of the house. There he paused beside the plain white pillars that contrasted with the brown deck floor. Beyond the front steps was the barn he had just come from, its weathervane now turned into the wind.

His gaze went beyond his own land, across the creek to a point beyond the neighbor's farm. To the south lay the little town of Whitfield with its spires from St. Martin's Catholic Church, just visible to his naked eye. From there he turned to the southwest and for the first time noticed the dark formations of the clouds.

Southern Indiana with its slight rolling hills could produce beautiful sunsets, but tonight there would be no such display. Angry dark clouds gathered low over the hill to the southeast. Trained to interpret such signs from his life spent outdoors as a farmer, he knew before long there would be at least a stormy evening if not night.

It was here, ten years earlier, that Melvin had followed his hunch that Sarah would return from New York City and had purchased the farm. Not only had his guess been correct, the purchase itself had proven to be a wise investment. The land was good, solid black dirt that grew the corn, hay, and beans he needed.

Not far from here was the place down by Dogwood Lake Park where he had found Sarah that day after her return from the city. His heart had never doubted her, but still it had been good to see her in full Amish attire. From the stories he had heard, there would have been many reasons to wonder if she really would come back, but his faith had been rewarded.

She had been looking out over the lake that evening with shadows gathering around her. When he had walked up, silently he thought, she had without turning around, as if she were expecting him, simply stated in her calm, delicate way, "You have come."

"You were expecting me?" he had asked, already sure he knew the answer, but wanting to hear her say it.

Her shoulders had tilted sideways as she turned around slowly. Her eyes said the "Yes" as she added softly with her voice, "I am back."

Turning away from the view of the approaching storm, Melvin headed towards the house door, mentally running through a checklist of the needs of the animals in the barn. *Got the back window and door shut, the front I can see. Fed the cows hay. Calves taken care of.* Melvin glanced again at the cloud bank growing taller by the minute. Things would need to be tied down as well as they could be for the night, but as far as his memory could go they already were.

Sarah heard him open the front door and called from the kitchen, "Supper's ready."

Going through the living room into the kitchen he found his two sons, James and Nelson, already seated at the table. James was seven, already in school, skinny for his age, but Nelson at the age of four was still a little chubby and, it seemed, growing in height every day.

"Hi dear," Melvin said to Sarah, who was setting a plate of fried steak on the table. "I just need to wash up."

She answered with a tired smile, pulling a chair out from under the table and seating herself. "Did you get the hayfield cut?"

"Just got the last row down," he replied, going out to wash his hands in the utility room off the kitchen, waiting for the warm water and then splashing it thoroughly over his hands and arms.

"It looks stormy tonight," she commented more than asked. "The hay going to make it?"

"It should," he told her, rubbing the bar of green lye soap on his hands. "A fresh cutting like that shouldn't be hurt too much the first night."

"It looks like quite a storm though from the way the clouds are building up." She half rose from the chair to look out the front living room window. "It's also making it darker in here than usual."

He paused, the towel just touching his fingers, water dripping off his arms. "Maybe I'd better light the lantern now. It will be dark before we get through eating, and I don't like getting my hands dirty during supper if I have to get up then."

"We might make it," she replied, with another glance at the front window, hoping he could eat now that he had gone to the work of washing up. "Depends, I guess, on how fast the storm comes up. It won't be really dark for another hour."

"The way that storm is coming, when I was coming in, we probably won't be able to see in fifteen minutes." He came out of the utility room, having finished wiping his arms on the towel. One glace was all it took to come to a decision. "I'll light it quickly, I think."

He stepped back into the utility room and opened the cabinet door to carefully lift the green Coleman lantern off the shelf. In the kitchen, Sarah kept glancing at the banks of clouds rolling in. The storm indeed was coming in fast.

James caught her anxiety and pushed out to the edge of his bench to see for himself. "Are we going to be washed away?" he asked, with visions of Noah's flood fresh in his mind, for Sarah had just told the story to the boys a few evenings prior for their bedtime Bible story.

She interpreted his language correctly, connecting it to the story he had heard. "No, James, it's not a flood. Just a bad storm, but the Lord will take care of us. He always does that for his children."

"Are we his children?" he asked, his voice trembling slightly, hope edging his voice.

"If we believe in him," she told him, an attempted smile on her face, though it came hard through her weariness. It had been a long day, and a stormy windy night was not exactly what she was hoping for.

Out in the utility room, Melvin shook the lantern slightly to test the gas level. The sound of the swishing in the tank told him there was still plenty left. Taking the side handle he began pumping air into the tank, holding his thumb over the intake hole until the desired level of firmness had been obtained.

Striking a match he lit the lantern, turning the knob enough to get a small flow of gas going. The flame lit with a pop, then burned and dimmed with a rhythm of its own until the metal had warmed up. When the light settled down to a smooth burn, Melvin walked out into the kitchen, hanging the lantern from the hook on the ceiling.

CHAPTER TWO

GOING TO WASH his hands again, Melvin glanced over at Sarah, seated there with the two boys waiting for him. To him, she still looked as beautiful as she had when he first asked to take her home. His eyes must have been talking, because she caught his eye and let her face soften, inviting, he thought, giving her heart into his hands. He felt joy deep inside him and a great unworthiness of such love from one he so admired. Why had God so blessed him, he wondered, as he had wondered many times before.

He came back from the washbasin and took the seat at the head of the table. As the wind picked up he found it hard to concentrate on the table of food in front of him, and his eyes traveled to the living room window, distracted. He could see that the clouds were increasing in size and strength.

"Can we have prayer?" James asked in the silence as they waited. "I'm hungry."

Sarah noticed his declaration, but waited until they had bowed their heads in silent prayer before turning in his direction with delight on her face. "You are?"

James looked strangely at her. "Of course," he told her. "I played all afternoon and hard at school too."

"That's okay — I mean that's good," she hastened to say, not wanting to alarm him, but an appetite was good news. Surely there was not too much wrong with him if he was hungry. She hastened to change the subject, preferring to not dwell on her fears, since they likely were unfounded, she assured herself.

James had his mind on other things anyway. "Are all the barn doors closed, Dad?" he asked, putting a piece of steak on his plate. Sarah comforted herself at the sight, at the same time wishing she did not need to be comforted. It was just a cut.

"Yes, they are," Melvin assured him, turning in James's direction. "The cows are okay too, as they can get inside through the back way, and they have hay. The horses too."

James seemed satisfied with the answer. "It's really raining anyway," he stated the obvious as the rain pelted the roof, the wind gusts creating a flowing sound across the shingles.

"Oh, that reminds me," Sarah spoke up, the thought coming suddenly to her. "Remember that leak in the house roof you worked on last summer, Melvin?"

He nodded as a gush of wind hit the house, this time bringing rain against the siding under the front porch.

"It's back again," she said gently. "I just noticed it the last time it rained, and forgot to tell you. Seems like it takes a strong wind to make it show up. Tonight might be one of those nights." She grimaced. "Sorry, to mention it now, but the weather just reminded me of it."

"Is it a big leak?" he asked, reaching for bread and slathering it with the thick homemade butter Sarah made from their one cow. Occasionally when the cow was dry, they had to buy butter, but at the moment this was not the case.

"I'm not sure," she told him. "If it's coming back already from the fix last summer, it must not be. It doesn't show up during the regular rain. Just when we had some strong gusts last week." She winced as another blast hit the house.

He nodded his head. "I'll see if I can do something about it tomorrow when it's hopefully dry. I still have some of those tubes of tar out in the barn I used last time. It has to be warm enough, reasonably so, for the tar to stick. Maybe by midday it will be. You have any suggestions for tonight, though, since it sure looks like it will leak with this much rain and wind?"

She shrugged. "It shouldn't be more than a few drops coming in. Hopefully, the bucket will do the job."

"What if it doesn't?" he asked, concern on his face.

"Well, if the bucket overflows it gets on the hardwood floor, which will make a big mess. Surely it won't do that."

"Let's hope not. Worst case, I guess, the hardwood buckles or someone could slide on the water and get hurt. The boys have to be careful." He glanced at James and Nelson. "So be careful if you see water in the morning or something, and don't go sliding in it on purpose."

James chuckled at the thought, but Nelson was too small to join in the mirth, not yet sure what sliding on the hardwood floors might mean.

"Do you have to think the worst?" Sarah asked him, not because she was startled by his description, but because it might prompt her to think the worst about James's strange cut.

"I probably am," Melvin assured her. "I just thought to mention it, for the boys' sake really, though I suspect they would have enough sense to stay off of wet hardwood floors anyway. Wouldn't you boys? "

They both nodded vigorously at his question, although it was still doubtful Nelson knew what he was assenting to.

With supper completed, the boys went into the living room to watch the rain lash against the glass, peals of thunder sounding in the distance, at times close enough that the flash and the boom sounded almost together. Sarah watched them standing close to the glass, looking out, hardly flinching at the sounds of the storm. "They are darlings," she whispered, half to herself and half to Melvin. "God has so blessed us."

"That he has," Melvin agreed, pushing his chair back from the table. "You seem concerned, dear. Is it the storm that's bothering you?"

"No," she shook her head, the tears threatening as she kept her face turned slightly away from him, lest he see. "It's James."

"James?" he asked, surprise in his voice. "He seemed fine tonight, or is it something at school?"

"He has a cut on his arm," she told him. "He showed it to me today. There was just something strange about it that keeps bothering me. He also complained about how he was feeling."

"Yes?" Melvin waited for her to continue.

"He says he hurts all over sometimes. Says he's tired. It's real strange I would say for a boy his age.

"Well, most boys have cuts and most boys get tired," Melvin said. "It happened to me all the time when I was growing up. This is a farm after all. But let me take a look at it.

"Hey, James," he called into the living room where the boys were still standing watching the storm. "Let's see your cut on your arm. Your mother said you hurt yourself."

James looked up at the sound of his name, then moved towards the kitchen when he heard the rest of the call. Stopping in front of his father, he held up his arm, now clean from dirt, and lifted one side of the bandage Sarah had put on his arm.

"Looks like a normal cut to me," Melvin said in Sarah's direction, putting his head closer for a good look.

"It's not the just the cut, Melvin. It's that I don't think it's healing up. *Sel iss letz*" (that's wrong).

Melvin raised his eyebrows, looking again at the bandaged hand. "What'd you mean? Won't heal up? Has it been bandaged long?"

"No," she told him, "I just put it on today, but it doesn't look like it's healing. The cut is still all red even this evening. Doesn't it look strange to you?"

Melvin moved back from James's arm, letting it fall gently from his hand. "I don't know. It doesn't look too bad. Maybe if we keep an eye on it, it will get better soon."

Sarah nodded her head reluctantly, thankful in a way that Melvin thought nothing serious was going on, but hating to not be alarmed if something really was the problem. "You think it's serious enough to take to the doctor?" she ventured.

JERRY EICHER

"I don't think so," Melvin shook his head. "Just keep an eye on it, and take it a day at a time."

"I sure am not taking him to Esther," Sarah declared out of the blue, provoking a raised eyebrow out of Melvin.

"You don't have to," he said. "I don't think it's that serious anyway."

"Mom would want me to," she told him, her eyes firm. "But I'm not taking him."

"It'll be okay," he assured her. "It'll probably be all healed up in a few days.

With that, he helped her clear the dishes off the table, then retired to the living room with the boys as she washed. A few moments later, when the stack of dishes filled the drainer, she called to him for help with the drying.

"We need a girl to help," he chuckled, holding a wipe cloth in one hand and stacking a dish in the cupboard with the other.

She leaned her shoulder gently against his. "That doesn't come from lack of trying, now does it?"

His soft chuckle filled her ear as the sounds of the storm surrounded the outside of the house.

"James needs to start helping," she announced suddenly. "He needs to learn too."

"Ya," he agreed, "but not tonight. I'm doing it tonight."

She turned her face up to his, the glow of the gas lantern backlighting her head, her eyes soft in the shadows as he bent over to kiss her gently.

About the same time, on the northern edge of Dog-

20

wood Lake at the home of Esther, the storm was raging too. Tonight she went outside onto her front porch, ignoring the lashing rain on her legs, listening to the thunder peal all around her. Only her tightly wrapped shawl gave shelter from the elements. "What weather!" she said out loud. "Strange times we are in, indeed they are."

A flash of lightening lit up the sky around her. "*Es druvvel komm*" (the trouble comes), she said softly to herself, since no one else was around.

As the thunder died away in the distance, she moved slowly back towards the house, letting the screen door slam behind her, its sound just a low thud in the raging storm.

CHAPTER THREE

Aᴛᴛᴇʀ ᴄᴏᴍɪɴɢ ɪɴ from the kitchen, Melvin seated him-self on the recliner and asked James to come over. "I want to change your bandage," he told him. "And take another look at this."

James, not too happy about all this bother about his cut, laid aside the first grade Pathway Reader Sarah had given him some weeks prior. Turning sideways in front of his father to make the cut accessible, he waited.

Gingerly Melvin took off the bandage, giving it one last quick jerk at the end. "It hurts less that way," he said, when James winced.

The wound in front of him did look red and puffy, cutting diagonally across the arm.

"Sarah," he called out to the kitchen, "could you bring some salve and a new bandage?" When she appeared with the items a few moments later, he motioned to James' arm. "It doesn't look like there is any pus. I think this problem might be coming from where the cut is located, right out here where everything is hitting it all the time. It is hard to keep a bandage on or the dirt out. I really think that's the problem."

Remembering the dirt falling from James's hands earlier in the day, she was not only inclined to agree with him but glad there was a reason to, as the alternative was so much worse. "I had thought of that, too." She smiled comfortingly at James, who clearly was tired of the attention and this disturbance in his life. "So James, just be careful how you use the arm. No rough playing for a while and don't get it dirty. We will see if that doesn't take care of it."

James shrugged. "I'm too tired to play hard at school and Nelson doesn't play rough when we're home."

"Well that's good." She stroked his hair. "It will be your bedtime soon."

He nodded, running his hand over the new bandage Melvin had just stuck on, then rubbing his hand on his pants to get rid of the salve that stuck to his fingers. Remembering, he glanced up at Sarah while quickly trying to rub the salve stain out of his denim homemade pants.

"It's okay," she smiled at him, gently. "They're your everyday pants. Just don't do that with your Sunday pants."

With that he was back to his book on the couch, opening it by memory to the last page he had read. "Do you think there's something wrong with him?" Sarah whispered softly to Melvin.

"He's just a tired growing boy," he assured her.

Outside the storm was in full force. The lightning showed the weathervane on top of the barn swinging furiously, first to the south and then back to the west. The trees in the yard towards the main road were bent nearly sideways, snapping back at the slightest lull, then forced down again.

"You don't think there are tornadoes out, do you?" Sarah asked Melvin.

"It doesn't act like tornado weather to me," Melvin replied. "Just a nasty storm. It's pretty widespread from what I could see earlier in the evening. I think tornadoes are more focused, but, of course, one never knows."

"If we had radios like the English do, maybe we could listen to the forecast and know what's going on," Sarah mused aloud, knowing she shouldn't be putting this forbidden thought of hers into words, but it had been a long hard day.

Melvin showed no alarm at her remark, simply assuring her, "We must trust the Lord. He will take care of us. If it is his will that a tornado comes we will be in His care. His will is the best. It is even better than being warned beforehand. Besides, I think he would warn us beforehand."

"You think so?" Sarah asked, as she laid her fingers on his shoulders, their eyes meeting intently.

"I do," he said confidently. "I even think he would give us a sense that we should flee from danger. Which in that case we could all go to the basement."

"Do you feel anything now?" she asked, concern flickering in her eyes.

"No, do you?"

"Not really, just tired from the day and my concern for James. Maybe the worst is over soon."

He glanced at the window before bringing his eyes back to hers. "Let's go take a closer look."

Taking her hand, he led her across the hardwood floor till they were standing in front of the glass. Comfort flowed through his hand into her heart, the feel of his calluses on the skin of her palm. She let her head lean against his shoulder, a faint smile on her face.

Out the window it did appear as if the worst was over. The weathervane, now lit by more distant lightning, had slowed in its gyrating dance. The rain, though, still came down in sheets.

"The wind has let up a bit," he murmured, his fingers moving in her hand.

She kept her eyes on the rain, letting her fingers respond to him. "It is good to see God send us rain," she said softly. "It would just be nice if He was a little gentler about it."

He chuckled, "Yes, that would be in our thinking, but then we are not God, are we?"

"You think He knows what's best?" she whispered, her eyes going over to James on the couch, fear stirring in her heart.

"He always does," his voice came to her over his shoulder, touched with softness on the edges.

Suddenly they were interrupted as a pronounced "drip, drip" behind them penetrated their consciousness. Recognizing the sound, Sarah felt irritation stir within her.

"Ah," Melvin chuckled, letting go of her hand and turning around at the same time she did. "The pesky little leak I see. Oh, why didn't I fix it right the first time? Now there will be water all over the floor."

"It's not your fault, it's just the leak," she assured him, letting her eyes meet his, their irritation showing but not meant for him, as she knew he would know. She raced out to the kitchen to get the bucket from the closet, careful to give the little spot of water on the floor a wide berth.

Melvin thought she looked lovely as she hurried away, her form thrilling him, her spirit so alive at moments like this. It was strange, he thought, that she so stirred him on a stormy night like this.

When she came back with the bucket to set under the leak, she held in her other hand a mop with a rag hanging on the side. He hid his thoughts, though he suspected she knew. That was strange, too, he thought, how she knew his mood even when she acted like she didn't — like right now, as she put the bucket in line with the drip from the ceiling.

"Let me have the rag to clean up the water," he told her, getting down on his knees to match his actions with his words. She gave him the rag as he positioned himself on the hardwood floor. Wiping up the water around the bucket first, he then lifted the bucket itself and wiped up under it.

He could tell that she was watching him. He could feel her blue eyes without seeing them, knowing they would be tender at this moment, knowing too that she wanted the rag herself, that it would be hard for her to stand there while he did this the most mundane of tasks. He knew, and he loved her for it.

"It's good to see a man who can clean up things," her voice came to him, a smile in it, conveyed without even trying to, as natural as if she had been doing it all her life. Maybe she had, he thought — not to him, of course, but simply preparing herself to love and to be loved. "Men should be useful around the house and not just at their work."

"Is that so?" he said in mock horror as he savored the moment.

"You can stop wiping now," she told him. "That's dry enough. I see there's still nothing like a woman's touch. Give me the rag and let me finish it."

Melvin got up slowly, giving her the rag and letting his fingers touch hers again before walking over to his recliner and settling into it. He pulled himself back up momentarily to reach for the Budget, then let his body go back into the comfort of the soft velvet padding. He had purchased the recliner a few weeks earlier and had brought it home on the old spring wagon he kept in the back of the barn. That had saved on the delivery charge, but it had done nothing about his feelings of guilt, which were coming back again at this moment.

Normally he felt no guilt about his decisions — if they were legally made, of course — but for some reason this one, which was legally made, still bothered him. He had never mentioned his guilty feeling to Sarah, even when she helped him carry the chair into the living room, choosing this spot for it to sit.

It had all come about just this past communion when the "church *ordnung*" had been changed to allow recliners of any kind. That was how such things needed to be done, legally, and Melvin had seen no danger in the rule change, voting then without any feelings of reservation. Now, though, finding how comfortable the thing was, his conscience was stirred, and he could see why there had been prohibitions for so long. Looking back, his body enjoying the luxury of this English invention, he half wished he had voted against it.

Not that it would have made any difference, he assured himself. *Bishop Amos was for them so it would have passed anyway.* Deep down, though, he knew that was not true. His dissenting voice, respected as he was in the community, would have made a difference. It well could have been the deciding factor in swinging the pendulum in the opposite direction.

"You know, Melvin," his conscience accused him, "if you had voted against it, the thing would not have passed. All it would have taken is one person, and you could have been that person."

Shaking his head, he listened to the rain outside, letting his wish that he had voted the other way do its work. Although nothing could be done about the vote now, or would be done about it, his wish soothed him, comforted him, caused his conscience to pull back at his expression of regret. The English recliner was still here, though, and would be staying here, so he might as well enjoy it. That is how it seemed to him, but he just could not stop thinking of its comfort as being quite English, even as he let his body relax back into it.

After reading a few columns in the Budget, he got up and walked over to get his Bible. He felt an urge to read the scripture, his conscience still stirring in the background, but since it just didn't seem right to read the scriptures in the soft recliner, he sat down on the old backless couch for his selected reading. Opening the pages, he figured he might as well face the worst, so he turned carefully to Psalm 119, beginning with the first verse.

"Blessed are the undefiled in the way, who walk in the law of the Lord," he read.

CHAPTER FOUR

H E KEPT GOING, letting his back lean against the wall, feeling its hardness, comforting to him at the moment. He faced the thought thoroughly that maybe he had wanted to walk in some way other than the law of God. Lifting his eyes from the page, he let his gaze pass over James and Nelson. Nelson was still playing on the floor with his little wooden blocks, building a house or something. James had the Pathway Reader on his lap, apparently deeply engrossed in what the story was saying.

Delight filled him at the sight of his boys, along with a desire to be a good father to them — to raise them in the fear of the Lord, to lead them, as it just said on the page in front of him, into the law of God. He sighed, wishing he could do better. He wanted to feel like he was doing it right, to know it with a certainty, but even in those moments when he was closest to being certain, the goal still seemed far away. And tonight he wasn't close at all to being certain.

It was a long psalm, and he read down to the middle of it, knowing what was coming because he had read it often before. It was King David's expression of delight in the law and commandments of God. The evil ones, according to the King, had fat hearts, but the godly took pleasure in God's ways. Melvin was not sure what it all meant, but it made him feel better just reading the words.

Sarah interrupted him when she came back from the kitchen, her blue eyes bringing back the rush of emotion he felt for her earlier. How was it that heaven and earth walked so close together, he wondered?

"It's time for the children to go to bed," she told him softly. "Come boys," she said in their direction, "it's getting late. Time for evening prayers."

They rose without hesitation, Nelson moving quickly to put his blocks back into their box, the house that had been rising into a magnificent creation in his mind reduced in an instant to a crumbled pile of little sawn pieces of wood, and James closing his book, reaching over to place it on the edge of the couch.

Sarah motioned Nelson with a sweep of her hand to take his place beside James, seating herself with Melvin on the couch. Looking up into Melvin's face, she asked him, "You have a song before we pray?"

He nodded without speaking because he already had the selection in his mind that fit how he was feeling. With his strong baritone he led as his family joined in the soul-stirring German words of *Näher Mein Gott zu Dir* (Nearer My God to Thee).

When they were done, he reached over to put his arms around Sarah's shoulders, pulling her close to him. His desire for God and her blended themselves together in a way he did not understand. Her body relaxed, she smiled over at James and Nelson as together, the four of them, knelt and prayed while the rain beat outside and the water dripped, dripped, into the bucket from the leak in the roof.

Sarah stood to see the boys off to their rooms, fussing one last time over James's bandage on his arm.

"I'm okay, Mom," he told her with annoyance in his voice as her fingers ran over his arm, probing the flesh above and below the cut. "You're just going to make it hurt worse."

"Okay, okay, I'll leave it alone," she said, pulling him close to her. He let his body fall into her embrace, too young yet to feel awkward or resistant to such intimate mothering.

Walking with them to their bedroom upstairs, she checked the windows and made sure they were settled in, taking one last look from the door at each of them nestled in his own twin bed. Gently she shut the door, love for her little boys and concern all running together at the moment. *Keep them safe, dear God,* she breathed a prayer on the way down.

Melvin was still settled on the couch, his Bible open again, trying to finish his chapter. She took the seat beside him, simply sitting there, watching the rain out the window, thinking about life and what it might hold. Not one to do that often, she wondered why she was tonight. Maybe the weather had something to do with it, she concluded.

"You ready to settle down for the evening?" Melvin's voice broke into her thoughts.

She looked at him, his Bible still open but his eyes on her. His manliness struck her afresh, causing her to pull in her breath. "You're still reading your Bible," she told him, the wonder of her pounding heart surprising her. It seemed like a long time since she had married him, and yet tonight it felt like it was yesterday.

"I think I love you," he told her, his eyes shining, his arms reaching out to pull her to him.

She let herself go, welcoming the feel of his strength around her shoulders, the comfort he brought, her fears lost for the moment in the wonder of his love.

Melvin was sure he had just dozed off into a dreamless sleep when he woke with a start, his senses alert for danger. Something was wrong. His sense of what time it was completely failed him, his mind searching for clues and finding nothing. Outside the bedroom, the rain still beat against the side of the house; it seemed louder now than it had sounded earlier.

It was quite dark in the room, with no light coming in the windows — only a glimmer through the door from the kerosene lamp in the hall. When Sarah had wanted the light in the hall he had objected to it, so now she rarely let it burn all night except on dark nights like tonight. So its presence gave him no clue either as to the time.

Then he noticed something strange about the light coming in from the hall. It was acting crazy, dancing wildly about, creating shadows that flew up and down the wall, going dimmer then brighter again, all within split seconds. Above the dancing light was the unmistakable roar of the wind.

He shook Sarah awake, whispering, "What is going on?"

She woke instantly, sitting upright in bed, listening. "The door is *uff*" (open), she whispered back.

"The what?" Melvin asked in astonishment, not sure he heard correctly.

"It sounds like the door is open."

"That can't be." He was positive. "What door?"

She paused, her head tilted to the side, her long hair touching the bed where it hung over her shoulders. "It's the front door."

"I'm not sure about that," he muttered. "Sounds mighty strange to me, but I will go see." He pushed the covers aside and got out of bed, stepping softly to the bedroom door to look down the hall. There was nothing to see except the dancing light from the kerosene lamp, but a sharp wind was blowing over its glass shade, coming from the front of the house.

"*Something's* open," he whispered back to Sarah, who swung her feet out of the bed to join him.

Stepping out into the hall he reached the corner of the living room and looked around it cautiously. Melvin could not believe his eyes. The front door was wide open, swinging back and forth on its hinges without a person in sight.

Through the door the rain was blowing in, each blast of wind driving it even though the porch overhang deflected the worst of it. In the middle of the hardwood floor the drip bucket Sarah had set out was nearly floating on the water puddle around it.

He felt the touch of Sarah's hand on his shoulders as she came around to look past him. "What is going on?" her voice came out in a half whisper tinged with fear and tension.

35

"The door's open," he said, stating the obvious, because nothing more profound occurred to his half-awakened brain. Gingerly stepping forward, he tiptoed through the water to reach the front door to shut it. Pushing against the wind, he brought the door around, then nearly fell forward when the gust stopped suddenly. The door shut with a thud.

In the ensuing silence, the drip, drip from the ceiling could be heard hitting the water in the bucket. The sound was hollow and full like it is when a drop hits deep water.

Sarah's voice from where she was still standing in the hall reached him. "Who opened it?"

He glanced around, then outside through the window, seeing nothing. Was somebody in the house? The thought brought a paralyzing fear, but he shoved it away. His gun was hanging in the utility closet, but it never crossed his mind to use it. He would trust God — that was his training and his faith — but he would need to find out if someone was here. The rest would be up to the Almighty.

"You think someone broke in?" Sarah asked, still in the hallway.

"I have no idea," Melvin said, speaking just loud enough so she could hear. "The door's not broken or anything — no one forced it — but I am going to look."

She seemed frozen to her spot as he walked towards the kitchen. Knowing where he was going did not make it any easier. He needed his flashlight in the utility room, but there was darkness in-between here and there.

Inspiration and courage came to her all at the same moment. Whatever the danger was, she wanted not only to help but to be by his side. She might not be of much help, but being with him seemed of great importance at the moment. Reacting, she moved quickly down the hall, picked up the kerosene lamp, and held its flickering flame low in front of her to keep it out of her eyes. It was not much, but it was better than the darkness Melvin had between him and his source of light.

The gratefulness in his eyes when she came after him with the light gave her another shot of courage. "I'm coming with you," she whispered.

He nodded his head. "I just need it to see to get out to the flashlight."

With her holding the lamp, they walked through the kitchen, their legs sending strange shadows across the cabinets. Reaching around the corner he found his flashlight and turned it on. The utility room was empty.

Melvin turned the light back into the living room. "There's nobody here. They wouldn't be back in our bedroom, and we already came through the other rooms."

"They wouldn't have gone upstairs, I don't think," Sarah whispered. "The door must have been opened from the inside."

"You think so?" he asked with skepticism.

"You weren't sleep walking or something, were you?"

Melvin shook his head. "I don't sleep walk."

"Then who could it have been?"

"It must have been one of the boys, you think?

"Let's go see if they are sleeping," Sarah said softly.

With that they went upstairs together, Sarah's lamp giving all the light they needed, Melvin holding his flashlight ready should the need arise. In front of the bedroom door they paused, then opened it and looked in. James's form could be seen clearly in his bed under the covers, sleeping soundly, but on Nelson's bed a little form was sitting up, covers wrapped around him, muffled sounds of crying reaching them.

Sarah stepped away from Melvin and handed him the lamp before walking across the floor. She sat on the bed beside Nelson and reached out to pull him towards her. His crying became quieter as he nestled up against her.

"Did you open the door?" she asked him.

His little voice trembled, "Yes."

"Did you do it all by yourself?"

His whole upper body went into the nod, his shoulders moving with the motion. "I wanted to see if the animals were okay in the barn."

"Were they okay?" Sarah continued probing, wanting to know how far he had gone with it.

"I don't know. I couldn't see anything. The rain came in like this...." He pulled his arm out from under the covers, the little fingers extended, moving his hand quickly in a horizontal motion. "Then I couldn't shut the door. The rain wouldn't stop coming in. I was scared, Mommy. Then I came back up to bed because I didn't want you to know there was rain coming in."

"Now, now, that's okay," she said, pulling him tighter to herself, wrapping the blankets tighter around him when she felt him shiver. "You should have come and told me. Daddy and I will take care of it, but you should always come and tell me about something like that."

He nodded again, his shoulders moving under the covers.

"You just sleep now, okay? Daddy has shut the door, and I am sure the animals are all right. You can see them in the morning."

Satisfied, he lay back snuggling in the covers as he pulled them up to his chin. She could see his face dimly in the flickering light, fear still around the edges but already heading towards the land of childhood slumber.

"Goodnight, Mommy," he said, moving his head on the pillow, settling in.

She stroked his hand before getting up to leave, glancing over at James, who hadn't stirred during the whole conversation.

"What a mess," Melvin said with a sigh when they got back down the stairs. "It'll be a mess to clean it up in the morning." He stood looking at the pooled water, holding the lamp up to cast its light as far into the living room as possible.

"We're cleaning it up tonight," Sarah's voice came to him near his shoulder.

"But there is no use making noise that will wake the boys. It can wait till the morning."

"It won't make any noise. Not much anyway. We can't just leave this water on the wood. I will get the dustpan and broom and we can pick up the worst of it."

Knowing she was right, but hating to miss more sleep than he already had, Melvin sat the lamp on the end table in front of the couch, then reached for one of the brooms she brought with her from the kitchen. Together they worked quietly and quickly, getting the water into the bucket and then out to the kitchen sink to dump it down the drain.

"Okay," Sarah pronounced with a sigh when the only thing left was a faint dirty wetness on the wood floor, "back to bed. I can do another mopping in the morning for the dirt. It's a good thing, though, you woke up when you did. Much later in shutting that door and this mess would have been a whole lot worse."

"I know," Melvin agreed sleepily, already heading for his warm bed. "I thought the leak in the roof was a big deal, but an open door makes a whole lot greater mess."

Sarah nodded, thinking out loud at his retreating back, "Who would have thought an open door could cause so much damage in so little time?" Fear threatened her as she followed Melvin down the hall. Was this a warning of what was coming? Was a new door opening in their lives, one that would bring trouble and destruction? "Please God," she whispered, quietly so Melvin would not hear, "give me the grace to bear what you are sending us."

CHAPTER FIVE

After breakfast the next morning, and a promise to
check the leak on the roof as soon as things were dry,
Melvin left for the fields. Sarah got the boys up for their
breakfast, packed James's lunch, and saw him off to school
at the end of the lane, where his cousins picked him up for
the ride into Glendale. The little one-room Amish schoolhouse stood on the east side of town, having been there for
ten years now, built on a piece of property formerly owned
by the town.

Usually Amish schoolhouses ended up out in the middle
of the country somewhere, but here, with the offered sale
price and the smallness of the town, plans were made for
the purchase of the land and the building of the school
right on the edge of town.

With James gone, Nelson stood outside looking at the
results of last night's storm, in wonder at the strewn pieces
of leaves and branches in the yard. Sarah noticed and hollered out the front door that he could pick up the branches
and place them in little piles. His great delight at the news,
which he obviously considered constructive playing, was
reward enough for her, since she figured his actual yard
cleaning abilities would be limited.

Refilling the bucket with clean water and adding soap, she finished moping up the floor, taking the time to remove all the traces of dirt streaks. The hardwood looked none the worse for wear when she was done, for which she was deeply thankful. Water stains would have been not only a nasty sight, but difficult to explain the next time they had church in the house.

Though the explanation of how it happened would no doubt be received by the other women with understanding, one's housekeeping reputation was always a thing to keep well in hand. Having a child wandering around opening doors in the middle of the night in a thunderstorm was kind of pushing it, she figured. Best that this never get around. It was also good that this was an old house, she figured. *Some of the newer wood floors would have been all buckled up with that much water on them.*

The crunch of tires on the gravel in the driveway, as she was putting away the mop, alerted her to English visitors, no doubt. Yet when she went to glance out the front window, lest whoever it was see her before she saw them, it turned out to be a familiar gray Bonneville — her sister Martha.

Swinging around the half circle of driveway, Martha parked out of the way, half on and half off the grass. As Sarah watched she got out of the car, her keys waving in her hand, and pushed the door of the Bonneville shut with a flourish. Clearly the Amish-raised girl was quite comfortable with her English ways.

Darker haired than Sarah but still blond, her slim figure was framed by a dark skirt and white top. At moments like these, Sarah could not help wishing things were different.

Martha had changed so much since she had left, but she was still her sister and Sarah was not one to cut family ties over church changes. With a quick step she headed to the front door to open it.

Martha was married to a Mennonite, Silas. Sweet on him for years, yet forbidden by their mother Deborah from dating him until she was twenty-one, she had wasted no time in tying the knot once she was of age. It had been five years since she joined the local Mennonite church, and Sarah figured she would never quite get over it. In her heart she had always hoped Martha would choose the same path as she and stay in the Amish world.

Martha bustled up the walks, all energy and good cheer. "Beautiful day, isn't it?"

"I guess so," Sarah smiled somewhat grimly, remembering the night before and James. "You sure are chirpy."

"So what are you out of sorts about?" Martha's cheerfulness turned into concern at the sight of her sister's face. "You look like you've been up all night."

"Nothing, really. We did get some sleep. I just got done moping up the hardwood floor from a lot of water that came in last night."

"Your roof leaks that much?" Martha raised her eyebrows. "I know you mentioned that leak last week, but you said it was a little one."

Sarah shook her head, for some reason feeling the need to lower her voice, even though no one else was around. "No, it wasn't that. Last night, after we were all in bed, Nelson opened the front door during that storm."

"Really?" Martha's eyebrows went up into her forehead.

"You had a kid wandering around the house, opening front doors during a thunderstorm?"

"I know it sounds like bad parenting, but when he told me why it does make a little sense."

"Oh, I didn't mean that." Martha quickly waved her hand sideways. "We don't have any children yet, but I'm sure you're a better mother than what I will be. Just that maybe there's something wrong with him. Is he sick?"

"No. After we were all in bed, he claims he wanted to know if the animals were okay in the barn. I guess the wind and all had him worried, and we did talk about the animals being safe at supper. Maybe that was what bothered him, although he didn't say anything at the time. Anyway, he couldn't get the door shut again, the little tike."

"Well that can happen." Martha was all understanding. "How did he take it?"

"We found him in bed crying after we shut the door. Melvin heard the wind in the house first. Otherwise I might never have woken up. Gives you a weird feeling in the nighttime, trying to figure out why your front door is open."

"I suppose so." Martha glanced up from the front porch to see Nelson standing in the barn doorway, his form framed by its vastness, accenting his boyishness even more.

Sarah followed Martha's glance. "Oh, there he is, in the barn. I told him he could pick up the branches from the storm last night, but I guess that didn't last too long. The play must have turned into work."

"Hi, Nelson," Martha hollered at him across the yard. "So what are you up to this morning?"

He shrugged his shoulders offering no reply.

"Come say hi to Martha," Sarah told him, her voice carrying easily to his ears.

He pushed some dirt around in front of the barn door with his foot, as if thinking the proposition over, then took off running towards the house.

"Oh," Martha said, wrapping her arms around him in a hug when he got within range. "You scared last night?"

"Yes," he said with wide eyes. "The wind" — he made a wooshing sound, waving his arm back and forth — "it came right in the door. I thought the horses might be cold."

"Well," she said with another hug, "that was a good boy, taking care of the animals, but next time you should tell your mommy about it. She is bigger than you are."

"A lot bigger," he said grimly, his eyes serious. "The door went back." He waved his arm again for emphasis.

"Ya," Sarah injected, "I think he will next time. Won't you Nelson?"

He nodded soberly.

"Well, you want to go back to playing in the barn?" Sarah asked him. "Martha can tell you goodbye before she leaves then. Okay?"

He nodded again, a little more cheerfully this time.

When Nelson was halfway down the walk, Martha turned to Sarah. "I want to ask you something out of his earshot. I wasn't trying to chase him off."

Sarah nodded. "I know, but I figured you wanted to talk about something. What is it, something serious?"

"Am I that obvious?"

"Well, we are sisters, I guess."

"Let's go inside where it's comfortable, then."

45

Ignoring Sarah's curiosity once they got into the living room, Martha headed for the new recliner and settled herself in it. "I am sure glad to see Bishop Amos got some sense into his head. This is a new recliner, isn't it? I never noticed it before. Bishop never let us have them when I was Amish."

"Well, times change. We did vote for it, too, so it was not just the bishop's doing," Sarah said, more interested in what Martha came for than recliner conversation.

Martha wasn't done though. "You can't convince me. Remember, I was Amish myself. Your vote would have gotten nowhere if Bishop was against it. But it is nice they let you vote on it. Now in our church, our votes mean something. Just the other night we passed a vote, and I am sure the pastor voted against it. That is how things really should be, I say."

"Quite disrespectful," Sarah said, horrified, "voting for something your pastor is against."

Martha shrugged. "Well, he didn't really say he was against it, but you could tell. Some of us women brought up the issue several months ago. I gave some really good arguments for it, if I have to say so myself. So we passed it with a majority 'yes' vote."

"You always were the spunky one, but that's overdoing it a little, don't you think?"

"I like it that way," Martha stated firmly. "Silas's church is really nice."

"Well, you can have it," Sarah told her firmly. "Now what did you say earlier you were going to tell me?"

Martha grinned. "What I came over for is the trip plans I mentioned last week. Have you given it some further thought?" She leaned forward in the recliner, expectantly.

Sarah searched her memory, not finding anything among the pressing concerns of yesterday and last night.

"You can't have forgotten, surely." Martha didn't seem too fazed. "I guess I did just mention it in passing, but the more I think about it the more brilliant the idea becomes. But" — Martha glanced around for any sight of Nelson — "I did want to discuss it with you first before the boys know anything about it. That way if nothing comes of it, they will not be disappointed."

"Okay," Sarah nodded her head, still not turning up anything from her dazed mind. "So what was it?"

"It is this. We want to take a trip out west — a real trip, to the real west. We need to go before it gets too hot. Not deep, deep west, like California or something, but maybe Colorado. Isn't that a great idea or what?"

"Yes," Sarah allowed, her mind producing the conversation from last week at long last. "It did sound interesting then and it sounds interesting now, but I haven't mentioned anything to Melvin about it."

Martha leaned even farther forward in the recliner. "Then do, please. That is the best part, really, if you and Melvin and the two boys go along with us. We want you to. All of us could fit into our van real well. Sarah, it would just be a blast, wouldn't it? Isn't that a great idea?"

Sarah, a little stunned now that she was fully looking at

the idea, gathered her thoughts. "I'd enjoy it, I think," she allowed. "Neither Melvin nor I have ever been out west, but what about the money? We don't have lots of it."

"It won't take lots of money. That's what's so wonderful about it," Martha grinned. "This is not like that paid New York City trip we took before we were married. Since we have to pay, Silas and I talked, and we know just how to do it. There would be the cost for gas, of course, which we could split. For nights we can take along two tents and stop at camping grounds. That costs maybe fifteen or twenty dollars per night. Most of the campgrounds have showers you can use. The boys can sleep in the van."

"But what if it rains or gets cold?"

"We talked about that, too," Martha continued confidently. "The weather should be warm enough by then to sleep outside, with sleeping bags. If not we could spend a night or so in a motel. If it rains, the tents we have are waterproof."

"What about food and meals, since we aren't in New York City with Maxey Jacobs paying the way?"

Martha never missed a beat, obviously having been over these details before. "We talked about that, too. Maybe one meal a day in the restaurants, something like breakfast, we thought. For lunch we can snack on things out of the grocery stores — those are not too expensive. And then for supper we can make our own at the campgrounds. It would be gobs of fun, Sarah. Come on, let's do it."

Sarah chuckled, letting the thought of it fill her mind. But then visions of vans and travel, clothing and boys needing attention sobered her. She hated to bring it up, but decided that it would be better. "James has been acting a little strange lately."

Martha looked up in surprise. "How's acting strange?"

"He just told me yesterday. Has been having these weak spells, he said, and showed me a cut on his arm that apparently has been there for some time and won't heal. I sure hope it is nothing serious."

Martha let herself lean back into the recliner, sighing in relief. "Oh, well, that doesn't sound too serious, does it? I know I don't have children yet, but we were tired too sometimes, growing up. Has he been getting the cut dirty? You know how boys are."

"It was dirty when he showed me yesterday," Sarah remembered, seeing again the dirt falling off his hand when he held it up. "He was playing in the barn."

"Exactly," Martha pronounced, "the exact place for all kinds of wired germs to hide out. He probably got one of those, and it will soon be over. Did Melvin look at it?"

"Ya," Sarah nodded, "he gave him good attention last night."

"And what was his idea?"

"He figured about the same as you. Something along those lines."

"Well, see, there you go. It's really nothing to worry about."

Sarah was not totally convinced, but she let relief come over her because she so desperately wanted it to be true. A little cut was just a little cut, and really she was making a big deal out of nothing.

"So," Sarah let a smile play on her lips, "when do we go?"

Martha's eyes sparkled. "In six weeks or so, Silas and I thought. That would give both of us, Silas and me, time to get our jobs in order. School would be out for James, and we also have some church meetings in four weeks. Those would be over. After that we should be free to go. You and Melvin would surely have time by then to find someone to do the chores. After that we would be ready to set out. Coming up, Colorado, here we come."

Sarah did feel little shivers of excitement running up and down her spine in spite of herself. It had been a long time since she had been out of Daviess County. "It does sound good to me," she allowed herself to say, because it did, and because the darkness from last night now seemed a little more distant.

Martha was ecstatic. "You will do it then?"

"I will have to talk to Melvin, of course, but he will probably want to go, too. He loves to travel when we go to see his family. It's not every day we get a chance like this. Many of the other church people have gone on western trips, so I doubt if there are church objections."

"Then it's settled, unless Melvin says no, which I hope he won't. Oh, I am so excited about it all! It will be the greatest fun, Sarah. I just know it will be!"

With that, Martha was ready to go, but took time to cover the news she'd heard recently. A cousin in Pennsylvania was due for a baby. Elmer Yost's wife in their church had just found out she had breast cancer, thankfully still in its early stages. Martha had been home that morning, where their mother Deborah was getting ready to leave for the sewing.

As she mentioned the sewing, Martha turned to Sarah

with questions in her eyes. "Why aren't you going? You go, don't you?"

"Of course I do, when I can. This morning just isn't one of those days."

"Well, I can take you, if you want. It would save time."

"And how would I get home?"

"Ya, that is a problem," Martha allowed. "I guess you can skip a month. I never cared much for them anyway."

"I do, but there's just too much going on at home at the moment."

The door behind them opened, letting in Nelson, his face red from running in from the barn, but his hands clean, Sarah noticed.

"So you had a hard night?" Martha asked him. "You were worried about the horses in the big wind?"

He soberly nodded, sticking his hands in his pockets after he shut the front door. "I can shut it now."

"Oh, the poor child," Martha cooed. "You didn't do anything wrong, did you? You were just trying to be a good boy."

He nodded again.

"You want to hear some news?"

His face lit up slightly, not quite sure what the news was about.

Martha noticed and chuckled, "Your mother and I were just talking about some plans for a trip. You want to go along?"

Nelson grinned, not totally sure what a trip was, but thinking he liked the idea anyway.

Martha ruffled his hair. "I have to go now. You pick up all the sticks in the yard yet?"

"I tried," he ventured. "There were so many of them. When is the trip?"

"Not too long," she told him. "Maybe about six weeks or so. We will have to see what your father has to say about it. Okay?"

"How long is six weeks?" he wanted to know.

Sarah laughed at that. "Now, now, too many questions. It's a long time for you, believe me. Just don't worry about it and it will come soon enough. Martha has to go now."

He grinned, pulling his hands out his pockets as Martha gave him a hug again on her way out. "No more nightmares, okay?"

With that she went down the walks, climbed into the Bonneville, waved, and drove slowly out the driveway.

After he came in for lunch, Melvin, much to Sarah's delight, climbed onto the roof to attempt leak repairs. He looked, calculated, lifted what looked like loose edges, and finally settled on a course of action. Squeezing his tube of tar in the caulking gun, he applied some in the appropriate place, did some more, then, concluding that the job was done, climbed back down.

"Already done?" Sarah asked him in surprise.

"Yes. Was it supposed to take a long time?" he asked, half amused and half irritated, knowing that it was supposed to.

"No, just as long as it's done right," she replied, skeptical but willing to allow that it might have solved the problem.

"I think it's fixed," he told her, "but I guess we won't know until it rains again. Those little leaks are the hardest ones to find it seems."

"Hopefully we won't have a storm like that again too soon."

"Probably won't," he agreed, making ready to return to the fields.

She for her part decided to wait until that evening to ask about the trip. It was not such a pressing matter that she would need to use his daylight hours to discuss it. Six weeks was a long time, and that night would be soon enough to know.

After Melvin got in from the fields that night and had his supper, Sarah asked him about the proposed trip, giving him the details while he sat in the recliner. As she expected, it did not take long for him to agree to it.

"I think it's a great idea," he told her. "We have never done a western trip before."

"Well, it wouldn't be entirely western, just to Colorado."

"It's a start," he shrugged. "You think James is able to go?"

"He seemed fine when he came home from school. I changed the bandage. It looked a lot better, I thought."

"A false alarm then?"

She winced, her fears not yet totally gone. "I hope."

"Let's do it then," he decided. "Let Martha know, and we can start the plans."

CHAPTER SIX

A LL THE SPARE moments of the next six weeks were spent planning, packing, and notifying the family. Sarah's and Martha's parents, Ben and Deborah Schwartz, were told at church on Sunday, as were Silas's parents. Melvin's parents, John and Mattie Yoder, lived in the north district close to Odon and had to be notified by mail. Nobody objected but thought it was a good idea.

That left the choice of a chore substitute yet to be made, one who would know what to do once they left. That entailed him coming over for an evening, watching and helping, getting a feel for what Melvin wanted done.

"You okay with Elmer?" Sarah asked Melvin at the kitchen table one evening, after she saw that Elmer had been there.

"Ya," Melvin told her, stabbing an errant corn kernel on his plate, the mashed potatoes giving him a backstop on which to catch the slippery little thing. "He's a good boy."

"The cow won't be dead when we get back?" Sarah asked, having no idea where that fear was coming from — it just was there.

Melvin chuckled, looking up at her, then sobering when his eyes caught her blue ones. "James isn't sick, is he?"

55

"No," she sighed. "I keep thinking he might be, but he's fine. The cut on his arm is already healed up."

"That's good. Is everything ready to go then?"

"I think so."

"When is the date anyway?"

"You mean you've forgotten? It's next week."

"Just teasing," he told her. "I knew it was sometime next week."

So it happened that Martha and Silas pulled into the driveway at five o'clock a.m. on the first Monday of June. An hour later they rolled south on Highway 57 heading toward I-64 west. The sun sent its first rays streaking through the back window of their van as they came off the ramp onto the interstate and hit 65 miles an hour.

"It is a beautiful morning," Silas said, settling his ample frame back into the driver's seat, his beardless chin still glistening from his morning shave. "We can stop for breakfast anytime now," he declared quite loudly, patting his stomach under the steering wheel.

"Would you be a little quieter," Martha told him, softly. "The boys are still sleeping."

"No, we're not," James piped up from the back. "I've been awake for a while already."

"See what you've gone and done," Martha told him. "You woke him up."

"I don't think I did," Silas protested, chuckling. "He's probably as hungry as I am. Besides he said he's awake. You heard him say it."

"Children always say they are awake when you ask them, don't they Sarah? You can't go by what they say, can you?"

"The boys are fine," Sarah smiled, knowing her sister's pleasure in arguments and her confidence in winning them, even when they were growing up.

"Well, I didn't intend to wake anyone," Silas insisted.

"I'm hungry," Nelson said loudly from the back seat.

"See, that proves it," Silas declared. "Nelson heard me mention breakfast, so he had to be awake."

Martha was not quite ready to give up. "Boys are always hungry. It doesn't prove anything. Anyway, what does it matter? We are all hungry. Find a McDonald's for breakfast."

"What do you say then, boys?" Silas asked, loudly directing his words towards the back, gleeful that he was winning. "Shall we go to McDonald's?"

There was silence from the backseat. "Boys," Silas tried again, "did you hear me? What about McDonald's?"

When they still said nothing, Sarah supplied the missing information. "I don't think they know what McDonald's is."

"Don't know what McDonald's is?" Silas's voice fairly boomed in astonishment. "Then it's high time. Don't you ever take them out, Sarah?"

"Hey," she informed him, "we're not Stone Age, just don't hang around McDonald's."

"Rather have meat and potatoes," Melvin got in quickly, a smile on his face.

"Well, you do have a point there," Silas agreed, patting his stomach again, "but there's no home-cooked taters out here, I'm afraid. Besides, it's morning."

James added his opinion from the back seat. "I want to go to McDonald's."

"Well, then," Silas told him, "McDonald's it will be. Your first time, and I will get to take you there. It's a good place to eat for little children, let me tell you, and grownups, too, of course. You will see. We have the Poseyville exit coming up next. They should certainly have a McDonald's."

Five minutes later the blue motel and restaurant roadside markers came up for the Poseyville exit, with McDonald's on the list. "Here we go, boys," Silas boomed, making imitation noises of his own motor as they slowed down for the exit.

Once out the van, little Nelson and James walked slowly through the swinging doors, their eyes wide, taking in the strange sights of food pictures, people, booths, and bright lights. "Why have they got all the pictures of food?" James wanted to know.

"That is so you know what to order," Sarah told him.

"I'll take that one," little Nelson said, pointing to a large picture within his sight, a sundae resplendent in all its swirling glory, whipped cream bubbling over the side of the plastic cup with a cherry perched on top.

"That looks good," James said. "I want that one, too."

"Now, boys," Sarah quickly interjected herself into their thoughts, "you have to eat what they have for breakfast first, then maybe ice cream, but I don't think they serve that right now."

"Well, I want one later then," James proclaimed.

"We will have to see about that. For now you can just look at it," Sarah told them, suddenly coming to her senses and deciding there would be no ice cream for breakfast.

The little group of Amish and Mennonites lined up in

the twisting aisle leading to the counter, Silas and Martha going first with the boys in between Melvin and Sarah.

A farmhand and his female companion got in line behind Sarah and Melvin. He was a big fellow with muscular arms showing off beneath his tee shirt, grease on his pants, a touch of a belly hanging over his belt. She was thinner than he, a little frail-looking for a farm girl, but from the windswept look of her face it was clear she was used to being outdoors.

When Sarah turned around to look at him, he asked without hesitation, "Are you Amish?" He said it with that way English folks have of saying it — the "A" with the long vowel sound drawn out for a split second longer than the next syllable.

Sarah put on her best smile. "Yes, we are, and this," she motioned her hand towards Martha, "is my sister and her husband, and my husband Melvin is behind me."

"We are just local people," the fellow said while the girl grinned, "farm folks. I am Parker and this is my girlfriend, Terry. We just love the Amish people though. Not that we get to see them often, but we have been to visit in Holmes County, Ohio. They are just great people."

"That's nice of you to say," Sarah said, wishing there wouldn't be such a big fuss made, but it was just the way it was. "It's always good to hear that people think well of you," she told him, because she figured it was better to respond that way than some other way.

The line moved forward as Sarah made sure James and Nelson stayed between the dividing bars. Behind her the girl was saying to her boyfriend, "Don't you think little Amish boys are so cute in their little hats? It's just adorable."

She wanted to chuckle at that, too, but figured they meant it well. Ahead of her Melvin was motioning for her to come up to the cash register to order. "It's our turn," he whispered.

Between the two of them the food was soon ordered. They watched while the people in the back expertly tossed the egg muffins and pancakes into the proper boxes, then at Silas's insistence found a booth where they could watch the van.

"Good policy," Silas muttered, explaining his choice while pulling out a chair to sit down. "Even a locked van can be broken into, and things carried off while you eat."

"It's not that bad," Martha told him. "You exaggerate a little."

"Maybe," he allowed, his two breakfast platters on the table in front of him, "but I like to keep an eye on things."

"Not something you think about much on the farm," Melvin commented dryly from across the table. "Benefits of country living."

"It's coming our way," Silas said with creased brow. "Cities moving in everywhere, pressing the farms in, bringing crime in with them."

"Kind of a dark picture of the world, don't you think?" Melvin eyed his brother-in-law, trying to get to know him, not having spent that much time around him.

"Can we have prayer?" Martha wanted to know, eager to eat and not that interested in the conversation anyway.

Silas nodded, cutting his gloomy pronouncement short

without any signs of regret. "Let's pray folks," he announced quietly.

Together they bowed their heads, the boys' and Melvin's hats on the floor, then everyone went to eating with relish, except James, whose half-finished egg muffin ended up back in the box.

"You're not hungry?" Sarah asked him, her fears, long dormant, now flaring in her chest.

"I can't eat it," he said, wrinkling up his face.

"There is something wrong with this boy," Sarah muttered hurriedly to Melvin, all kinds of things running through her imagination. "What boy doesn't want breakfast?"

"I don't know." Melvin looked at James carefully. "He looks okay to me. They've just never eaten McDonald's food before. Maybe that has something to do with it. Or it might just be nervousness."

"You think so?" she asked, wanting desperately for it to be true.

"Let's take the boys out to see the playroom. That might help distract him," Melvin suggested.

"Would you like that, James?" Sarah asked him, not sure if he had been listening or not, hoping he had not.

"I'd like that," he said, and she knew he had heard, but it didn't seem to bother him, for which she was thankful.

"Has he been sick?" Silas asked in a surprisingly quiet voice, his concern showing.

"Not really," Sarah told him quickly. "We just had some concerns a few weeks ago, but he's been doing well since then."

"About the time we planned this trip," Martha offered, to fill in the gaps. "I think it was just a false scare myself."

"That's what we hoped, and still do." Sarah got up. "Let's get out to the playroom. I suppose we should soon be on our way."

"A few moments." Silas glanced at his wristwatch. "We can't lose too much time this early in the day."

With that, they put the wrappings and James's half-eaten meal into the disposal can by the door, slid their trays on top of the stack, and took the boys to the play area.

"What do you think of this?" Melvin asked Nelson and James when they all walked into the room of multi-colored slides and climbing decks.

Looking at the slides, the boys' faces showed signs of recognition, but the big box with the four-foot deep pile of small balls was another matter.

"What is this, Mommy?" James asked with a puzzled expression in his voice.

Sarah thought she knew, but decided they would wait and see. "Watch what the others do," she told him. In a moment another little boy, his mother with him, came by. The boy dived in, disappearing completely from sight under the ball pile, coming up giggling with delight a foot from where he went down.

"That is what you do with it," Sarah told James. "You want to try it?"

"There is no way I am doing that," James informed her, shaking his head.

Watching the demonstration, Nelson had no such reservations, slipping past James and diving in.

James muttered half to himself, "That's not safe," even as his brother's head broke the surface of the pile of balls, laughing with delight.

Sarah took Nelson's hand to help him out as Silas stuck his head into the play area. "Time to go, boys. Got to get on the road."

"You hear that?" Sarah asked, reaching for both of their hands. "Time to go."

Five minutes later they were at the entrance ramp of the freeway, Silas having to wait his turn to get into the westbound lane, but soon they were accelerating off the ramp. When they had reached a comfortable speed, Silas set the cruise control and leaned back against his seat with a sigh.

CHAPTER SEVEN

THEY PASSED THE Illinois state line at the Wabash River, noting it for both James and Nelson's benefit. The hours and miles passed by quickly as they crossed the Illinois landscape: Burnt Prairie, the Mt. Vernon exit, Richview, New Baden, and soon after noon, the skyline of St Louis. Off to the north the arch of St. Louis's main feature could be clearly seen.

"That," Silas proclaimed with enthusiasm, "will have to be our first sightseeing stop. You have to see the Arch. It is called the Gateway Arch. We stopped in there when I was still with the young folks."

"The Arch? We are stopping there?" Sarah spoke up.

"Yes," Silas answered, not sure what the tone was in her voice. "You've never been up it have you?" Outside the traffic was quickening as the van crossed the Mississippi river.

"You'd better watch your driving," Martha told him, glancing at the loose way he was holding the wheel. "This is Saint Louis and the traffic can get bad."

He absentmindedly brought his other hand up, placing those fingers lightly on the bottom, keeping his eyes on the road.

"I think that would be a great idea," Sarah told him,

going back to his question. "I've never been up, but this would be the time for it, with the whole family along."

Glancing in Melvin's direction, she saw that he was nodding his head.

"Gateway Arch it is then," Silas stated, his attention on the road at the moment.

Switching lanes and following the signs, Silas managed after multiple loops and turns to pull into the designated parking lot for seeing the Archway. "Not one single wrong turn," he pronounced loudly, letting go of the steering wheel and pulling out the keys.

"That's one thing you're good at," Martha assured him, giving him a generous smile. "I married you just for your driving skills."

"You did not," he retorted in mock indignation. "You better had not."

"No, it was because you were Mennonite."

"That's just as bad," he muttered, opening the van door. "At least I got you," he added, chuckling at his own joke.

Melvin grinned at this exchange, fully enjoying the humor and spontaneous outburst of his two in-laws.

"Some brother-in-law," Sarah said in his direction, noticing his reaction. "Don't worry, they're not divorcing."

"I didn't think so," he said, getting out.

Silas and Martha were already waiting and led the way to the visitors' lobby, where they stopped in front of the brochure display. Taking one out Silas read in a low voice for all of them: "This beautiful national park is here to remember the spirit of the country's pioneers, and stands as a memorial to Thomas Jefferson, our third President. He dreamed of the spread of freedom and democracy from 'sea to shining sea.' Central to the park is the Gateway Arch, a symbol of what this city of Saint Louis was to the opening of the West. From the dizzying height of 630 feet you will catch a stunning glimpse of the St. Louis area."

"Sounds interesting," Melvin said.

Silas continued, "Many people are interested in the construction of the Arch. The total cost came to $13 million. Of that amount, $11 million was for the Arch itself. 75% came from federal funds and 25% from the city of St. Louis. The remaining monies were spent on the Arch transportation system and were financed by Metro. During construction it was estimated that 13 people would die of construction accidents. Instead everyone lived to see the day when on October 28, 1965 the Arch was completed."

"Okay, okay," Martha nudged Silas's elbow, "what does it say about falling? Anything about it falling down?" She had suddenly developed fears at the sight of this three-sided, stainless steel tower, not that she was close up to it.

Silas moved on down the page and then turned it over. "Here it says, ya, right here. 'The Arch is designed to sway as much as 18 inches. It takes a 50-mph wind to move it 1 inch. Overall it is estimated that the Arch can withstand 150-mph hurricane conditions. Normally there is no sway to the Arch at all. The Arch is also built to withstand a strong earthquake.'"

"There you go," Melvin said, "safe as can be."

Martha seemed satisfied with that explanation, drawing in breath again as if it had been in short supply only moments before. Leaving the lobby together they all got in line for tickets. After collecting them, Silas gave James and Nelson their own to hold as they went through the gate for the ride up. Nelson insisted that he go first and proudly held out his ticket to the ticket agent, his three-inch rimmed hat balanced on his head as he tipped his face up and grinned.

The agent reached down, took the ticket, and then wiggled the hat back and forth in a playful manner. "So what have we here?" he asked. "A little Amish boy. How are you today?"

"Just fine," Nelson said in his little boy voice, unashamed and unafraid in this great unfamiliar English world.

Sarah wished Nelson would ask, "And how are you," but he had not learned that yet. Not that there was much chance for practicing, since the Amish do not use such English greetings among themselves.

James gave his ticket next and the others followed. With room for four in each car the group had to split up, Martha and Silas going with two other people they did not know so that Melvin, Sarah, and the boys could be together.

The ride started with a faint whooshing noise, proceeding up as the car gently adjusted itself horizontally for the tilt of the Arch. Sarah saw the boys' faces tighten in fear. "It's okay," she told them quickly. "See, this is the car that we are in." She held the palm of her hand out horizontally. "As we go up the car stays level, but since the Arch tilts on an angle" — she held up her other arm to show the contrast — "the car changes its position as we go up. When we get up to the top, though, it will look like this, like we are in a tunnel, because the Arch has come together." She held both of her hands straight with each other.

James nodded his head, but Nelson just hung onto the edge of his seat. He relaxed a little when the car slowly came to a stop, a red light coming on followed by a clicking sound of something locking in place.

"You may now disembark," a voice came over the speakers in the ceiling, the car doors opening automatically. James let out his breath in one long whoosh as they stepped out with Sarah holding to the boys' hands, one on each side of her.

"See, it's level," Sarah told them, "just like walking on the ground, and yet we are on top of the Arch."

Walking forward briskly, the four of them rejoined Silas and Martha, who were closer to the front of the car. The viewing windows were a short walk on up, and from there they could go up a small step, lean next to the glass, and look at the St. Louis skyline. They found themselves available windows and did so. Before them stretched the city for what looked like miles. It was a clear afternoon, with the Mississippi River running past the base of the Arch on the east side and a view of distant farmland beyond the city buildings.

When the two men crossed over to the west there was nothing but city as far as their eyes could see.

"It's all town now," Silas said in a hushed voice. "There was a day and time when it was not like this. When our country was founded, this was the place where the trappers, settlers, and adventurers gathered for the push west. At that time it was just a little town, a town where great dreams were put to the test as men and women started perhaps the greatest journey of their lives.

"They crossed here for some reason, when they could have crossed to the north farther up in Illinois, or even to the south. Yet they chose here. Maybe it was because it was easier, or maybe it was just that people like to do what everyone else does. Whatever the reason, they gathered here until it became known as the Gateway to the West. What is it about men, Melvin," he asked, glancing at his brother-in-law, "that causes them to be drawn to central points, to gather at gateways, to want to push through doors ever onward? Isn't it something?"

Melvin was looking at the skyline. A tall office building to his left had reflecting windows in which the sunlight cast a thousand images up and down the street. He barely heard what Silas was saying. "This really is something!" he finally offered, knowing he needed to give some response, wrapped up in the view before him. "Sounds like there's quite a history to the place."

"There is," Silas said quietly, his frame leaning forward into the little cubicle to get a still better view out the window.

They were interrupted in their musings when Sarah and Martha with the two boys joined them after getting their fill at the other side, mostly in fascination at the Mississippi River.

"Ready to go?" Martha asked, everyone nodding in answer, having seen what they came up for. On the way back down, James and Nelson rode the side-slipping cars with less fear, almost enjoying the feeling of the quick descent on their bodies.

Once down, Silas suggested they find a Shoney's for

supper, to which there were no objections. Half an hour later on the outskirts of west St. Louis they found one. After the meal he suggested they spend the night at the Motel Six across the street.

"We can hardly find a campground here at the edge of St. Louis," he explained as logic for his suggestion, even though none was really needed. "I'm too tired to drive much farther," he added for good measure.

Melvin glanced at Sarah before saying, "It's fine with me. I guess it won't cost too much for a motel, just for one night. Tomorrow evening we have to find a campground."

"It's decided then," Martha declared, relieved that camping was not on the schedule right away. "Motel Six it will be."

CHAPTER EIGHT

THE MOTEL SAT on a little knoll off the interstate, along with a McDonald's and an Arby's, its driveway circling around gracefully to the front entrance covered with a small canopy. Most of its rooms were laid out in the building farther to the right, over which the evening sun bathed the city line of St. Louis in red and orange.

Silas pulled up and stopped under the canopy, putting the van in park but leaving it running. Together he and Melvin went in, returning quickly to report that rooms were available and they had arranged to be next door to each other, numbers 201 and 203. Martha picked 203 right away, and Silas got back in the seat to drive to the rooms.

Sarah said she did not care one way or the other when Martha gave her a quick look. "A bed's a bed," she said wearily.

"Don't be so sure about that," Martha told her. "All motel beds are not the same. Believe me, I know from experience."

"Motel Six is good, though," Silas added quickly. "There shouldn't be much difference between two rooms in the same motel. We have stayed with them before, and these are nice people."

So it was that one weary group of travelers opened the

doors to the rooms around eight o'clock that evening and found the clean rooms and beds a welcome sight.

The last thing Silas told Melvin before shutting the door was, "Be sure and lock the door. This is still the edge of west St. Louis."

"You're just all doom and gloom," Martha declared, hearing the comment. "Don't worry, Melvin, he's just thinking the worst."

"Just trying to be helpful," Silas said, sticking the key in his door.

"I'll be careful," Melvin said to his retreating back as he picked up their two suitcases. Sarah already had their door open.

It did not take long, after their baths, to settle the boys down for sleep in the bed away from the front door. Sarah insisted on that, tenderly tucking them in and watching as they dozed off quickly.

Heading to the bathroom, she looked back in annoyance as the phone on the little desk by the bed started ringing.

"Who do you think that is?" Melvin asked sleepily, already stretched out on the bed, fully clothed.

"You'd better answer it," she told him, waiting by the bathroom door to see who it was.

"Why is it ringing? No one knows us and if they do, how do they know we are here?" he asked, still making no moves to answer it.

"Maybe I should answer it."

"No, leave the thing alone. It could be anybody," Melvin said from the bed, not sure he liked this city life with its ringing phones right in the room.

"But we have to answer it," Sarah insisted.

The phone rang for the fourth time. "Okay, I'll see who it is, but who would be calling us at a Motel Six in Missouri?" Melvin reached out to pick up the phone. "Hello?"

"Hey, Melvin," Silas's voice came through loud and clear, "just thought I would call to make sure you have locked the door. Use the bar chain, too."

"Ah, how are you calling us? You're next door. How do you know this number?" Melvin was not sure what to make of it.

Sarah whispered from in front of the bathroom door, "Who is it?"

He mouthed back, "It's Silas."

On the other side of the wall Silas chuckled. "I didn't scare you people, did I?"

"Well," Melvin said, "we weren't sure what was going on. How can you call like this?"

Silas chuckled again. "Sorry, I forgot that you might not know. See, each room has a phone. Ask Sarah about it. She probably knows about such things from being in New York. You can call from room to room by dialing the other person's room number. That's what I'm doing."

"Isn't it kind of expensive to call?" Melvin wanted to know.

"No," Silas told him, with noises like he was moving around his room coming though the phone earpiece, "the service comes with the room. It doesn't cost anything, really. But hey, what I was calling about. I just thought to mention that not only should you lock your door, you should put the chain in the chain lock."

"What is a chain lock?" Melvin wanted to know.

"It's a chain hanging on the door frame. You take the end of the chain with a little round knob on it and slide the knob into a keyway on your door. It keeps the door from being opened even if it should become unlocked."

"So that's what Sarah was doing with the door, but why would the door become unlocked?" Melvin wanted to know.

"I don't know. Big cities have pickpockets and such. Maybe they know how to open doors without keys. Just use the chain lock, and I will feel better, okay?"

"Okay. Well, good night then," Melvin said. "The boys are asleep already, but I will get up and check the door again. I'm sure Sarah did the chain thing, but if not, I will put it in."

"Okay, good night, then," Silas concluded, hearing Melvin hang up the phone on the other end. He put the receiver back, saying aloud to himself, "Why am I worrying about this stuff? No one bothers people at a Motel Six, do they?"

Martha was already sleeping and so didn't respond. Silas grunted, stretching himself out on the bed, finally falling asleep with a final thought: *I need to quit worrying about this stuff. It never happens anyway.*

❧

Some time later Melvin awoke with a start, hating the sudden awakening and his sense of complete bewilderment. Where was he anyway? Then he remembered, the low glow of lights through the front window shades bringing back the memory. They were at the Motel Six just outside of St. Louis.

He looked around the darkened room, his eyes searching for anything that might have awakened him, his ears listening for a noise that might be out of place. It was hard to tell with the hum of the city in the background, its unusual sounds assaulting his ears. The light through the shades from the streetlights caught his attention again. *Did no one ever sleep in this town?*

Everything seemed normal. Why did he wake then? It seemed to be more than just the normal waking, his subconscious telling him loudly he had heard something. Listening quietly again he heard nothing but vehicles going by outside and the breathing of Sarah and the boys. They seemed to be sleeping fine in this strange place. Why couldn't he?

Then he heard it again, certain it was the same sound that had awakened him. There was a movement of metal on metal as if someone was gently moving the two together, then a soft thud. He listened intently. It came from just outside, over by the windows that were letting in the light from the street — or was it from the door itself?

On the farm he could have told for sure, but here the sounds were strange, coming from different sources and directions and running all together in his brain. He listened, and softly it sounded again, this time becoming more insistent and intense, he thought. Someone must be trying to get in the door, just like Silas had said.

He shook Sarah gently. "Sarah, wake up. Someone is trying to get in."

She moved slowly. "Is something wrong?"

"Shhhh. Quiet. Someone is trying to open the door."

She did not move as she listened. "You are dreaming, Melvin. No one is trying to get in the door. Silas is just scaring you."

"Yes, there is. I just heard it."

She was fully awake now and listening. Neither of them moved in the silence. There was no noise, and then it came — a moving of metal on metal, and followed again by that thump.

"There is something," she whispered, her eyes wide, their blueness glowing in the low light from the street.

"I'm going out to look," he announced, swinging his legs out of the bed.

"No don't," she clutched his arm. "This is the city."

"So what am I supposed to do? Maybe they can't come in and maybe they can, but I'm not just going to lie in here all night listening to this. Maybe they're stealing things from the van."

"There's nothing in the van to steal," she whispered. "Call Silas and Martha's room and tell them. They might know what to do."

"Silas," he echoed, sounding skeptical. "Maybe they're stealing the van."

"That's possible," she still whispered. "Call them. Silas knows the city better than we do."

"Okay then," he decided. "What was their room number? I don't remember."

"Let's see. Ours is 201 and theirs is 203. I'm sure because Martha said that was the one she wanted. Just pick the phone up and punch in the numbers."

Melvin moved over in the dim light to the white phone — pausing when the noise outside the door sounded again, this time even louder — and then lifted the receiver. All the numbers on the face of the phone lit up as he punched in 2-0-3.

It rang once, twice, and then the third time. Silas's sleepy voice came on the other end at the fourth ring. "Hello?"

"Hey, Silas, this is Melvin, over in the other room. Someone is trying to get in our front door, I think. What are we supposed to do?"

"Someone tried to do what?" Silas's voice was groggy, his mind searching for thoughts.

"They're doing something outside our door," Melvin told him, "but we have the chain in place like you said so I doubt if they can open it."

"You're making this up, right?" Silas's voice was skeptical, memories of tricks played on him and tricks he'd played on other people running through his mind.

"No, I'm not," Melvin said. "The noise just happened again, and I think we ought to do something about it. None of us is going to be able to sleep over here until we do."

"Okay, okay, I believe you. Let me call the front desk and see what they can do."

"No, no," Melvin's voice was insistent, "not that. They might call the police and we don't want to be involved with them. I have a better plan."

"Like what?" Silas was really skeptical now.

Melvin took a second to finish working out his plan and then was certain. "Put your phone down the same time I do, and then, let's see ..." — there was silence as he calculated the distance to the front door — "... count slowly fifteen seconds. You know how to do that."

A grunt confirmed that Silas did.

"So after we have the phones down, we'll walk towards our front doors, going to fifteen thousand."

"And then what?" Silas was breathing deeply.

"We'll quietly unlock our doors, and on fifteen thousand we'll both rush out together. Whoever is out there will be so surprised they'll be into Saint Louis in no time."

"You want to holler?" Silas's breath was coming in short jerks.

"No, but you can. That would be perfect. One noisy, the other quiet. It will be really unsettling."

"Okay, let's do it. Phones down together."

There was a click on both ends.

"You're not going to do that," Sarah said, having heard the conversation on her end, putting the rest together by deduction.

Melvin said nothing, walking slowly towards the front door, counting under his breath. Arriving at the door, he felt the lock turning softly under his hand as he removed the chain with his other hand. He half expected a force to hit the other side, a rush of robbing fury to enter the room.

There was nothing but silence, though, as he reached fifteen and jerked the door open, leaping outside in a huge silent bound.

Later he was sure that Silas's bellow and his night clothing flapping from his own leap scared him worse than anything the two cats sitting on the hood of the van felt. They expressed their contempt at the intrusion of their night's session by spitting in rage and flying off in opposite directions.

Melvin caught himself just before he smashed into the van. Faint lines of claw marks lay in front of his eyes, traced all over the hood of the van, glittering in the light of the street lamps.

Silas, pulling his own stop against the van, glared at the scratches, then at Melvin, his breath coming in short jerks. "We'd better get inside," he gasped. "Do you know what we look like if someone sees us?"

"Like two idiot farmhands who got lost in the city."

"Something like that. Confounded cats, scratched the hood all up."

To their left came the distinct sound of a door opening. "Let's go," Melvin said, his voice trailing off.

Silas pulled his eyes away from the hood scratches, gathered himself together, and with what dignity he could find walked back to his room, his eyes looking anywhere but at the lady staring out of her front door at him, the front of her nightgown clutched in both hands.

Melvin made it inside his own door just after Silas closed his, completely overcome with a silent fit of laughter as he locked the door and slid the chain back into place.

"Have you two lost your minds?" Sarah asked from the bed, unable to see the mirth in the situation.

Melvin made it to the bed, holding his sides, finding relief in being able to sit down somewhere.

"So what was it?"

"Two cats," he said, when he could get the words out without an overabundance of noise.

"Cats?" she asked, still not finding anything funny after being awakened in the middle of the night in a strange motel room in fear of someone breaking in.

"Ya, just two cats," he said, calming down. "Silas's hood is all scratched up. They did a pretty good job of it. Must have been jumping up and down, falling off, that sort of thing."

"So it was nothing but cats," she muttered. "Do you think we'll get any sleep now?"

"I hope so." He was getting his last laughs out of his system. "That's some man your sister married." He choked up a moment with a fresh fit of laughing. "You should have seen him coming out that door, his night clothes flying — almost looked like a flying, hollering, feed bag."

"Hey, you shouldn't make fun of him. Martha did marry him."

"I wasn't making fun of him, just laughing, that's all. It was funny."

She rolled over on her side of the bed, tired of the conversation. "Goodnight," she told him sleepily.

He only chuckled as she drifted off to sleep.

CHAPTER NINE

WITH ALL THE excitement from the night, Sarah still woke at six o'clock, nudging Melvin till he stirred. She was a little surprised he was not up yet. At home, he would have been out and doing the chores already. For a moment he looked dazed, then sat up looking first at her and then at the two sleeping boys, wrapped up in their blankets. She saw the memories of the night slowly coming back to him as a grin spread across his face.

She ignored the grin, her memory not being as amusing as his. "We'd better get up," she told him. "Silas said last evening he wanted an early start. I suppose he still wants to, even with last night's boyish shenanigans from you two."

"Hey," Melvin protested, "it did sound serious."

"Well, I guess so." She softened as he leaned across the bed to kiss her. That too was different from home; he never kissed her in the morning. "Be careful," she whispered as she heard stirrings in the other bed. "They'll see us. Maybe you'd better go see if Silas still wants to go early?"

"I will do that," he yawned, reaching for his clothing, then heading out. Moments later the sounds of knocking came from next door. Sarah couldn't hear what they said, but Melvin was back in a moment. "He asked why I didn't call instead of knock, and said he still wants to go early, that we have a long ways to go — especially with monsters after us."

"I see he thinks it's funny too," Sarah told him dryly. "Did he say anything about breakfast?"

"No."

"Just like a man, I suppose. Well, let's get loaded then. Silas probably has plans to eat somewhere."

Thirty minutes later the van was on its way, the occupants having said their good-mornings sleepily to each other and taken off without breakfast. The skyline of St. Louis was soon behind them as Interstate 70 to Kansas City rolled out beneath the van wheels.

Sarah was still thinking of breakfast, especially for the boys, but decided she was not going to be the one to bring it up. She would see how long it would take before anyone mentioned it. If they wanted to drive all the way to Colorado without eating, that was just fine with her. Musing on her grouchy feelings she was surprised, as she normally felt quite cheerful in the mornings.

Martha finally brought it up. "Food," she exclaimed, looking over at Silas silently driving the van, his hands gripping the wheel. "What about breakfast? I can't believe how hungry I am." She laughed softly. "It must come from all those cats I chased around last night."

Sarah, her mood instantly elevated, joined in, the old family spirit coming back. "Maybe we should have gone out too, Martha, and burned up a few more fat calories than usual?"

Martha, poker-faced, turned around to look at Sarah. "You know, why haven't I thought of that? I could use it as a weight-loss device. Just turn cats loose to run around outside the house. I could chase them all night."

Sarah caught a glimpse of one of Silas's hands on the wheel. It was splotchy, with red and white in different areas. He was saying nothing. She decided not to look at Melvin in order to keep her straight face. "I never knew a cat could get two grown men so worked up."

"Ya," Martha grinned, "yelling like little boys. I'm glad we're never seeing those folks from next door again."

"Okay," Silas said, his voice letting go in a profusion of ventilating air, "you two can just be ungrateful and unthankful wives if you want to, but we were the ones willing to risk our lives for our families."

"Knights in armor," Sarah whispered to Martha, leaning forward in her seat.

"Wooden swords in hand," Martha whispered back, as they both dissolved into giggles.

"You going to help me out here?" Silas asked Melvin over his shoulder. "They're killing us here, and we the brave souls that we were, daring to face evil men with only our bare hands."

"Well, I suppose we did look pretty foolish coming out of those doors," Melvin allowed, a grin playing on his face. "You should have seen yourself."

"Why, how did he look?" Martha asked, alarm suddenly in her voice.

Silas noticed and decided to push his advantage. "Ya, how did I look?"

"Pretty funny when you made that leap. Think you scared me worse than the cats."

"He was in his night clothing, wasn't he?" Martha's eyes grew big as a vision of her husband appeared to her. "He jumped out of the door like that, didn't he?"

"Ya." Melvin was proceeding cautiously, not sure where this was going.

"And the lady next door saw you, right?"

"As we were going back in," Melvin said slowly. "She didn't get to see too much."

"Men," Martha proclaimed in exasperation. "Now I am glad we are going down the road, hopefully someplace far, far away."

"You said you wanted breakfast," Silas ventured, hoping to steer the conversation somewhere else.

"I suppose so," she muttered. "I think I do need some nourishment, now that I know what you were doing to our reputation. It kind of takes your strength away."

"Oh, honey," Silas tried his hand at cooing. "It wasn't that bad, and we were really brave boys."

Martha glared at him, then had to chuckle in spite of herself. "So where are we going to eat then, big man?"

He stuck his nose in the air, assuming a commanding posture. "There's an exit with a McDonald's coming up. It also has the Graham Cave State Park. We can get our food, stop in at the park and eat there."

"Isn't that too far out of the way?" Martha asked him, skeptical of his motives at the moment.

"Not really," he replied. "The cave is just a little way off the interstate."

"And why do you want to see the cave this morning?"

He shook his head. "For no particular reason. Just a nice place to eat. Better than indoors at McDonald's."

"You're not chasing any cat there are you?"

"No," he pronounced as both Sarah and Martha glanced at each other and dissolved into conspiratorial, sisterly laughter.

Silas lifted his nose into the air again, although a smile played on his cheeks. "You can assault me all you want, lowly souls, but I am the one who charged the evil in the nighttime to save the damsels from danger."

"Ya, cats," Martha muttered.

"It's the idea that counts," Silas declared, turning on his turn signal for the McDonald's exit. "The idea is the big thing."

Martha reached across the van to stroke his arm. "My brave little David with his sling shot," she said, bursting into laughter again.

"Okay," Sarah said, coming to his rescue, the older sister taking charge. "Let's get these boys to a restaurant — all four of them. My two youngest ones have got to be starving."

Silas already had his turning signal on for the right hand turn, pulling into the McDonald's and finding a parking space close to the front entrance. "Not too many people here," he commented as he put the van in park. They all climbed out.

"Are we still ordering and then taking it to the park?" Martha wanted to know.

Sarah and Melvin found that agreeable, nodding their

heads. Once inside, though, and the food ordered, Nelson and James wanted to eat at once.

"I'm hungry," James said. "Why can't we eat now?"

"Just wait a little," Sarah told him. "We are going to a park to eat."

James made a face but then seemed okay with the plans. Sarah turned to Melvin, whispering over his head, "Did you hear that? He said he's hungry."

Melvin nodded. "Yes, I noticed," he said, a smile on his face. "Our fears must be as groundless as that cat chase last night."

"Hey," Sarah's face lighted up, "you know, that might just be true." A great sense of relief flooded through her. Maybe God was sending them a message, showing them how groundless their thoughts of danger were. "Maybe this trip is doing him good," she whispered again.

Martha, who had turned around when they mentioned the subject and heard despite the whispering, told them, "I sure hope so. I was really worried about him."

"He's hungry this morning," Sarah concluded, feeling like a load had rolled off her shoulder as they followed Silas back out to the van and drove towards the park.

When they got to the park it turned out to be a low hill with a paved road going straight up it. Hollowed out under the hill was an open cavern, wide and high enough to hold several vehicles easily. "This is it," Silas announced. "Graham Cave."

Turning into one of the designated parking places, Silas stopped the van. About twenty feet away were picnic tables that were empty at this early hour. "Just perfect," Martha said. "Nobody else around. Pile out everyone and let's get this breakfast underway."

After the Egg McMuffins and Big-Breakfasts had been eaten, they walked over to the cave for a quick look around. Overhead the sky was clear and the air scarcely moving. Bright sunlight streaked through the trees at an angle, casting long shadows towards where they stood. At the entrance of the cave Melvin looked up over the edge of the overhanging lip of earth. "What a beautiful morning," he said aloud. "God's creation is a wonder."

"Yes, it is," Silas agreed with him. "To see the handiwork of God reminds me of how great He is. Sort of puts things into perspective at times."

Melvin quietly agreed with a "Yes," then added, "but I think it's time we should be going. Not that I want to rush off, but we have a ways to go yet, don't we?"

"Just like a man," Martha said from nearby. "Always wanting to get on down the road. I was still enjoying the place."

"Hey," Silas came to Melvin's defense, "I was enjoying the beauty just as much as anyone, but we do need to get going. We weren't planning on staying long anyhow."

"I guess so," Martha allowed, in that understanding tone of voice one uses when things are just the way they are. "We can keep an eye out for more places to stop and see, though, can't we? We have three days to get out to Colorado, right?"

"Right," Silas agreed. "We can take our time to look around, if Melvin and Sarah want to. I guess we'll just see things as we go along."

With nods Sarah and Melvin agreed, and five minutes later they were all on the interstate again. The next signs gave the distance to Columbia, Boonville, and Kansas City. Silas made himself comfortable in the driver's seat, adjusting the tilt and sliding it back all the way.

"Looks like you're settling in for a long haul," Martha commented, glancing at him. "I was hoping we could stop somewhere soon again."

"Just making myself comfortable," he told her, grinning. "I'm ready to stop whenever you are." Then he looked sharply at the road and the car ahead. "Oh no, I need to pass, I see." He turned on his left signal, a semi-trailer close behind him half blocking his turn. "Thank you," he said under his breath as the semi noticed the signal and pulled back to give him room, the car behind the semi following suit.

"Surprisingly heavy traffic for this time of day," Martha commented, noticing his maneuvers. "Probably the closeness to Kansas City that's doing it."

"You're probably right," he muttered, concentrating. "This makes me glad we aren't tackling Kansas City during the rush hour. This time of day should be about right though, even if Interstate 70 goes straight through downtown."

As he concentrated on the traffic, Martha reached down for the map beside her seat, opened it and began scanning for interesting spots to stop and see. Finding none at a glance she kept looking.

"Not finding anything?" Silas asked her, knowing what she was looking for.

"No, nothing interesting, but I'm still looking," she told him, disappointment in her voice.

When she said nothing for five minutes or so, he suggested, "If you can't find any places today, we can just drive on through, make some time, and then do more stopping tomorrow."

"We might have to," she told him, then turned around towards Sarah and Melvin to consult with them. "I'm not finding anything interesting for some distance, from what it shows on the map. If it's okay with you two we can just drive all day and then see more things tomorrow maybe."

"Fine with me," Melvin said, Sarah nodding her head in agreement.

"See if you can find a campground for the night," Silas suggested before Martha put away the map. "That way we don't have to look for it later."

She bent back over the paper, following the interstate into Kansas. "I don't know for sure," she told him, "but Bunker Hill looks interesting. It's on the other side of Salina. We could probably eat there right next to the Wilson Lake State Park. Ought to be campgrounds around there and the distance is about right to drive in one day."

He nodded his head. "Sounds good to me."

So they drove the hours away, chatting about family and church. Silas mentioned a difficult construction job he was on at the moment, which led to a discussion between him and Melvin about square footage, clear spans, and the maximum load bearing of overhead trusses.

Sarah and Martha tuned out rather quickly, turning to another matter. "Do you remember the meetings I told you we were having?" Martha asked Sarah.

Sarah nodded, "Revival meetings." She knew the term,

having heard it before from her sister, although never having been to one.

"We had them just two weeks ago, a real special time for us."

Sarah was astonished at the sudden springing up of tears in Martha's eyes. Her own face softened in sympathy as she asked, "Oh, what where they about?"

Martha wiped her fingers under her eyes. "Nothing in particular I guess, as far as the subjects go. Just the usual revival sermons."

Sarah waited, knowing there was more coming.

The tears welled up again. "This one evening he spoke on the family. Usually those subjects are on child training and that kind of thing."

Sarah nodded, not really knowing but sympathizing.

"Anyway, he spoke on barrenness" — the tears flowed freely now — "of God's grace to bear it, and how He gives blessings in other ways to those people. I know it was supposed to be comforting, but I just never thought I would be one of those people."

Sarah sat in silence, absorbing the news. So this was the reason. She had often wondered why Martha and Silas did not have children, but had never asked why. Seeing the tears on her sister's face, she wished they were both at home right now so she could get closer to her. Since they weren't she did the next best thing, reaching out to touch her arm across the space between them.

Silas and Melvin must have heard the turn of the women's conversation, because they fell silent and the talk of construction ceased. In the silence, the rhythmic pattern of the road was their companion, pa-ruummn, pa-ruummn, pa-ruummn.

Martha wiped her tears with her fingers again. "I'm sorry, it just came over me."

"Is there anything you can do?" Sarah found her voice, venturing to ask tentatively, bits and pieces of fertility jargon going through her head.

"We already tried," Silas said, shaking his head. "Outside of a miracle, there is nothing that can be done."

"We'll find the grace to bear it, somehow," Martha was quick to say, blowing her nose with a Kleenex she produced from the glove box. "God will give us only what we can take."

Silas didn't seem so certain, Sarah thought, glancing at his face and wondering what he was thinking. Did it bother him that he would never have any sons? She looked over at Melvin, his face sober — what would he think of a life without sons? The thought ran through her like cold water, a terror and an emptiness she could not even contemplate. Why was she blessed with two sons when her sister had none, not even a girl? The question was at once too complex, too frightening in its implications, too fragile for any man to handle with his own hands.

"We're just approaching Salina, I think," Silas broke into her thoughts without answering her questions. "The sign was back there about five minutes ago."

James and Nelson in the back seat finished the transition by announcing, "We're hungry, Mom," almost with one voice.

"I am too," she said wearily. Life was much too difficult

at times, she thought, but yet it called one back to it with the simplest of tasks, as if trying to help out, keeping things easy when the going got difficult.

"We'd better eat," Martha said, wiping her last tear away with the Kleenex. "Salina's probably as good a place to stop as we'll find before settling down for the night. How far is Bunker Hill?" She quickly reached down and unfolded the map again. "Another hour or so on the other side. It looks like there's a nice campgrounds there though. It should have a grocery store too, I would think, where we can buy supplies."

Silas said nothing, letting the motor of the van idle down as he touched the turn signal, pulling into the Salina exit lane.

CHAPTER TEN

WHEN THE SUN rose the next morning, casting its first rays through the trees onto the Wilson State Park campgrounds, just south of the Wilson Reservoir, it found the Yoder/Mast families already up with Silas bent over the fire pit. He lit the match on the third try, blowing on the little red flicker till it got going and greedily reached out for fuel to feed its hunger. A few minutes later, Silas perched the pan over the metal grill as the flame touched the bottom, turning sideways with little puffs of smoke as if it did not like the taste of metal.

"Eggs quick, someone!" he boomed, his voice carrying across the campground. "Bring me the eggs, please; the pan will soon be hot!"

Martha brought him the carton, shushing him in the meantime. "This is a campground and it's early. Some people might still be sleeping."

"I guess that is a thought," he said in a quieter tone.

"How can anyone be hungry with as much as we ate last night at Shoney's?" Sarah asked no one in particular from where she stood by the van, getting the two boys up and dressed.

"It was the tossing around on all those rocks last night,"

Silas put in his opinion of the state of affairs.

"I think it was the cats I was chasing," Martha stated with a straight face.

"Okay," Silas said, not amused. "That was yesterday, this is today. It really was the tossing and the night air."

"I didn't hear anything," Martha informed him. "You slept quite soundly when you were inside with me. You sure you didn't slip out to look for cats?"

Silas said nothing, intent as he dropped the eggs into the pan, ignoring her.

"It's an old joke now," Sarah commented from over at the van, supplying sisterly help.

"It is," Silas agreed, his hearing suddenly restored while he still concentrated on the task at hand. He grabbed another egg, cracking it into the pan. "I sure hope someone checked the dates on these eggs last night at the grocery store. They're acting strange. It's going to be hard enough to fry them without having old eggs."

"Maybe it's you?" Martha asked, deciding to leave the cat subject alone.

Silas looked up, cooing at her, "You know I'm an expert camper, egg maker, tent sleeper. It comes natural, in the family kind of thing."

"It does," Martha muttered, reluctantly. "Sure nothing of the family thing in me anyway."

"You can say that again," Sarah added her agreement. "Why did we never go camping growing up?"

"Probably so I could be embarrassed when I went with my husband and all his family experts to the campground," she stated firmly.

Sarah laughed at that explanation, so like her sister's perspective. "All families are different," she added comfortingly.

Silas was concentrating on his pan, cracking another egg open on the edge and gently dropping it in. "Hey, this one looks good," he proclaimed, as the round yellow yolk stayed together, sliding around on the butter.

Ten minutes later they were all gathered around the picnic table, their breakfast of eggs, bacon, orange juice, and semi-toasted bread in front of them on plastic throw-away plates. The morning mists surrounding the campground were fast lifting as the sun made its first serious attempt at breaking through.

"Pretty good, isn't it?" Silas commented on his own food as they began eating, confident in what the answer would be.

"Good enough for me," Melvin told him, while everyone else answered by their wholehearted eating.

"Looks like they like it," Silas congratulated himself. "Good food if I must say so myself."

Martha glared at him.

"Hey," he grinned, "it's not your fault you grew up in a non-camping family. You at least were smart enough to marry into one though."

"Does he ever stop?" Sarah asked, her sympathies totally with the non-camping side of the argument.

"He has nice qualities too," Martha assured her as if Silas were not around.

Melvin grinned, more to himself than anyone else. This was all new to him, having never seen Sarah and Martha like this before.

"What are you grinning at?" Sarah now glared at him, ready to defend the family in event of attack from another quarter.

"You have a nice family," he said sincerely, completely disarming her. "Really nice."

Martha raised her eyebrows. "My, somebody likes us. You hear that Silas?"

"Oh, I like you too," he mumbled, his mouth full of eggs. "You just can't camp."

"I think we'd better just leave this one and the cats alone, don't you think?" Martha asked him, her eyes in his direction. "Shouldn't we, honey?"

He grinned wickedly but nodded his head.

On either side of them, people began to stir. One fellow jerked up the zipper on his tent and stuck his sleepy face outside. Sarah could clearly hear him say to his wife back inside the tent, "Nough ruckus going on around here to raise the dead. You'd think people could make breakfast without this much fuss. Fellow can't find any peace on this earth."

Sarah grinned at Martha. "About as peaceful as staying at Motel Six with the cats, don't you think? I think I'll head back to the farm."

"Shhh, he'll hear you," Martha whispered, "and we're not mentioning cats anymore."

"Well, it's time to get up and go anyway," Sarah replied, but not too loudly.

"It is," Silas pronounced firmly, "before these women really get us all into a lot of trouble. Don't you think so Melvin?"

He nodded his head in agreement, getting up from the table and heading over to their tent. A few minutes later, the women had the table cleared off and the men loaded the last of the luggage into the van, packed around the tents. Silas made sure everything was tight before closing the rear hatch door.

"By the way," Sarah said to Melvin when they got into the van, her voice sounding a little strained, "in all the excitement of the morning I forgot to tell you that James has another cut and it was bleeding again, right through the bandage I put on yesterday. You think there's something serious going on?"

Melvin frowned at the news, glancing at her with concern. "I sure hope not. Maybe it will heal like the other one did. Remember, we decided this all might be just a scare."

"But what if it's not?" Sarah asked him, unable to keep her fears at bay, even with her earlier resolve to do so.

He thought about that for a moment. "I tell you what," he stated firmly, "as soon as we get back home, I think we should get him to a doctor and have this looked at. I don't think there's anything to it, but I would hate for there to be a real problem and we just ignored it."

"Why would a cut bleed all the time?" Sarah wondered out loud.

"I don't know," he admitted. "I guess that's what doctors are for."

"So what are we doing with the day?" Silas asked from the front seat, changing the conversation. "Everyone still feel like seeing some of the sights, or shall we head straight for Colorado?"

To the surprise of Melvin and Sarah, the two boys spoke up from the back. "Let's see something," James said, with Nelson seconding him.

"That sounds good," Melvin said and whispered to Sarah, "He must not feel too bad."

"What about you two?" Martha asked them, turning around.

"It's fine with me," Melvin told her while Sarah nodded her head, still thinking about James but deciding not to pursue it any further. Her fears could well be just that, fears.

"Okay, then," Silas said in Martha's direction. "Start checking the map when we get on the interstate."

As Silas reached I-70 at exit 199, Martha found the atlas and started looking at their route, running her fingers back and forth as she searched.

"Finding anything?" Silas asked, chancing a glance off the road towards her.

"Ya, just ahead is the Cathedral of the Plains. That sounds interesting. Not too far off the road. Want to try that?" she asked over her shoulder.

The others nodded, and fifteen minutes later Silas had pulled the van onto State Route 257 towards Victoria.

They saw the beginnings of the cathedral well before arriving, the front graced with two gray four-sided rooftops on massive square red brick turrets, the peaks reaching well over a hundred feet into the air with crosses on top.

The front of the cathedral was a high wall that rose to the full height of the building with a large oval stained-glass window in the center overlooking three arched doorways.

Behind the front turrets, the building itself stretched out its full length, completely faced with red brick, its Romanesque design on full display with supporting columns and arched windows.

"Looks Catholic to me," Sarah said, wrinkling up her nose.

"I believe it is," Silas commented. "It's got really good workmanship though, as usual I must say. Catholics seem to specialize in building."

"I wonder who laid all those brick," Melvin mused, giving the high walls a good look. "Can you imagine that? All that work and the scaffolds it must have taken."

"Might have some information inside," Silas guessed, "who built it and all."

They got out of the van and strolled toward the center doorway, the building looming larger and grander the closer they got. Above them, the oval stained-glass window cast colored light back to the sky from the early morning rays.

Martha craned her neck to see the tops of the turrets with their crosses. "What a place, and three ways in at that!"

As they entered, Silas paused to pick up a brochure. Opening it, he read, "Cathedral of the Plain — built by Volga-German immigrants at the beginning of the 20th century to give them a feeling of home. Its real name is St. Fidelis Church, but it was christened Cathedral of the Plains by William Jennings Bryan during one of his campaign stops when he was a candidate for President of the United States."

"So, it did take German labor to build the thing?" Melvin chuckled. "Why am I not surprised?"

"Good builders the Dutch are," Silas said, bending his arm around to pat himself on the back. "Good people too."

Other than chuckling, the others made no comments on his actions, moving forward to enter the main auditorium. Its arched ceiling rose high into the air with ornate columns on each side for support, the open expanse vast.

With Martha in the lead they started up the center aisle. Rows and rows of brown benches stretched out before them, climaxing in the distance in a raised platform supported by its own set of pillars.

Pausing in front of the platform, they looked up at the painting hanging above the pulpit that depicted a scene from the sufferings of Christ, enhanced by two ornately carved chandeliers suspended from the ceiling. A massive candle and holder stood on the main level in front of the raised platform. Here and there people sat in the pews, facing the altar in silence, meditating with bowed heads.

The room cast a unique spell over them. They stood for a few minutes in their own silence before filing back down the aisle and out the door, turning for one last look at the brick structure before getting into the van.

"Quite a church," Silas remarked as he pulled onto the interstate entrance ramp, accelerating the van into the flow of traffic. "So what's next?"

Martha was already opening the map, finding the Kansas page. She studied it for a few minutes. "The next place would be about, oh, twenty minutes, I'd say. It is the Chrysler Boyhood Home and Museum in Ellis, Kansas."

Martha paused, thinking, then asked, "Why would we want to stop in there?"

"You know — cars, inventions, and that sort of thing." Silas's voice was full of interest.

"Well, all you will see is his house, probably. Where he was born."

"It says museum too."

"Ya," she conceded, "if it's got cars, but who wants to see cars?"

"I do," Melvin put in his vote. "It just might be interesting."

"Okay," Martha folded the map, "let's see it then."

"You haven't asked me yet," Sarah told Martha dryly.

"Like it would do any good," Martha muttered, "would it, sister of mine, and why are you piling on me? You're supposed to be on my side."

Sarah had to chuckle at that. "No, it wouldn't, because I want to see it too."

"So, see, why would I ask you then?"

"Because it's good manners, maybe."

"We're sisters, what has that got to do with good manners?"

"You do have a point," Sarah agreed, still grinning.

Silas turned to Melvin with an exaggerated motion of his hand, waving it as far back as he could with his other hand still on the steering wheel. "Aren't you glad these two are now finally apart, safe from each other's claws. How did they ever survive until we came to the rescue?"

"I would leave cats out of it if I were you," Martha glared at him.

"I think you'd better," Melvin grinned. "That's not a very shining mark on our record."

"Oh, it's shining all right," Sarah informed him, jumping in the fray. "Just glittering with ignorance."

"Oh my, oh my," Silas bellowed in his best voice, waving both of his arms around in the air, ramming his knee up against the steering wheel to hold the van on a straight line, "she fireth both barrels. Have we been on the road together too long, or am I just imagining things?"

"Much too long," Martha whispered at Silas, laughing softly. "Now where were we?"

He put his hands back on the steering wheel, not answering her question.

"The Chrysler Boyhood Home and Museum," Melvin said, highly amused. This was definitely more interesting than the farm.

OVER THE HUM of the van tires on the pavement, the conversation turned to what might be happening at home, then to James. "Didn't I hear you and Melvin say something about taking him to the doctor when you got home?" Martha asked, shaking her neck to loosen the kinks from all the turning around she was doing in the front seat.

Sarah nodded. "We were thinking of it, at least letting a doctor look at him. I just can't keep my mind off the thought that he might be having a problem."

Turning around in her seat again, bending her neck, Martha looked back at the boys. James was leaning sideways with his head hanging awkwardly off the top of the seat, sound asleep. "He looks kind of white, doesn't he? Why's he trying to sleep this time of the morning?"

"See what I mean," Sarah said, "it's little things like that."

"You women might just be making a big thing out of nothing," Melvin reminded them quietly. "We'll just let the doctor look at him when we get home."

"Well, might as well stop worrying then," Martha sighed. "He's probably okay anyway."

"We're at the exit," Silas announced, slowing down and

pulling into the lane. The car behind him pulled left, whishing past.

A few turns later their destination came into view, the white, front gable of the home sticking out towards the street with two lower-level windows and one upper.

"That little story-and-a-half bungalow was his home?" Martha exclaimed. "Not much for the great car maker, I would say."

"We all have humble beginnings," Silas informed her in a exalted tone. "Take me, for example. Little carpenter, but destined for greatness."

"Ya, that's why I married you," she snapped right back, "all for the good ride."

"Tust, tust," Silas clicked his tongue on the roof of his mouth, "how she barks, but her lips are sweet."

Martha glared at him, then burst out laughing, unable to keep a straight face.

"See, she likes me!" Silas proclaimed triumphantly. "Now what have we got here?"

What they had was a small house, the front porch recessed in at the door, a dormer on the upper roof lined up with the porch window below, and in the yard a large American flag.

"So what did you expect?" Silas asked. "A mansion or something? He wasn't born rich after all."

"He just got rich after he was born," Melvin commented dryly.

"Ya, like me," Silas said, hope in his voice, but everyone ignored him, climbing out to head towards the house.

Once inside a young man in his early twenties greeted

them with a big smile. "Welcome to the Chrysler Boyhood Home and Museum. I will be your guide when you are ready to begin the tour."

Silas nodded for them all. "We're ready."

Holding out his hand their guide began his chatter: "Built in 1889. Just your typical nineteenth-century home in a midwestern style. Walter P. Chrysler's father lived here with his family from the time he built the home until 1908. This is the kitchen. It features an iron cook stove, cooking pots, and utensils from the era. Here in the living room we have an old pump organ, and in the bedroom a high-backed walnut wooden bed. It is matched by a marble-topped dresser."

The tour downstairs lasted for ten minutes, the young guide concluding his explanations at the base of the stairs, announcing, "And now the upstairs. When you are ready?"

"Ah," Silas cleared his throat, "I think we will pass on the upstairs. Can you tell us where the museum is?"

"Sure, right out the back here," the guide motioned towards the rear door, not moving from the stairs, though.

Silas started in the direction given until Martha punched him in the back, whispering, "You need to tip the guide. The tour was not self-guided."

"Ah, yes," Silas mumbled, fumbling for his wallet. Taking some bills out he gave them to the guide.

"You need to tip him, too," Sarah whispered to Melvin.

Melvin made a face, discreetly of course, but produced some bills and handed them over.

"Thank you," the guide told them. Whatever feelings he

was having about these visitors he kept to himself, disappearing towards the front of the house.

"We'd better get out of this place," Melvin told Silas as they walked out back to the museum. "They are going to rob us blind. We'll never get to be rich at these rates."

"I think the tipping's over," Silas grinned. "The museum's self-guided. At least I think we can enjoy it without having to shell out money."

Entering cautiously, on the lookout for any guides waiting to pounce, they walked through the exhibits. There was the shotgun Walter P. Chrysler had used for hunting, some of his books and photographs, as well as the executive desk he had used in his office at the Chrysler building in New York. What the men found most interesting, though, was the 1925 Chrysler previously owned by Walter's great-grandson.

"Come on," Martha told them after they had been standing in front of the Chrysler for a full five minutes, "it's time to go."

"Just a minute," Silas told her. "This might be a once in a lifetime experience. Look at these wooden spokes on the wheels. Those headlights sticking out like fog lights. Can you imagine today's people driving something like that?"

"No I can't, nor are you going to," she told him firmly.

"Something old-fashioned like that," Melvin chuckled, "we could almost drive it."

"Amos would never let you do that," Sarah informed him. "Now it's high time we get out of here if you start having ideas like that." She pulled on his arm. "Come on."

He made a mock showing of allowing himself to be led

out the door, then shook her off once they got outside. Chuckling, he then took her hand as they walked to the van.

Glancing behind her, she saw that Silas and Martha were doing the same. "Maybe we ought to go on trips more often," she whispered over his shoulder.

"I suppose so," he agreed, pulling her hand to his side, his fingers tightening on hers as he looked into her blue eyes.

She would have kissed him then and there if they weren't in public, but they were already back at the van anyway.

Once on the interstate again, they decided that the Prairie Museum of Art and History, just outside of Colby, Kansas, would be their last sightseeing stop of the day. Silas thought they could get there, see the place, have supper somewhere on the road, and still drive a little ways before stopping for the night.

They rode up to Colby through a balmy 78 degrees on the flat Kansas prairie. I-70 stretched out in a straight line for miles and miles with only slight changes in elevation. The signs for towns read Ogallah, WaKeeney, and Voda.

After Voda, Silas couldn't contain his curiosity. "What is it with these strange names anyway? How do people come up with this stuff?"

"They're quite interesting towns," said Sarah without hesitation.

"You know something about them?" Silas wanted to know.

"Of course — they're interesting towns."

"No, I mean, do you really know something about them?

"Well, I know a little, like Ogallah and WaKeeney are both in Trego County, which was first surveyed in 1867."

"Come on now, Trego County is easy. You probably saw it somewhere. But where is the 1800 stuff from?"

"We studied about the state in school. I still remember some of the towns and their backgrounds."

"That's an awfully long time to remember something."

"Not if you really like it. I took an interest in the Kansas prairie and some of the towns associated with the railroad. Warren Keeney and his railroad company out of Chicago selected the site for the town of WaKeeney. The name came from the first two letters of Warren plus his last name — hence, WaKeeney."

"Well, that's interesting," Silas allowed, a little exasperated at her. "What about the town of Voda?"

"I don't remember anything about it."

"Maybe the railroad didn't go through it."

"Could be."

Silas cleared his throat. "We have the town of Quinter coming up here. You know anything about it?"

"Would you quit pestering her," Martha admonished him. "She's already told you enough."

"Hey, this is interesting stuff," Silas insisted. "You don't even have to pay an entrance fee for it, like that robber's lair back there we just came through."

"Don't pay any attention to him, if you don't want to," Martha said, turning around to look back at Sarah, rubbing her neck from another kink.

"No, that's okay," Sarah said with a smile. "The Quinter history concerns the Brethren church. In the spring of 1886, two men from a colony of Brethren came by covered wagon and purchased land in the town, but had some trouble with it. A new town company finally straightened everything out, renaming the town after one of the Church of the Brethren's noted ministers, Elder James B. Quinter. So we have the town of Quinter."

"Well, who would have thought that?" Silas said, impressed.

"You could be nicer about it, couldn't you? She did tell you," Martha reminded him.

"I will remember that next time," Silas replied, keeping his eyes on his driving. "Colby is coming up in about an hour, and I won't need any information about it," he added as if it were an afterthought.

The Prairie Museum of Art and History turned out to be north of town, containing the Cooper Barn built in 1936 as part of the Foster Farm Operations and a Presbyterian Church first located in Gem, Kansas, and then moved to the current site in 1988. There was a one-room schoolhouse, a sod house, and the Eller house built in the 1930s as part of a farmstead. Artifacts included clothing, furniture, and objects from 1930s farm life.

After wandering around, the tired group returned to the van, headed south on highway 25, and then proceeded west on I-70. "So what's the plan now?" Silas wanted to know, yawning, his hand over his mouth.

"Let's get out of Kansas," Martha suggested. "I've seen enough sites for one day." The others silently agreed.

With the late afternoon sun in his eyes, Silas kept the van at the maximum speed allowed, making good time.

It was the boys' hunger that stopped them for supper. They bought food from the drive-through and kept going. Martha made that decision, after warning the boys to be careful with their food in the back.

They crossed the Kansas line into Colorado and, seeing a sign for camping outside of Burlington, Silas suggested they should go there. He reminded the others that he hadn't seen a camping sign in quite a while.

"Sounds fine to me," Melvin agreed. "I'm tired enough to stop for the night anyway."

"Tomorrow it will be Focus on the Family, then," Martha announced for all of their benefit, as Silas took the exit.

CHAPTER TWELVE

THE FEW TREES around the campground on the flat plains did little to give shelter, and piercing rays of sun shone through the lower trunk line on the horizon, waking the weary travelers before they were quite ready. However, the sun did nothing to scare off the buzzing mosquito outside Silas's screened tent window. He had heard the sound during the night and, confident he was safe, had ignored it.

Silas now glared at the tiny insect. "Did the sun catch you without breakfast, my little honey? Well, to a short hungry life for you, my little pest."

"He's just a mosquito," Martha protested.

"If he comes inside now, I can swat him," Silas said maliciously, his eyes shiny with intent. "He's probably afraid to since the sun is shining. Only does his dirty deeds in the night when no one can find him, the little, lowdown rascal."

"He's bigger than the ones at home," Martha observed wryly. "Maybe they grow larger and aren't as scared on the plains."

Hearing Melvin and Sarah stirring outside the tent, Martha and Silas left the mosquito to his own devices. Breakfast was prepared, blessed, and eaten in short order. They packed the van were back on the interstate by 7:30.

Following Martha's instruction to come in on the north side of Colorado Springs, Silas passed the exit for Highway 24 and instead took the next exit, heading across the state on route 86 through Kiowa and Franktown. Picking up Interstate 25 at Castle Rock, he turned south, keeping an eye out for the Focus on the Family sign. Ten minutes later he found it, slowing down to take the exit.

"It's not a very big sign," he commented to Martha.

"I like it," Martha told him. "They are a large organization, but it just shows they don't need to make a big show of things. Look at some of the billboards we've been seeing. Large signs don't mean the businesses are all that great."

"So what is Focus on the Family again?" Sarah asked, curious now that they were close. "You told me a little about it at home, but that's all I know."

"It is headed by James Dobson," Martha told her, "a man we have learned to appreciate. He reaches out to families with radio programs and books on child training, marriage instruction, and compassion for people in general. Dobson's father was a Nazarene evangelist."

"Here's the Welcome Center," Silas announced, pulling up to the parking lot in front of a low-slung assembly of red brick buildings, set against a backdrop of distant mountains. Lines of off-white limestone lay across the red brick, shining with regal dignity.

They all walked toward the door, a conspicuous sight in their Amish and Mennonite attire since the parking lot was almost empty.

"I thought there would be a lot of people around,"

Martha said, holding the swinging doors open for the others.

"It might be the time of day," Silas suggested quietly as a security guard approached them. He shook their hands, informing them the next tour would be at the top of the hour and introducing them to Cindy, who would serve as their guide.

A tall girl in her early twenties, Cindy greeted them and wrote down their names on a tablet, then left to return a moment later with nametags for everyone.

"Put these on, and we should be ready for the tour when it starts," she smiled. "Where are you folks from?"

"Indiana," Sarah told her. "My sister here is well-acquainted with the organization and suggested we stop in during our trip."

"We are glad you did," Cindy smiled again. "We have people stopping in from all over. Later in the afternoon it is usually quite busy around here, but at this time of day there are not as many visitors."

Cindy stayed with them until the tour was to start, welcoming a few other visitors as they arrived. She then led the way further into the building, explaining how the Welcome Center came to be. When friends in Michigan became aware of what a distraction it was for the staff to have only the Administration Building for tours, they gave a four-million dollar donation to build the Center.

"Now we have tours both here at the Welcome Center and at the Administration Building," Cindy said, pointing through one of the windows at a building in the distance.

"Focus on the Family is first and foremost evangelical in nature," Cindy continued. "Dr. Dobson always stresses that our number one goal as an organization is 'to cooperate with the Holy Spirit in spreading the Gospel.' We give daily 'Focus on the Family' broadcasts. There is a kids' program, 'Adventures in Odyssey.' We make videos for teens and have several magazines covering the entire family. Our goal is to minister to people's needs."

Sarah was moving forward to follow Cindy when she was interrupted by James pulling on her arm. "Mom," he whispered, "I don't feel well."

She stopped, looking at him with concern, feeling his forehead. The group separated to go around her as Cindy continued talking. Melvin noticed her absence and went back to check on her. The three of them standing away from the group caught Cindy's attention, and she walked back to them.

"Is there a problem?" she asked, concern in her voice.

"I don't know," Sarah said quickly, not wanting to make a fuss. "He says he feels sick. He's been feeling tired, but we thought he was doing better."

Not paying much attention to what Sarah was saying, Cindy looked James over. "He doesn't look well," she commented, then asked James, "How do you feel?"

James shrugged his shoulders. "It hurts all over, like. My head feels funny."

Cindy laid her hand lightly on James's head and studied his face from closer range. She turned to Sarah. "Do you want me to call for medical help?"

"You mean like an ambulance?"

Cindy shrugged. "It could be that, or you could just take him to one of the local hospitals."

Sarah didn't know what to say, glancing at Melvin, who simply nodded his head. Martha, too, nodded her affirmation. It was Sarah's fears, though, rooted in a conviction that something was wrong, that decided the matter for her. "I guess so, but won't that be a big problem? I mean, it might not be something serious after all."

"It could just be the flu," Cindy agreed, "but a doctor might be able to help with that too, and it would not be a problem at all. The hospitals are right close to here."

Melvin glanced at Sarah, then turned to Cindy. "We'd really rather not go to an emergency room. Is there a doctor in town we could take him to?"

Cindy thought for a minute, running the options through her mind, then told them, "Wait a minute and I will see what I can do."

They waited, a little self-consciously, appearing even more conspicuous in their distinct clothing as they stood apart from the others. Before things got too uncomfortable, though, Cindy returned with another tour guide to carry on with the others while she turned her full attention to them, concern written on her face.

"There's a Dr. Bradshaw downtown," she told them. "He's associated with Doctors' Hospital. We just called his office about your situation, and he can see you if you come right down."

"Okay," Sarah sighed, deeply thankful. "We can't thank you enough for this, though I so hope it's not too much bother. We really are sorry about this." Sarah glanced around nervously at the strange surroundings, which suddenly seemed even more unlike home than they had only moments before.

"It's fine," Cindy assured her, distracted by all the thoughts running through her head. She then turned her attention back to James. "Now, little boy," she said, kneeling down in front of him and laying her hand on his shoulder, careful not to disturb his hat, "let's go see what the doctor can do for you, shall we?"

He nodded his head, his face a little pale, and they followed her to the front of the Welcome Center. Sarah expected Cindy to give them directions to the doctor's office; instead she offered to go with them, saying it would easier if they just followed her. It was not far away, she assured them, just down on East Pikes Peak Avenue.

Sarah could see that Melvin was not comfortable with this arrangement. It was all a little too much for him, she knew, as she watched him approach Cindy. "We don't want to be a bother," he said, clearing his throat. "If you just give us directions, I'm sure Silas can find the way down there."

"It won't be any bother," Cindy assured him. "That's what we're here for, to help people. Besides, I'd just as soon be doing this than giving tours," she chuckled. "Not that that's not interesting too, but I'd really like to see what this little fellow's problem is. If I just let you go down by yourselves, I may never know." She smiled at James.

Melvin was still uncertain, Sarah could see, but Cindy's obvious willingness and kind words were overcoming his hesitation. "Okay, then," he said, accepting her offer.

The ride downtown went quickly enough as they followed Cindy's white Buick, pulling into the tiered parking lot and finding a spot on the second deck. Cindy led them briskly to the elevator, where they stood quietly while being lowered to the next level.

Entering a large office complex, Cindy seemed to know her way around, because she continued without checking the directions on the large board of doctors' names by the front entrance. They took another elevator to the fifth floor and a few turns later arrived at door 550.

Cindy entered without knocking and was told by the secretary that Dr. Bradshaw would soon see them, that they were to wait in the small waiting/playroom.

CHAPTER THIRTEEN

WITH MELVIN ON the other side of the room and the boys shifting in their seats beside her, Sarah noticed Cindy studying her. She remembered that Cindy had looked twice at her before, but she had thought nothing of it. Now, in the silence of the doctor's office, she began to feel very self-conscious.

"Excuse me for staring at you," Cindy said, not at all nervous, which helped, "but you somehow look familiar."

"Really?" Sarah was both surprised and puzzled.

"Yes, I'm sure you do, but I didn't know this girl was Amish."

Sarah was even more puzzled, and it showed.

"I'm sorry," Cindy said, a little embarrassed now. "There is no way it's possible, but you look like a girl who modeled the Densine Line for Maxey Jacobs, many years ago. I was younger then and really liked their designs. I still have a few of the dresses. It's funny how people look alike."

"I did model for them," Sarah told her quietly, the memory of it coming back fresh in her mind.

"Are you serious?" Cindy exclaimed. "You're Amish. Amish people don't model, do they?"

"Normally I suppose they don't," Sarah allowed, "but this one did in her younger days."

"You really did?" Cindy was enthralled. "Then you also dated the owner of the company, what was his name? Phillip, yes."

Sarah chuckled, "Well, we didn't really date."

Cindy was not put off so easily. "Tell me more about it. How did you get the chance?"

"Through one of my mother's friends," Sarah told her. "Her son knew Phillip and told him about me. They invited us, me and my sister" — Sarah motioned over to Martha — "to New York City. One thing led to another and I worked for Maxey Jacobs about six months."

"Did he propose to you?" Cindy wanted to know, leaning forward on the chair.

"Phillip?" Sarah laughed, "No, it never got to that point. We both knew we weren't meant for each other's worlds. He was a wonderful young man, though. The story was published in a book called *Sarah*. He married a short time later, and his wife had connections with a publishing house."

Cindy's eyes were shining. "That's quite some story. I never thought an Amish girl would have such an opportunity."

"Life takes unexpected turns sometimes," Sarah said, becoming sober again at the thought of James.

"I'm glad to have met you," Cindy said, noticing her shift of attention, and turned to watch Nelson, who had now gone into the playroom.

Martha, seated two chairs over, leaned across, lowering her voice so the others would not overhear. "Your past coming back to haunt you?"

Sarah made a face. "It's not haunting me. I did nothing to be ashamed of."

"You sure about that?" Martha looked Sarah sideways in the face. "You were up in New York by yourself for a long time."

"I didn't — now stop thinking such thoughts. You know better than that."

"I suppose so," Martha nodded her head, leaning back in her own seat. "Sister Saint."

Sarah thought she heard the remark, but chose to ignore it. There were more important things pressing on her mind.

⮞

A nurse soon came, introducing herself as Melody, and took James back, inviting Sarah and Melvin to go along. After getting them settled in one of the rooms, she left with James to weigh him, then returned to check all his other vitals and left them with a promise that the doctor would be in soon.

Five minutes later an older man with white hair came through the door, his stethoscope dangling, a smile on his face. "I am Dr. Bradshaw," he introduced himself. "How are you today, James?" He paused to acknowledge both Melvin and Sarah. "So we are having some problems, are we?"

James shrugged his shoulders, his eyes on the floor.

"Well then, why don't you come up and sit on this table, James, and we can get started. You're from Indiana right?"

James allowed himself to be helped onto the table, nodding his head in affirmation.

"So tell me the history," Dr. Bradshaw said to Sarah after James was seated, giving her some basic questions about when she first noticed any problem.

Sarah soon had the whole story out, going over the bleeding, the weakness, the loss of appetite, and the cuts that wouldn't heal. Dr. Bradshaw grunted but made no comment, moving to get a good look at James, asking more questions as they occurred to him. He finally wanted to know if he could take a blood test.

"Sure," Sarah said. "Is there a problem, you think?"

"There might be," the doctor said, "so I would really like to examine his blood."

Opening the door into the hallway, Dr. Bradshaw quietly called for Melody, standing by when she came in to draw the blood sample. When Melody left with the test tube, he told Sarah she could take James out to the waiting room and she would be called when he knew something more.

Going down the hall after Melvin, who was protectively keeping James near him, she saw the back of Dr. Bradshaw retreat into what was obviously their lab. Out in the waiting room, as they took their seats, Martha grabbed Sarah.

"What did the doctor say?" she whispered.

"Nothing, yet. He's taking a blood test."

Martha winced, Sarah noticed, and said quietly, "Surely it can't be anything that serious."

"I don't know, but I want you to be with me when he brings back the results," Sarah told her, reaching out for the familiar ties of family comfort.

"I'd be glad to," Martha assured her, settling back into her seat.

"Okay, then," Sarah told her, "just come back with me and Melvin when they call us."

Melody appeared ten minutes later, leading the three adults back to the office, closing the door with a gentle smile. "Dr. Bradshaw will be right with you."

When Dr. Bradshaw arrived, concern on his face, he looked surprised at finding an extra adult in the room. Sarah noticed and quickly introduced Martha. "She's my sister. I hope it's okay. I just wanted some family support if the news was really bad."

"That's okay," Dr. Bradshaw assured her, taking his seat on the three-legged stool by the countertop full of syringes, bottles of medicines, and test tubes. Then he asked Sarah, "Has your boy been examined by a doctor in the last six months?"

"No," Sarah told him, "there was no reason to that I could see. We normally don't go in just for the flu, unless it gets serious. Although with this problem we were planning on having him checked out when we got back home." She glanced at Melvin, who nodded his head.

Dr. Bradshaw pressed his lips together. "I don't want to break this news to you before I know for sure, but I believe your boy is quite sick."

"Sick with what?" Sarah asked, her voice strained, her heart pounding.

"Like I said," Dr. Bradshaw wrinkled his brow, "I would prefer to send this blood test out for confirmation. Maybe you could come back in the morning and we can talk more."

Sarah glanced at Melvin, who shook his head, confirming her feelings. "Really, doctor," she quickly told him, "I would really like to know what you think now. If you want us to, we can come back tomorrow for the verification, but I would like to know what you think is wrong with my son."

Dr. Bradshaw shifted in his chair. "Okay, but just to let you know that it will ultimately take a bone marrow sample to confirm this. It looks to me like your son has leukemia."

"Leukemia!" Sarah exclaimed, weakness going through her whole body.

"Yes," Dr. Bradshaw said quietly, "acute lymphocytic leukemia."

CHAPTER FOURTEEN

S ARAH SAT IN the doctor's office in stunned silence, unable to move, her mind numb, Melvin standing beside her equally still. Caught in the horror of the moment, they looked like deer frozen in headlights.

Dr. Bradshaw looked at them with concern. "Are you okay? I know the news is kind of abrupt if you had no prior warning. I'm very sorry for your son."

Martha was the first to move, coming over to place her arm around Sarah's shoulder. She said nothing, though, for what was there to say at such a moment? "It will be okay" or "I'm so sorry" seemed out of place, inadequate.

Ultimately, it was the tears that pushed Sarah to move. They rolled slowly down Martha's cheeks in twos, then in threes, dropping on Sarah's hair and forehead. To Sarah's stricken mind, the gentle splats felt like great blasts of energy, awakening her. With the awakening came the first waves of pain, reaching into every part of her body with almost physical force.

"Will my son die?" she asked Dr. Bradshaw with as firm a voice as she could muster.

"I don't know," he said. "The disease seems, in my opinion, to be in its early stages, but your son really needs to be examined by a specialist in this field. A lot of advances have been made lately with treatment for leukemia."

"How are we going to get him home?" Sarah wanted to know. "How sick is he?"

"I believe you still have time for the trip home. Most leukemia does not progress that fast. Come back tomorrow morning for the results from the lab. Then get the boy back home as soon as possible and to a specialist in Indianapolis. I will give you a referral," he said, scribbling on his pad.

"Thank you, doctor," Melvin finally responded, taking Sarah's hand. "Let's go," he told her softly.

"Just a minute." Dr. Bradshaw motioned for them to wait while he went to the waiting room where Cindy was waiting with the others. He came back with her in tow. Addressing Melvin and Sarah he said, "I have asked Cindy if she would, and she will be taking care of arranging your lodging needs for the night. We don't want you having to wander all around Colorado Springs."

Cindy nodded in agreement. "I can, if you want, take you all back to the Welcome Center where arrangements can be made."

Melvin was stunned again by their kindness, not sure what to say. "That is very kind of you, but haven't we been enough of a bother already?"

"It's not a problem," Dr. Bradshaw assured them. "Cindy will be glad to do it for you."

She nodded her head, soberly, seeming to share in their shocked sorrow. "Why don't we go on back to the Welcome Center and we can make some plans there, okay?"

There was really nothing to do but assent, as their strong

sense of justice would forbid the turning down of compassion during such a time of need. Trained by religion and custom to care, they were equally taught to accept, though not to ask for the same.

They returned to the Welcome Center, where, in short order, reservations were made for them to eat at a restaurant and sleep at a motel for the night. Both were nearby and came with deep discounts for both families, courtesy of Focus on the Family.

Although it seemed incomprehensible that they would feel like eating, they all went anyway. Sarah was hoping James would not notice anything unusual, as the last thing she wanted was to answer questions right then. On the few occasions she had taken James to doctors or dentists, he usually was more concerned about getting back home to his routine than about what such medical experts had to say.

Sitting there in the restaurant waiting for their food to come, she knew this time would be different. He would ask, and she knew she would tell him. That was why she wished the conversation would never start, yet she knew it had started already, without her consent or knowledge. They were but two people, a mother and her child, caught in the middle of an ongoing drama they neither controlled nor could end. By that connection of the heart, he knew that something was wrong.

"Mommy," James asked her, looking up from unrolling his spotless knife and fork from the napkin, "am I going to die?"

She found to her own surprise that the stark question was a relief, that it cut through the suspense and the fog to her heart, and found it ready with an answer. "I don't know," she told him. "Only God knows that."

"It's bad then?" he asked, the blue eyes he got from her turned towards her. She wondered how something so innocent could be assaulted with something so evil, as tears threatened her composure, but she resolved to remain strong and simply nodded.

She could tell what he was thinking and she waited for his next query. "Will I ever be better again?" he asked finally.

"I think so," she said. "We will have to take you to a good doctor when we get back home."

"Can he take care of it?" he asked, his brow knitted in concentration, wondering if something as bad as this must be could ever be overcome.

"We hope so," she said, and then knew the answer was not good enough, but it was all she had.

"Will I go to heaven then?" he asked. "It's a nice place, isn't it?"

She wondered how he knew to ask this stuff. Martha, who had been listening silently, forsook her attempts at hiding the now tear-soaked napkin and openly dabbed her eyes.

"Yes," she told him, "it's a very nice place, because Jesus will be there."

Where did that come from? she asked herself. Her religion did not go out of its way to teach that angle of things. Looking down at his face raised towards her, she knew where it came from. It came from her heart. How could she say anything else? Did she not love him with a force that ached inside? Was there not a God? Was not the face of that God the face of Jesus? Had He not formed love out of his own heart? She blinked her eyes rapidly lest her tears come in front of James.

"It'll be all right," he said, nodding his head. "I'll be okay."

He's comforting me, she thought. *Isn't that strange? Maybe he knows that he's gone already. Maybe heaven has already come close to him to welcome him home.* Her heart beat wildly in her, stunned at the thought of it. *Please, God,* she pleaded, *don't take him from me! He's still so young, and I want to see him grow up.*

She reached out, running her hand across his head as the food arrived. To her surprise, he ate hungrily, as if in relief, and stayed that way throughout the meal. After they left the restaurant, the rest of the evening was uneventful as they gathered their thoughts together the best they could.

Melvin made a point of kneeling down for prayer with Sarah and the two boys before she tucked them in. As Melvin was about to begin praying, his hand around James's shoulder and Sarah and Nelson on the other side, Silas and Martha tapped on the door. When Sarah answered they first apologized for interrupting and then joined them at the bedside.

In the morning they got up early and were back at the office complex on Pikes Peak Avenue by seven. Walking through the front door they were surprised to find Cindy waiting for them.

"You're up early," Sarah told her.

"Well, I wanted to be here when you came back," she told them. "Dr. Bradshaw is waiting for you."

"Did he tell you what the results were?" Sarah asked.

Cindy hesitated. "Yes, he did, but I think he's supposed to tell you."

She led them quickly to number 550, opening the door for them, then followed Melvin and Sarah inside. While the others waited on the plastic chairs, the nurse took Melvin and Sarah back to the same office room they had been in the day before. Dr. Bradshaw soon opened the door and greeted them quietly.

"The results have been confirmed," he told them. "From what we can tell from a blood test, it looks like some form of leukemia. My guess is Acute Lymphocytic Leukemia in its initial stages, but none of that is sure until they do a bone marrow extraction. Here is the name of the doctor in Indianapolis and referral information," he said, handing them the papers. "If you have any problems, please let me know. There should be none, though, as Dr. Watkins in Indianapolis specializes in leukemia and lymphoma. He's a good doctor."

Melvin and Sarah both rose to their feet to thank him for his time and concern.

He simply nodded, expressing his best wishes and God's blessings to them, as he held the door open for them. "We will all hope for the best."

At the office door, they turned to thank him again before walking down the short hall to the waiting room. Cindy saw them coming and stood up, then approached with a question: "We were just wondering if you would come with me back again to the Welcome Center. I have been asked by Dr. Dobson to convey an invitation to you and everyone in your group to join in our devotional time this morning. We would be very glad to have you."

"Ah," Melvin said, clearing his throat, "but we don't know Dr. Dobson." He looked puzzled. "We really shouldn't bother him. You people have already done plenty for us. The food and lodging last night were worth much more than what we paid for them."

Cindy shrugged. "We were only glad to help. But we really want you to join us this morning. I shared your story with Dr. Dobson last night and with some of the other staff. They have been praying for you. We would be honored to have you join us this morning."

It seemed strange to Melvin that these strangers should care. Why it was so, he could not figure out, yet even with his feelings of discomfort, he felt compelled to accept. "I suppose so," he finally nodded his head in agreement.

Gathering the group in the waiting room, Cindy led the way down the halls and out to their vehicles. When they arrived at the Center, little was moving in front of the beautiful red building with its turreted entrance. Over the mountains the sun had just risen, bathing the Center with warm light.

"It is sure beautiful around here," Silas remarked as they got out, to which Sarah and Melvin numbly agreed, the beauty not fully impacting them at the moment.

Once inside Cindy took them to a door marked *West Conference Room*, where she held the door open and motioned for them to enter. Inside, a small group of around twenty-five people stood up to greet them, with a tall, well-built man stepping forward and extending his hand.

"I am so glad you could come," he said, with warmth and a soft smile playing together on his face, reaching out to shake first Melvin's and then Sarah's hands before turning to Silas and Martha.

"I am James Dobson," he said, directly addressing Sarah. "We heard about your boy last night. Is this James?" he asked, squatting down and taking James's right hand in both of his. "I am so sorry to hear that you are sick."

James looked at him, down at his same level, with his serious blue eyes, blinking a few times. "I think I am going to get better soon," he said bravely. "Mommy said we're going to see a good doctor. If he can't help me then maybe I'm going to see Jesus."

James Dobson didn't say anything for a minute because he couldn't. "You have a good mommy," he finally said before releasing James's hand and rising to his feet.

Cindy then stepped in quickly to complete the introductions, since none had been made up to that point. Sarah wondered how in the world James Dobson knew who James or the mother were, then received the answer with his next statement. He said that Cindy passed on to him the night before about an Amish couple's young son who had just been diagnosed with possible leukemia.

I guess we do look quite different from them, Sarah thought as she glanced over at Silas and Martha.

Dr. Dobson cleared his throat before continuing. "I hope you don't mind her telling us that? When I heard that you were going back this morning to Dr. Bradshaw's office, I asked Cindy to meet you there and invite all of you to our devotional. We would count it a privilege to pray with you before you leave."

Melvin and Sarah both shifted nervously on their feet but nodded, taking the seats offered them within the circle of people. No one seemed to notice their discomfort. Once settled, Dr. Dobson wasted no time in getting started. "I would like to read the 145th Psalm," he said, opening his Bible as did the others.

Someone passed a Bible to the visitors, and Dr. Dobson then read the entire psalm about how David had exhorted the people to bless forever the name of God. "...The Lord is gracious and full of compassion; slow to anger, and of great mercy. The Lord is good to all: and his tender mercies are over all his works.... The Lord upholdeth all that fall, and raiseth up all those that be bowed down. The eyes of all wait upon thee; and thou givest them their meat in due season.... He will fulfill the desire of them that fear him; he also will hear their cry, and will save them...."

Closing his Bible, he said, "We don't know why trouble happens to us. Yet we can know that God will always love and take care of us. He is a God of great compassion who in the end will make all things turn out right. We here at Focus want to pray with you that you might walk in that love during this time of trouble, that God would strengthen your faith and that you would always feel him nearby."

With that, they bowed their heads, with various ones in the group praying aloud and Dr. Dobson closing. Neither Melvin nor Sarah offered to say anything, because they didn't know what to say. It was all a bit overwhelming, this open display of religious expression by English people, with little differentiation between the women and the men.

When Dr. Dobson rose to his feet, Melvin and Sarah did too, Melvin finding his voice to thank Dr. Dobson for his concern and time.

It was James, though, who broke through the awkwardness of the situation. Going up to Dr. Dobson, he held his little black hat with his left hand, and with his intense blue eyes he looked straight into Dr. Dobson's face. "When you talk to Jesus again," he said, his little voice strong and steady, "tell Him I could use some help."

The room went silent at the mention of His name by a heart so young and broken. Many of them cried openly, reaching across the religious barriers that no one can ever quite remove, as they felt the oneness of the Spirit of God pulling their hearts together. Dr. Dobson knelt down and pulled James to his chest with both arms. "I will do that," he said, his voice choking.

Melvin, to his own surprise, yielded to the impulse of the moment and offered his hand and a hug to Dr. Dobson. Silas followed suit and Dr. Dobson then turned to Sarah to shake her hand. "Now you take good care of this boy. We will be praying for all of you."

Sarah smiled though her tears that came despite her best efforts to hide them in front of these strangers. Finding her voice, she managed to say she was glad they had come, which was true, as much as it surprised her.

Cindy led them back out to the front entrance and wished them well as they left. The clock on the dashboard said 8:15 when Silas pulled the van onto Interstate 25 North. They drove all day and all night, through Burlington, Hays, Junction City, Blue Springs, Columbia, St. Louis, and many more. They stopped only for food and essentials, and late the next afternoon they arrived in southern Indiana.

CHAPTER FIFTEEN

EARLY ON THE first day back, Melvin and Sarah reluctantly got out of bed at their regular times. Although their aching bodies would have liked more sleep, there were chores to do and plans to make. The person who had been doing the chores in their absence would not be back this morning, since they had arrived before he was done the night before. Once home, it made no difference how tired they were, they were expected to do their duty.

Even without phones, computers, or instant messaging, word spread quickly in the Amish community that Sarah and Melvin's boy had leukemia. Even those living among the Amish are not sure how such news gets transmitted so efficiently. By the weekend a hundred and fifty people would not only know but would care deeply about the matter. By the next weekend the news would have reached all the Amish communities in the bordering states and, soon afterwards, all the other places where the Amish newsletter, "The Budget," was widely distributed. Undistracted by modern entertainment and celebrity gossip, the Amish remember how to care about real people and real problems.

At ten o'clock, Sarah went down the lane to the phone

shack to call the number in Indianapolis. A woman's voice answered quickly: "Dr. Watkins' office. May I help you?"

With heavy heart, and uncertain how to talk about such a weighty matter, Sarah began tentatively: "I am Sarah Yoder from Whitfield. I was told to call this number about our boy who might have leukemia."

"Were you referred to us?" the voice on the other end asked, the faint scratches of pen on paper reaching Sarah's ears.

"Yes," Sarah said into the phone, wishing she could see a human face, bothered by the bareness of the black plastic in her hand. "Yes, a Dr. Bradshaw in Colorado Springs, Colorado, referred us to you. We saw him just two days ago on our trip out west. He told us to call you when we got back home to have our son's illness looked into. We just got back yesterday afternoon," she finished, hoping she had said everything correctly.

"Just a minute," said the voice. "I will be right back."

The line clicked and Sarah thought for sure she had been hung up on. *What am I going to do now?* She looked at the phone in her hand in uncertainty, then decided to wait, resting the phone back on her ear.

About the time she was ready to give up and put the receiver back on the metal hook, she heard the click again and the voice came back on the line. "Ah, Mrs. Yoder, I have found a note saying that you are to come in immediately. Your son's name is James, correct?"

"Yes, it is," Sarah said.

"This is a little unusual," the voice said, "since we are usually booked for at least six weeks, but the note says you are to come in as soon as you can. Let's see, when can you be here?"

Sarah's mind was whirling. "Well, I guess we can come anytime."

"How would Friday at eleven sound?" the voice asked.

"That would be in two days," Sarah thought out loud, then added, "Yes, that would be okay, I think."

"Have you got a pen ready?" the voice asked her.

Grabbing the white legal pad of paper and pencil kept beside the phone, she said, "Okay, I'm ready."

"These are the instructions, okay? Our offices are located in the Indiana University Medical Center, 2302 West 10th Street. Just follow Interstate 65 North into town and take the second Indiana/Purdue University exit."

Sarah wrote the information down carefully, asking the woman to repeat the street address.

When Sarah had that down, there were more instructions. "In case Dr. Watkins agrees with the preliminary results from Colorado, your son will need to stay overnight at the hospital for a bone marrow extraction. You should come prepared for that, just in case."

"An overnight stay," Sarah said, her mind whirling.

"Yes, at the hospital."

"Will I be able to stay with my son?"

"That's hospital policy, but I would assume so," the voice told her helpfully. "We will see you on Friday, then."

"Yes, and thank you," Sarah replied, her eyes dimming with tears. Only a few weeks ago her world had been so stable, so blessed, and now she was calling doctors and talking with their secretaries about admitting her son to a hospital. Her mind couldn't grasp it, and try as she might to remember that God was still in control, all such beliefs seemed distant now, lost in the turmoil.

Replacing the phone, Sarah looked up the number of Mr. Bowen, who did some driving for the Amish, and proceeded to dial it. His wife answered, and Sarah made plans with her for Mr. Bowen to make the trip to Indianapolis on Friday, with a possible return trip on Saturday if a hospital stay was required.

In the midst of her confusion, Sarah remembered to check on one essential fact, a concern drilled into Amish children from their youth — cost. "Is his rate still thirty-five cents a mile?" Sarah asked Mrs. Bowen. "It's been some time since we have used taxi service, that's why I ask."

"It is now thirty-eight cents," Mrs. Bowen told her, sympathy in her voice, knowing what such things meant in Sarah's world. "He had to up his rates last week because of the gas prices."

"Do you think they will be up for long?" Sarah wondered. "We may have to make quite a few trips to Indianapolis."

"I don't know," Mrs. Bowen told her, the sympathy still there. "Things are not likely to come down much, I doubt. You know how the oil prices are."

"Yes, that's true," Sarah agreed, not really knowing, but understanding. "Let's just plan on Friday once and then we will see what the doctor says from there."

"That'll be okay, dear," Mrs. Bowen told her sweetly. "Ah, may I ask what your son's illness is?"

Mrs. Bowen's voice, full of concern, brought the tears again as Sarah told her about the possible leukemia.

"Well, God will help you, darling," Mrs. Bowen's voice came to her clearly. "We'll be praying for you."

Sarah thanked her the best she could, still finding it hard to talk about things so close to her heart with people whose voices came out of a black piece of plastic.

Sarah left the phone shack and walked home along their dusty lane, back to her duties of the day. There was still all the unpacking to do from the trip and the washing to get caught up on, which produced a full line by one o'clock with two washers yet to go. Melvin was already back in the fields working a full day's load, plus more she was sure, as things always seem to back up on farms when one leaves them. In her rush, she was still glad to see Martha's van pulling in the driveway towards evening.

James and Nelson, who had been playing quietly all day, came out of the barn to meet Martha as she got out of the car. From the front window Sarah watched them as they talked, the boys standing on each side of Martha, all of them no doubt catching up on their day apart, more familiar with each other from the trip west together.

"You can't even tell he's sick," Martha remarked to Sarah when she came inside and the boys were out of earshot.

"I know," Sarah agreed, "but yet he is. I'm sure of it — seems like I can feel it. But like the doctor said, it's just in its early stages."

"Did you make an appointment with the doctor in Indianapolis?"

"Ya, on Friday."

"That quickly?"

"They just did," Sarah shrugged. "The woman who

answered the phone seemed surprised, too, but said they were supposed to take us in right away."

"That's awfully nice of them. It must be because of that doctor in Colorado."

"I think so."

"Do you have a driver for Friday?" Martha asked her.

"I called Mr. Bowen and made the arrangements with his wife." Sarah shook her head. "My the prices are steep, don't you think? He's charging thirty-eight cents now. I told Mrs. Bowen we might have to make quite a few trips, so I don't know what we're going to do. I'll see what Melvin says about it, I guess, but we have to make whatever trips the doctors want, with treatment and all."

Martha nodded in agreement. "Things are quite expensive. You know that I'll help out when I can. If it comes to that, I can take off from work. This Friday I can't, though, because the bakery would need more notice than that with their tight staff schedule."

"I know," Sarah told her. "That's why I didn't ask. We'll just have to see what news we get once we go up there. I guess we can always ask Rebecca, if worst comes to worst. She might be willing to help drive some of the trips. I suppose with treatments, there would be quite a few trips. None of the drivers will be able to do everything," Sarah sighed, sitting down on the couch. "This road may just be a long one to travel, I'm afraid. I always thought God would be with us, and I'm sure He is, but I'm already starting to feel very alone. Whoever thought there would be so many things to do when your child gets sick."

Martha took a seat beside her sister on the couch, not

really finding the words to say what she was feeling, her heart pulled in all directions. "You just never know what life will bring," she finally ventured. "Who would have thought this would happen when we were girls? Us, with our plans and dreams of marriage and children, husbands who loved us — well, at least we have that."

"There's always something to be thankful for," Sarah agreed, feeling like she was just saying words that needed to be said, wishing she really felt them, ashamed that she did not, but having to settle for what she could do, speaking them, because they were true.

"You know," Martha said, glancing out the window, tears welling up in her eyes, "What if James does go? I'll be so glad we had that trip together. It was such a precious time with him. Maybe God was giving us such a time before we have to bid him good-by."

"You don't mean that, do you?" Sarah's face was pale at Martha's words. "Do you know something about his dying that we don't? Is he really going away from us? Oh, Martha, if he is, I just don't know if I'm ready to let him go. I just can't."

Martha glanced at Sarah's face in alarm, reaching out to grab both of her hands in hers. "I'm so sorry, I really am. I didn't once think about how that would sound when I said it. No, no, I really don't know anything, Sarah, please I don't. I was just thinking out loud, lost I guess in my own sorrow. I really am sorry. Please, I'm so sorry. I don't know that James is dying."

They held each other's hands for a moment longer, lost in their own thoughts, wondering where God was when the heart was so broken.

Martha finally glanced at the clock, knowing that she needed to go. "Let me know right away what the doctor says in Indianapolis," she told Sarah, heading out the door. "I'll be checking in later, okay?"

With that she was gone, Sarah watching her drive out the lane before turning to the kitchen to begin the final supper preparations.

CHAPTER SIXTEEN

NOT LONG AFTERWARDS, as dusk was approaching, Sarah saw Melvin come down the lane from the back field, his steps slower than usual, tired she figured from both the day's work and the after-effects of the trip west. As Melvin was unharnessing the team behind the barn, Sarah noticed two buggies coming up the lane. As they got closer she saw that the front one was her parents, Ben and Deborah Schwartz, coming no doubt for an evening visit. The buggy in the rear was not that familiar to her, so she would have to wait until it got closer to see who was in it.

Her heart was comforted, though, at the sight of her parents. Their coming on the first evening showed their great concern and desire to be of aid in whatever way possible. Sarah stepped out on the porch to watch them come, hungry for the sight of familiar family faces in this their time of trouble.

Her father's stern face was weathered brown from a life of farm work, his dark beard splattered with streaks of silver on the edges. It was as if his beard was the site of a final stand against the demands of encroaching age. So too was the man. The horse he now drove pulled too far to the left, almost into the ditch. Bouncing through a rough patch of dirt, the buggy leaned precipitously towards the field, Ben sawing hard on the left line.

"Whoa, Henry," he hollered to his horse. "*Vella noch uff da vayk bleiva.*" (Let's yet stay on the road.)

Bouncing around on her side of the buggy was Sarah's mother, Deborah. Her body, rounded and soft, showed the effects of years of good Amish food. She countered her husband: "*Vel, van du net so un hutshligha gaul headscht, dieda ma fliecht un layba blieva bis ma alt vadda dieda.*" (Well, if you didn't have such a high-spirited horse, we might live till we got old.)

Indeed, Ben's horse was not a calm one. When Betsy, their old plodder, got too old to keep to the road, Ben went to the auction to buy another. He wasn't sure what came over him. Maybe it was seeing all the racehorses grown too slow for the track jerking their heads into the air and pulling on the lead ropes. Maybe he was reminded of winter nights in his dating youth driving home from the singing with Deborah sitting mere inches from him in the buggy. Perhaps he felt again the lines taut in his hands and heard the rubber buggy wheels humming on the pavement, his horse blowing white steam sideways from its nostrils, while he overtook the lead buggies with one of the fastest horses on the road.

Whatever it was, Ben purchased a spirited horse. When the auctioneer said the name, "Whispering Wind," at the start of the bidding, it gave Ben a start, sealing his desire for the horse. But he quickly wiped the name from his mind once the purchase was made. When he brought the horse home, he told Deborah its name was Henry. Technically it was, since Ben had renamed it on the way home, but he left out that little detail. Nor did he tell Deborah what he ended up paying.

Sarah shook her head as she watched them come up the lane, smiling in spite of herself. Always stubborn was her father. *What in the world is he doing with a horse like that? Well, Mom will take care of him if he gets too out of hand,"* she figured.

The two buggies pulled up to the hitching post by the barn, one behind the other, Sarah by now having recognized the rear buggy as that of Melvin's parents. Ben got out quickly to tie Henry, while Deborah waited, holding the reins. She obviously did not like or trust this horse.

Following them in on the right side, Melvin's father, John Yoder, stopped and pulled his horse over slightly to turn the buggy wheel away from his wife's side, making it easier for her to alight. Then he straightened the horse up to the hitching rack and got out himself. He got out slowly, as if to say there was no reason to hurry since his horse was a plodder and quite content to stand anywhere.

John Yoder still had very little gray hair for his age, a calm man with his middle well filled out. However, when such thoughts as losing weight occurred to him, John quickly put them out of his mind, lest they lead to places he did not want to go. His wife Mattie could still bustle around all day without getting tired, but when she mentioned a certain diet to her husband that might be healthy for people their age, he told her that things were just the way he liked them. That was not entirely true, but he felt it was better than trying to change.

Although they did not belong to the same church district, both couples knew each other well through the mutual family connection. They exchanged slight nods as greetings out by their buggies. With a sick grandchild in the house, anything more would violate their deep instinct of Amish piety and soberness in the face of tragedy.

With Ben and Deborah leading, they walked quietly together towards the house where Sarah waited on the porch. She greeted them as soon as they were in earshot, first with a smile and then with words, that she was so glad they had come.

"How is he?" Deborah asked quietly, glancing around to make sure James was not within hearing distance.

"You can't tell really," Sarah responded. *"Ie gukk noch gutt."* (He still looks good.)

All four grandparents nodded their heads in understanding, stepping up onto the porch. "Some things take more time to show than others," Mattie suggested.

"What says the doctor?" Ben wanted to know.

"The one in Colorado said that the leukemia is likely still in its early stages. That is good, I guess, to catch it early. There are a lot of new treatments they have now. He seemed hopeful, I thought, but they really don't know anything for sure until they do a bone marrow sample."

"Do you think he's hopeful just because he is a doctor?" Deborah wondered, searching for hope herself, and wanting to know how well grounded this one was.

"I don't know. He seemed like he was telling the truth," Sarah responded.

"That's how these English doctors are," Deborah told

her, setting herself against the chance of finding hope in that direction. "They don't like to tell things the way they are. Jake's Mary just told me the other day how the one in town smiled at them the whole time their boy was so sick with the flu. He said that things would turn around in a few days. Mary said the boy nearly died on them. Makes one wonder if these English doctors smile when passing the deathbed, too?"

"Now, Mother," Sarah said, sticking up for what she had seen, "maybe some of them are that way, but this one was really nice. He was good, too, from what I could see. I would say he has good reasons to be confident in his opinion."

"Well, I have my doubts," Deborah replied, then showed her real intent. "I wish you would take James to see Esther."

"Why would I want to do that?" Sarah asked in astonishment. "A little herb treatment isn't going to take care of leukemia, if that indeed is what James has."

"You never know." Deborah wasn't one to give up easily, nor did she intend to this time. "Sometimes these natural treatments are much more effective than the modern medicines they dope you with."

"You haven't talked to her already, have you?" Sarah was suddenly suspicious of her mother.

Deborah dropped her eyes sheepishly in view of her daughter's blue-eyed gaze. "Well, I know you've never really liked her, but I did meet her in town today. Just happened to run into her, by chance — now that's the truth — and I did take the opportunity to tell her about James."

Sarah continued to gaze at her mother. "And what did she say?"

Deborah shrugged. "I was a little surprised. She was not only willing, but said to bring him right over tomorrow. She would get a special treatment for him right out of her garden. Said the herbs are doing extra well this year, that she had exactly what was needed."

"Oh, she did?"

"Now you don't need to get sarcastic, Sarah. I know you don't like her, but she can cure a lot of things."

"Yes, maybe some little things. I mean the natural method isn't worthless, I agree, but a herb garden can't quite heal this problem."

Ben snorted through his nose, half in amusement and half because he was tired of the conversation. "*Vella na shvetsa vayyich ebbes shunsht.*" (Let's now talk about something else.) He shared his daughter's low opinion of the local Amish woman and her herb garden. "She's good for some things," he attempted to conclude the argument between mother and daughter. "She just might not be able to take care of this one, even if she wants to."

On the sidelines for the moment, yet nonplussed by this vigorous exchange, John and Mattie chose to stay out of it. First, they were from the other side of the family, and, second, they had no real opinion in this matter.

When things seemed to have settled down, Mattie thought she should say something, so she tried a compliment on Sarah's present choice. "It sounds like you have a good doctor," she told her.

Sarah nodded. "The one in Colorado was. Let's hope the one we are going to in Indianapolis is good, too."

"Oh, so you already have an appointment with a local doctor?" Deborah asked, picking up on Sarah's slight mention.

"Yes, on Friday."

"I still wish you'd see Esther," Deborah insisted, then changed the subject before Sarah could respond. "I called Mark today and left a message at his neighbor's place they use for emergency phone calls."

Sarah nodded in gratitude, relieved that her mother had taken the initiative in notifying her older brother.

"Where is Mark now?" Mattie wanted to know, not remembering any recent mention about his location.

"Pennsylvania," Sarah told her.

"He's married, right?"

"Ya — what have they got, Mom, five children?" Sarah volunteered, figuring on saving time since the conversation would no doubt go there anyway.

"Is he coming out soon?" Mattie directed this question to Deborah.

"There was a return message for me earlier this evening when I called the neighbors. Mark said they would visit as soon as things could be arranged at their farm. I guess they don't expect anything to happen too quickly," Deborah offered as explanation.

CHAPTER SEVENTEEN

HOLDING THE DOOR open for her family, Sarah let them inside single file, her father and Melvin's dad taking their hats off and laying them on the floor just inside the door.

"You'll have to excuse the house," Sarah told them. "We just got home last night, plus if you take a close look at the floors you might see water stains. They got wet in that storm awhile back, before we left on the trip. Melvin thinks the wood has settled down, but I keep thinking I might still see stains."

"It looks fine to me," Mattie commented, glancing at the wood.

Ben was a little more interested in the subject, letting his eyes sweep across the hardwood floor and then kneeling down to examine the boards up close. Their moments of piety now paid, even with a sick grandchild around life always went on for them.

"Get up off the floor, would you," Deborah told him. "You're way too old for those kinds of positions."

That comment produced quite a chuckle from John, his stomach vibrating slightly as he laughed. "Yeah, Ben, you should have heard what the young boys were calling you the other Sunday after church."

Deborah, not knowing where this was going and not liking it either way, demanded, "Don't tell him, John. He has enough in his head already."

This only produced a deeper chuckle from John, which drove Deborah to think further. "Does this have something to do with that horse we've got?"

John still chuckled, acting like he would say nothing, driving Ben to where he could stand it no longer. "Come on now, John, come on, let's hear it. News like that shouldn't be kept from an old man. Tell me, what are the boys saying?"

"Ben, you should be thoroughly ashamed of yourself even wanting to know," Deborah declared before John had a chance to respond, hoping to use shame to head Ben off at the pass, now thoroughly convinced it had plenty to with the horse she so disliked. "I tell you," she stated firmly, "you are going to take that horse right back to the sale barn tomorrow, no questions asked. That thing scares me every time we drive it. It's a danger on the road, a risk to life and limb. Why, I can barely get into town by myself now without taking my life into my own hands."

Ben ignored her, chuckling in anticipation of the news. "Come on, John. What are they saying?"

John Yoder, grinning wide, said, "They call you *da schteik* (the fast) Ben Schwartz."

"Ah...." Ben smacked his lips from his position on the hardwood floor, grinning himself. Deborah shared disapproving looks with Mattie. "What is wrong with them?" she asked, sighing in hopelessness.

154

"Nothing," Ben declared, though he hadn't been asked. "We're perfectly normal."

Shaking her head at the antics of her elders, Sarah led the two women from the living room to the kitchen. "Where are the boys, by the way?" Deborah wanted to know."

"They're out in the yard playing," Sarah said. "I thought it would be good if they spent as much time outside as possible. Shall I go call them to come in, since you're here?"

"No, don't" Mattie and Deborah both insisted. "Let them come in when they want to. They need all the time outside they can get. Now, even more than ever, with James not well."

"You're all staying for supper, aren't you?" Sarah more stated than asked, glancing in the oven where she had a roast going. Through the window she caught a glimpse of Melvin coming in from the barn.

"I brought something along," Deborah assured her. "I wouldn't expect you to cook with all that's going on."

Sarah nodded, grateful, knowing that she really did not have enough food for four more people.

"I have a casserole along," Mattie volunteered. "It will keep, if we don't eat all of it tonight."

"Then I'm glad I brought dessert," Deborah declared. "I wasn't sure what to bring, but knowing Sarah and all, I figured she would be making something wholesome in the time she has to cook. So sweets might be just what she needs."

"You were right," Sarah smiled, tired and grateful for her mother and the care she was getting on this the second evening home.

Hearing the outside door open, Sarah glanced up as Melvin stepped in the utility room doorway. "Everybody settled down?" he asked her, bending over to remove his boots.

"Ya, they're here," she told him, then added, "I think we need some light before too long." He nodded before sticking his head out to say hi to his mother and Deborah, then retreated to the pressing task of banishing the rapidly approaching dusk.

"Want me to get your dad to help with something?" Mattie asked him, from where she was sitting at the kitchen table.

"No, I'll be done in a minute," Melvin told her, lifting the gas lanterns from where they sat on the shelf. Picking up the first one, he shook it gently to check the gas level. Finding it satisfactory, he did the same to the second. "Should be enough for tonight," he said under his breath, making the gas level calculations from long experience.

Taking the air handle between his fingers and thumb, he pumped air into each lantern, then turned the rod to lock it in place. Lighting a match, he proceeded to let a little gas out while sticking the flame through the bottom shield. The lantern ignited with a small poof of exploding gas, then slowly flickered into a steady flame as if deciding whether or not to burn.

When the other was lit, he hung one on the hook in the kitchen ceiling and carried the other into the living room, greeting his father and Ben as he walked in. The illuminated room made the outside look even darker than it had before.

Drawn by the light from the lanterns, James and Nelson

came through the front door. "Well, there they are," Deborah raised her voice upon seeing them through the kitchen opening. "Come to your grandmother for a hug, will you?" she asked, stepping into the living room. Mattie came behind her, reaching out her arms as well. "Did you boys like your trip?"

Ben and John did little but nod at the boys as they walked towards Deborah and Mattie, taking turns hugging their grandmothers. They quickly tired of the attention and wanted to see what was in the kitchen, but the questions held them in check.

"So you have a sickness, James, I hear?" Deborah said, getting right to the point.

"That's what Mom and the doctor say," James responded. "I feel pretty good today. It could be real bad, though, but maybe I'll get better, too. We don't know yet."

"So you're feeling okay now?" Deborah asked him.

"Kind of tired right now, from playing with Nelson, but today I felt pretty good. It's nice to be back home."

"We hope the doctors can treat you," Mattie joined in the conversation, giving him another hug.

James nodded. "That's what the doctor on our trip said. He's a doctor a long way from here in a nice big building. A really nice man prayed for me, too. I asked him to tell Jesus about me when he talks to him."

Deborah hid her shock at this pronouncement by saying, "Well, you'll be better soon, I hope. Are you boys hungry?"

They both nodded their heads, and Sarah sent them to clean up at the utility sink basin. After they were gone and the adults could hear water splashing, Deborah turned to

Sarah. "How could you, Sarah? What is this about a nice man praying for him? What have you been doing? Where did he learn such English talk about Jesus?"

"Now, Mom," Sarah held up her hand, "there's nothing to worry about. A Dr. Dobson prayed for him, and we all believe in Jesus, don't we? I even talked about it at the restaurant with James on the first night after we learned he was sick."

"Oh, well, that's different," Deborah declared, a little mollified. "I didn't know this English man he was talking about was a doctor, but you still shouldn't give him that thing about Jesus. You know we believe in him too, but we just don't say it quite like the English do."

"I know," Sarah nodded, "we are different. In that situation, though, with us just finding out how sick James really was, it seemed like the right thing to do to let Dr. Dobson pray for him. Don't worry, Mom. I'm not going English. I know we have a lot of good things, too."

"I'm glad to hear you say that," Deborah told her, then decided to press her advantage. "Surely if you let an English man pray for James, you will think about Esther, won't you?"

When Sarah said nothing, Deborah glanced at her before retreating a few steps. "Well, maybe we should stop fussing and get some supper on the table, don't you think? Let me go get what I have and then we can set the table for these hungry men."

That was fine with Sarah, who was tired of the verbal sparring and more than ready to eat, hunger having made itself known to her some time ago. When Mattie and her mother returned from the buggies with their food, the table was set quickly. After calling the men in from the living room, they all bowed in silent prayer before beginning the meal.

When they finished, they retired to the living room to discuss the grave matters at hand. Later, with the hiss of the gas lanterns in the background, Sarah and Melvin listened from the front porch to the sound of buggy wheels on gravel as both their parents left for home, the red taillights on the buggies disappearing into the darkness.

Going back inside, Sarah took the boys upstairs to bed, then joined Melvin, who seemed lost in thought on the couch. She leaned up close against him, reaching out for his strength and calmness. "Mom wants me to take James to see Esther sometime, I think tomorrow already," Sarah told him, resting her head on his shoulder.

"Are you going to?" he asked her, not that interested in the subject but placing his arm around her.

"I guess you know what's going to happen if I don't," she told him. "Mom will be quite upset."

"I wouldn't be too scared," he shrugged and said, "we are the parents, right?"

Sarah sighed, ignoring that argument and advancing her own concerns. "I just don't know about Esther. You know, I never liked her, plus I don't think her stuff will do any good. I mean, it's just a waste of time."

"Yeah, I suppose so. My parents never had much of an opinion on that kind of thing either. We never went to her so I don't know much about it. I guess it's up to you what you're going to do."

"I'll have to think about it." She sighed again. "I'm just not sure her herbs will do much either way, good or bad, as far as that goes, but Mom seems to be so set on me going."

In the light of the gas lanterns, Melvin nodded his agreement to whatever her decision would be, pulling her even closer to him. Together they sat there, thinking their own thoughts about what had happened so far and what might lie ahead. When Melvin moved to kneel for the evening prayers, Sarah followed quite willingly, knowing they needed the help of the Almighty now more than ever.

CHAPTER EIGHTEEN

HAVING GONE TO sleep well enough, Sarah woke with a start, gripped with fear. Death pressed upon her with visions of James white and still, dressed in his best clothing, a wooden box around him, ministers speaking at his funeral.

The house itself was deathly silent and very dark, as if waiting, ready to show her what lay ahead. She usually left the bedroom window open at night, enjoying the sounds of life stirring even in the summer's darkness. Now, though, all was utterly still; not even a breath of air could find its way through the screen.

Her first thought was to calm herself and check the time. She turned her head slowly, overcoming the fear of movement, to look at the wind-up alarm clock on the wooden stand beside the bed. Its glow-in-the-dark hands faintly said quarter after five.

"Almost morning," she thought. "Then why is everything so quiet?"

She listened for any noise that might have awakened her. Lifting her head, she strained her eyes in the darkness. The eerie quiet sent chills down her back.

The world, it seemed, was hanging in the balance, as if waiting for something to happen. Her mind raced — was she imagining things or was there really cause for alarm? Was death as real as it seemed right now?

Then she heard Melvin's breathing coming in regular rhythms beside her. At least that was the way it was supposed to be, but why was the rest of the house so quiet? Was James really going to die? Was this a sign of what was coming, a foretaste of the awful shutting down of such a young life? Again she felt her skin tingle in the stillness. Then a stifling heaviness began to wrap around her heart.

She was at the point of waking Melvin when a cricket chirped by the window. The little screech reverberated throughout the bedroom, growing into song, relieving the tension.

The rest of the world seemed to respond as a slight breeze moved the curtains, stirring the dead air in the room. She felt deep breaths coming back into her lungs. It was a dream, she told herself — yet she was sure she had been awake. As if to put the dispute behind her, the wind-up alarm clock restored all normalcy by emitting a soft click, followed by a clanging racket.

She still didn't move as Melvin's hand came out of the covers and shut the thing off. Under the covers seemed the best place to think about what she had just felt.

"Five-thirty already?" Melvin muttered, more to himself than anyone. "And we just went to sleep."

She ventured an "I know," doubting if he would hear her in his grogginess, but wanting to hear the sound of her own voice. Was James dying? She pulled the covers in closer, the question persistent even with the fear dissipated, and she was uncertain what to do with it.

When Melvin's feet hit the other side of the floor, she moved to get out too, sliding the covers aside. He rummaged around on his side of the floor as he always did, finding his clothes and getting them on in the darkness. Was he afraid too, she wondered. Had he felt anything?

Tempted to ask him, she decided not to, letting things continue in their usual routine as Melvin left in the pre-dawn light for the barn and his chores. She got dressed and headed for the kitchen to prepare breakfast. With the late night last night, she would let the boys sleep in until Melvin had left for the fields.

At the breakfast table, after prayer, she decided to approach the question. Melvin was just stirring sugar into his oatmeal and reaching for the milk when she asked him, "You sleep okay last night?"

"Sure," he nodded without hesitation, but not sure, she could tell, why she was asking.

"I had a lot of fears this morning," she explained, watching his face to see how much information he wanted. "I woke up just before the alarm clock, and the house was pretty quiet. Do you think James is dying?"

He dipped his spoon into his bowl. "Fears are pretty normal during times like this. I wouldn't worry about it. We must just let God's will be done. He will know what is best."

She felt like saying more, asking for comfort, but stopped, supposing he had enough on his plate already. The thought of the cost of all this had worried her last night too — medical bills when she went to the doctor on Friday and driving miles for the taxi service. He really didn't need to be bothered further with her nightmares. She would keep them to herself. Yet they continued to weigh on her mind, even now that the sun was shining outside.

"You going to see Esther today?" he asked, remembering the conversation from the evening before.

She found a degree of comfort in the question itself. The fact that he remembered, had cared enough not to forget, warmed her. "Oh, you did remember," slipped out of her mouth, with thankfulness in her voice.

"Well, I don't always," he admitted sheepishly, "but I can get the horse ready if you are."

Suddenly, as if out of the blue, she knew what she would do about going to Esther. His question opened her mind. Why not try Esther? Her mother wanted her to, and maybe Esther knew something she didn't. The morning fear was giving way to hope. Maybe there was a miracle hidden in herbs that modern doctors were not willing to accept, as her mother seemed to think, and it certainly would cost a lot less than the English doctors would.

"I think I will go," she told him, relief on her face from having arrived at a decision. "Mom wants me to, and I should at least try it." That money was also a consideration she didn't mention, since she figured he would not think that worthy of playing a part in her decision. Yet she wanted to help out in every way possible, and perhaps this was one way she could.

"What time do you need the horse?" Melvin asked, finishing his oatmeal.

"In about an hour," she told him, getting up from her chair and starting to clean off the breakfast table. "I'll get the boys up before too long."

"I will get the horse ready, then." He moved for the utility door. "Do you want me to see you off?" he asked.

"No," she smiled at him, "just leave the horse in the barn. I can get him hitched up, since I have plenty of time."

"I want to see you off," he insisted, knowing full well Sarah was quite capable of hitching the horse by herself. Even getting the horse into the traces was not a big problem with the one they had now. Their previous horse had always balked halfway through the process, leaving one stranded with little recourse, but when the children came along Melvin took extra care to find the right driving horse.

"That's nice of you," she insisted with equal firmness, "but I'll be okay. There's no reason to delay your time in the fields just for a trip to Esther's. If you get the horse ready, that will be more than enough. Okay?" She stepped towards him, glancing towards the stairs first in case one of the boys had walked up unnoticed, then pulled him close, burying her head on his chest. "I'm so scared, Melvin," she whispered. "What if James dies?"

His arms were tender, tightening around her back, his voice reaching out to her. "God won't give us more than we can bear, Sarah." He lifted her away from him, stroking her face with his callused fingers.

She rubbed the tears away, nodding her head, drawing him to herself again. God at the moment did not feel very close, but Melvin did — a fact she was not about to tell him as she clung to him.

"I have to go now," he told her gently. "The work of the farm, it seems, still needs doing regardless of what happens. I wish I could stop, but I can't. Just let me know when you come back from Esther's if you need anything."

"You'll be in for lunch?" she asked, certain that he would be, but wanting to hear the sound of his voice more than the answer he gave.

"Ya, will you be back by then?"

"I'll make sure I am," she nodded.

With that he left for the barn and harnessed her horse, leaving him ready for her. By the time she got the boys downstairs and finished the breakfast dishes, he reappeared with his team on the other side of the barn, heading for the hay field.

"You don't need Sunday clothing," she told the boys, "but we are going to Esther's pretty soon here."

"Don't I get to play in the barn today?" Nelson wanted to know, his face concerned.

"Maybe you can play in Esther's barn," Sarah told him, inspiration hitting her — that solved both his problem and her own on what to do with him while she and James were with Esther. "Or," she added to cover the bases, "if not, you can play in ours when we get back." That seemed to satisfy him as he worked on his breakfast.

Her glance caught James's face. "You okay?" she asked him. "How did you sleep?"

"I don't know," he ventured, distracted. "Why are we going to Esther?"

"My mom wants her to treat you with some herbs." She touched his shoulder, squeezing it.

"Will it make me better?" he wanted to know, looking at her face. "Can she talk to Jesus like the doctor could in Colorado?"

Not sure how to answer him, surprised by his questions, Sarah ventured, "I suppose she can." Then she quickly added, "See James, this is medicine, same as what the doctors will have to give you too. We don't know what medicines will work, so we try them, okay?"

He shrugged, pushing away his half-empty bowl. "That's all I can eat," he said softly. "My stomach hurts."

She gathered him in her arms, the tears pushing but held back by her desire to be strong for him. "It'll be okay," she told him softly, as Nelson looked on, not fully comprehending but concerned.

So that he would not feel left out, she gave him a hug too as he wiggled in embarrassment.

CHAPTER NINETEEN

S HE MADE THEM stay in the house to spare their clothing until she was ready, then led the way to the barn.
In the distance she could see Melvin cutting the hay field,
heat already rising from the horses, the grass falling in even
lines as he kept the horses in the row.

James offered to help push the buggy out, and she didn't
have the heart to tell him no. The tears threatened, though,
when she noticed his hard breathing after they were done.

She brought out the horse and got him in line, holding
on to his bridle with her right hand. Each person devel-
ops his or her own technique for "getting a horse" into the
shafts, since two people are rarely available for the task.
While facing the buggy with the horse at a right angle, the
person must lift the double-pronged shafts with the left
hand while guiding the horse's head under them with the
right, swinging the horse sideways to bring in the rest of the
body. This has to be accomplished with only two hands and
some fancy footwork if necessary — a task Sarah, as well as
her sister Martha, had mastered while still at home.

James and Nelson were climbing in by the time she was
done, ready for the trip — at least Nelson was. James laid his

head wearily back on the seat. Sarah was using the single buggy, easily fitting both boys in, because it was lighter and easier to drive than the surrey with its front and back seats. With a slap of the lines she took off, driving out the lane, wondering if this was all a wild goose chase.

She drove down their blacktop road, taking care to pull over a bit on the curves where the cars usually had trouble passing a buggy. Glancing at her boys seated on either side of her, she found images from her childhood coming back to her of the times her mother would take her to see Esther.

She couldn't remember whether or not the homemade remedies really worked — only her feelings associated with the experience. Her anxiety about the unknown had been coupled with a sense of helplessness as her mother insisted she quit complaining, saying she was going to see Esther whether she wanted to or not.

Some twenty minutes later there was a feeling of seriousness in the air as she descended the hill towards Esther's place. Her son's life was at stake, threatened by an illness unlike anything she had ever experienced.

When she pulled in the driveway, Sarah saw Esther in the yard. Of average height, a little plump around the middle, she was dark-skinned from all the time she spent out in the sun. She wore a black head covering, typical of Amish in these parts who wore black on weekdays and white on Sundays. But Esther's black covering was larger than that worn by the others. Uniformity was a big issue in Amish circles, with everyone asked to wear the same. Sarah did not know why exceptions were made for Esther. Her larger covering was pulled forward almost past her forehead hairline, its strings tied tightly under her chin until they disappeared into the skin.

The sight of Esther in her weekday environment evoked within Sarah memories from her childhood. She winced but shoved the thoughts away in the urgency of the moment. If Esther could help, then she must be allowed to help.

With a bucket of water on the ground by her feet, Esther was working on a horse tied to the fence in front of her. She repeatedly dipped a heavy washcloth in the bucket and scrubbed the horse's hindquarters, water running down its legs and pooling at its feet.

"*Vee gehts*" (How goes it) was Esther's cheerful greeting as Sarah got out of the buggy to tie her horse.

Sarah's "*Goot*" (Good) in response was her only answer, as she found the tie rope under her seat and secured the horse.

Esther continued her work with the washcloth on the horse's posterior. "You brought him, I see," was her next comment, as the washcloth splashed into the bucket of water. "I saw your mother in town, and she told me James was not well."

Sarah only nodded her head. What else could she say?

"We will go to the house," Esther said after a moment more, dropping the washcloth in the bucket. "I have got some things ready for him."

"Did you know we were coming?" Sarah asked surprised, reaching in the buggy to help Nelson down as James got out the other side.

Esther shrugged. "No, but it is a bad year for things like this."

"Really?" A shiver ran down Sarah's spine, making her feel like a little girl again being told to swallow bad-tasting spoonfuls of liquid in Esther's kitchen.

"Yes," Esther continued, "I have known it for some time already. Ever since that bad storm we had about two months ago. That night I knew there would be much trouble this year. People would get sick, but I had hoped the children would be spared. The next morning I began to grow the special herbs needed for their healing."

"Have there been others?" Sarah asked, not sure she wanted to know, but unable to refrain from asking.

"Yes," Esther nodded soberly. "Last week Paul Raber's kidneys started acting up again, and I had just the thing for him. He told me, after taking two cups of my tea at home, there was no more problem. Then there was Clara Miller's youngest child and her niece, too. They came in together. Terrible flu, they thought they had, and it had already gone into the lungs. It was really bad. Both of them were well the next week after they were here. She told me so herself last Sunday."

"I see." Sarah was not convinced, but what could she say? A testimony was a testimony, passed around from mouth to mouth until most everyone heard about it. These she had not heard, but maybe it was because, as Esther said, there were so many of them.

"Is your boy a serious case?" Esther wanted to know. "It's the oldest, James, right?"

"Yes," Sarah nodded her head, then whispered to Nelson: "You can run to the barn and play if you want."

It didn't take a second telling before he was off, happy

in his chance to explore a strange barn, which promised to hold untold fascination for a young boy. It also held untold dangers, yet rare is an injury among Amish children from such playing, perhaps because of their exposure from the earliest years to such an environment, which freely punishes foolishness and rewards caution.

"We can go inside," Esther told the two of them when Nelson had disappeared into the barn door.

"Okay," Sarah agreed, taking James's hand as they followed her inside.

"You can sit by the kitchen table till I wash my hands," Esther informed them. "Then I will take a look at the boy. I have the water heated already." She motioned with her eyes towards the wood stove where the tea kettle was putting out a little trickle of steam.

Figuring that Esther must have a lot of patients to have water heated in the middle of the day, Sarah waited, wishing they hadn't come. She could almost taste the bitter flavor of various liquids drank in her childhood, nearly on this very spot.

It didn't help much when James asked her, "What's she going to do, Mommy?"

"I suppose," she whispered to him, "she's going to give you something to drink. That's what she always gave me when Grandma brought me."

"You came here?" James's eyes were getting bigger, having seen Esther in church on Sunday since he was old enough to remember, but never in this setting or connected to his mother.

Sarah saw him relax as he looked her over, probably

figuring that if his mother made it through whatever lay ahead, he could too. "Just drink what she gives you," she told him. "It tastes bad, but it won't hurt you."

He wrinkled up his forehead, wearily, she thought, but resigned to his fate. The thought occurred to her that drinking nasty tea might be nothing to what awaited them at the doctor's office in Indianapolis. There was that talk about the bone marrow sample at the hospital, whatever that was. Surely, with modern medicine having progressed so far, the English must have figured out a way to make such things painless.

Yet doubt filled her. What if they had not? From somewhere her memory revived stories about the pain still involved in such rare procedures. Maybe it was good that they came here today? If Esther could help them it sure would save a lot of trouble.

Coming down the hall from her washroom, Esther interrupted her thoughts. "Well, well, let's take a look at the boy."

She walked up to James, stood in front of him, and placed her fingers first on one eyelid then the other, lifting them to look underneath. "Not good," she muttered, "not good at all, but I have just the thing for it."

James watched her, rubbing his eyelids as soon as she let go of them, shaking his head a little and then running his fingers through his hair.

"So you have something for him?" Sarah asked, real hope running through her for the first time.

"Yes, yes, this will do it," Esther told her, pouring water into a metal cup. "Let's see" — she proceeded to open several containers of tea, picking and choosing among them, dropping them into the hot water — "that should do it." She stirred the mixture with a spoon she took from the cabinet drawer.

Returning with the cup, she set it in front of James, smiling. "As soon as it cools off a little you can drink it."

Sarah could not help but sniff the air at the sweet smells coming from the metal cup in front of James. "It smells good," she half said, half asked. "Mine never tasted good."

"*Ach,*" Esther waved her left arm in the air, "those were the old days, when you were a child. Nowadays things are a lot different. We now have vanilla tea and jasmine to cover up the bad-tasting stuff. Makes things a lot easier. Can you drink it?" she asked James. "It should about be cool enough."

"Vanilla?" Sarah asked, never having heard of that in a tea.

"Yes," Esther smiled, watching as James tested and then proceeded to drink the cup empty rather quickly.

"It tasted good," he pronounced, obviously surprised but pleased.

"Well, that's done," she said. "That should do. It was simple enough. He should be well now."

"Well?" The question just came out of Sarah in a burst of astonishment. "You're not sending anything home with us? I mean, James is really sick, the doctor said."

"I know," Esther nodded, looking wise. "That's what they said about Clara Miller's youngest too, but they don't know everything. James was sick, sick enough to need what I just gave him, but he's better now."

175

Sarah, having felt hope only moments before, now felt dashed to the floor, broken in pieces by this flagrant display of Esther's. There was simply no way this could have done anything. Esther must be making fun of her on purpose, right in front of her. "You can't be serious," she found herself exclaiming, her anger rising as she glared at the woman. "The doctor said he was really sick, and that doesn't go away just by drinking a cup of tea. So why did you even try?"

"It was to heal him of his sickness," Esther said solemnly, reaching over to take James's cup and then rising to set it back on the counter.

"You didn't do anything!" Sarah was surprised at the anger that found its way into her voice. She tried to control it, knowing that if she could not she would have to answer to her mother.

"It makes no difference what you think," Esther said, not looking at her. "The boy will be well now."

Sarah felt a real frostiness creeping over her but decided not to pursue the subject further. She just wanted to get this over with and James out of there. "Will there be a charge?" she asked, because she faintly remembered her mother asking that question when she was a girl.

"You know the custom," Esther told her. "You can just give me what you can, and since you and Melvin just made that trip out west, I suppose there should be plenty of money around," she said without a trace of a smile on her face.

"Okay." Sarah took a deep breath, keeping her anger in check, pulling ten dollars from her pocket that she had brought along just in case, placing it on the kitchen table.

Esther glanced at it, then without the slightest emotion in her voice said, "I wouldn't go up to that doctor on Friday,"

Sarah paused in astonishment, not sure she was hearing correctly. "But we have to take James to the doctor. What do you mean?"

"The boy is well. You should not doubt the old ways."

"Uh, we are taking him to the doctor," Sarah told her quickly, reaching out for the doorknob, suddenly having had all of this she could take and knowing she had to leave before she said something she would regret later.

Esther said nothing more as they left the house and went to the barn to collect Nelson. He made a face at having to quit his playing but came at Sarah's insistence. Driving out the lane, Sarah saw that Esther was standing just inside the front door watching them, her black head covering drawn even lower over her forehead than before.

CHAPTER TWENTY

S ARAH WAS ALMOST shaking as she took the buggy out of the driveway, her suppressed anger made worse by the raised hopes only moments before. How could she have been so dumb, she thought, to believe that Esther could do anything for James? And now there was the aftermath to worry about. No doubt Esther would not hesitate to tell it around, especially to her mother Deborah.

As they swung back on the road, the sun was just at the point of radiating its full warmth, rising above the morning clouds that scurried across the horizon. Mid-morning shadows, cast from her buggy and the trees along the road, chased each other over the blacktop as she drove by. James and Nelson sat quietly beside her on the seat, sensing her unrest, uncertain about its cause, waiting for it to show its hand before they ventured forth with anything.

She pulled into their driveway, thankful to see Melvin come out of the barn to meet her as she approached. He caught the horse's bridle, held on to it until they climbed out, then unhitched the traces on one side as she did the other.

"What are you doing in from the fields this time of the day?" she asked him, the edge still in her voice.

"Oh," he raised his eyebrows at the tone, "the mower

broke, but I've got it fixed now, thankfully without having to go into town. What's wrong with you?"

"That woman!" she steamed. "I'll never go back to her again."

"Now, now," Melvin chuckled. "What did she do? It couldn't have been that bad."

"Gave him some tea!" Sarah exclaimed. "Charged me ten dollars for it, then had the nerve to tell me not to go to Indianapolis to see the doctor. Isn't that bad enough?" she finished, her eyes blazing.

Melvin raised his eyebrows again. "That doesn't sound too good, but she can't charge you for anything. You must have offered it to her."

"Well, something like that." Sarah gave the horse a little slap to get him out of the shafts as Melvin lowered them gently to the ground. "Mom always offered when I went with her, and so I did the same thing. Ten dollars seemed like the right number, but it was all for nothing. I had myself actually thinking that she might be able to help." The tears were pushing again.

"So that's the problem," Melvin said softly, walking over to take the horse from her and pulling her close to him with the other arm. "You did okay, and if it helps anything, I wasn't expecting too much."

She nodded her head, more comforted that he cared than with his low expectations.

"How are you feeling?" he asked James, letting go of Sarah to place his hand tenderly on his son's head.

"I don't know," James said seriously, then smiled a little. "Her tea tasted good."

"I don't care," Sarah snapped again, her anger returning. "I'm never going back there again!"

Melvin was not sure what he should do about this, but decided he had better deal with his wife's agitation in some way. "So why did you go, then?" he asked, only succeeding in making things worse.

"I went because Mom wanted me to," she told him, her anger now directed towards him, "and because I couldn't be sure that it didn't work. What if it had worked and I had not gone? Would you want to be responsible for that?"

Melvin, a little confused by her outburst and unsure how to respond, still ventured another attempt. "So, now we know, right, so that's the end of it? Look, I'm not blaming you."

"It was awful!" Sarah replied, a little mollified but still disturbed by the entire episode. She could still hear Esther's parting instructions to her.

"I can't believe she had enough nerve to tell us not to take him to a doctor," she added out loud.

"I can't either." Melvin put his arm around her again, seeking to comfort her, feeling a need to bring this to a conclusion. "You take James to the doctor on Friday. We will follow their advice about what to do, okay? Like the doctor said in Colorado, they have a lot of new treatments today, and hopefully, if it is the will of God, they will work." He reached out to touch James on the shoulder. "It's going to be okay, I think."

James solemnly nodded his head, then said, "She never talked with Jesus. I liked the big man out west better. He said he would talk to Jesus for me."

"I'm sure you're right," Melvin assured him. "You don't ever have to go back to Esther, okay?"

"Oh, I don't care," James said quickly. "Her tea was okay, I guess."

"You're not going back," Sarah declared, her lips pressed together firmly.

Taking Sarah by the hand, her fingers trembling, Melvin led her into the house with James and Nelson following at his side. Sitting down on the couch with Sarah beside him, he got the boys to sit on the floor in front of them.

He pondered for a moment, wondering what to say. Simply saying that he believed things would be okay did not seem quite sufficient at the moment. Finally, he realized he felt like singing, so he began. It was a song they all knew from Sunday morning, *Oh Gott-Vater wir loben Dich*, to one of the faster tunes.

For a moment he thought he and the boys would be the only ones singing. Then, weakly, Sarah joined in, her voice rising above the boy's clear, child voices. By the time they finished one stanza, Sarah had stopped her trembling.

"I feel a little better now," she said quietly when they were done. "Thank you for spending some time with us out of your busy day." The tears gathered in her eyes again.

James added his opinion from the floor in front of them: "I'm glad we sang that song, Dad." He shifted around on the hardwood floor, trying to find a more comfortable spot for his thin body. Sarah noticed and pulled him up on her lap as Melvin left to return to his fieldwork.

When he returned an hour later for lunch, James and Nelson followed him in from the barn, ready for the sandwiches Sarah had prepared. She seemed to be doing okay, he thought. He headed back to the field, worked the rest of the afternoon, then returned with the team of horses when the sun dropped low in the sky. Sarah had supper ready, and the evening continued in as routine a manner as they could make it.

After the boys were in bed, she sat down on the couch, wearily letting her body sink into its softness.

"So what time are you going to Indianapolis on Friday?" Melvin asked from the recliner, the gas lanterns hissing above on the ceiling, darkness already well settled outside.

"First thing," she told him. "Mr. Bowen wants to have plenty of time to arrive ahead of the traffic. He said if he gets there early, it won't matter, that we can wait easier than having doctors wait for us."

"You may have to stay overnight," he stated more than asked. "Do you want me to come up the next day when Mr. Bowen picks you up?"

She smiled soberly at him, warmed by his offer but declining it. "You have plenty to do already on the farm. If I have any problems I'm sure someone at the hospital will know what to do about it. Mr. Bowen should be fine picking us back up the next day, and I suppose the doctor can tell me what time that needs to be. I'll let Mr. Bowen know before he leaves."

He nodded his head, relieved he had such a capable wife, but added just to be sure, "I'll be glad to come up or help if you need something. I guess you can try our phone at the end of the lane, but I doubt if I would hear you."

"Just love me," she told him, the tears spilling over. "This is such a hard time for me."

"That's easy to do, dear," he assured her, going to her and taking her hand. "God will surely help us, if we ask Him."

Sarah awoke in the dark with a sudden jerk, uncertain what had awakened her, her heart pounding and throat dry from intense fear. The ticking of the wind-up alarm clock came from the little footstool by her bed. Without moving her head, her eyes found the outline of the clock hands. It was 4:30. "Almost morning," she thought.

All the doubts she had kept at bay during the day seemed gathered around her, watching with eyes she could almost feel. Death seemed so real, so possible, so close, that she wanted to cry out for help. But who was there to call to?

Would Melvin understand if she screamed? What good would that do? He would say she was having a nightmare, pushed to the edge by the trouble gathered around them. Was she having a nightmare? Blinking her eyes, she was uncertain. People could blink their eyes in their dreams, couldn't they?

She wanted to reach out her hand, to touch another person, to feel his comfort … but would it be comforting? No longer sure, she froze, afraid to move, afraid to look at Melvin, afraid of herself, afraid of her doubts.

God seemed far away as the stillness hung over the house like a heavy blanket. She could almost taste sickness, its evil bouncing off the walls of her mind, as the ticking of the alarm clock bounced around the room in the silence.

Maybe she was dying and not James. The thought brought a fresh wave of fear, pulsating through her, penetrating her faith in the goodness of God, in the goodness of anyone. Would Melvin love her if she were dying like James was? Would he still look at her the way he did now if some vicious cancer robbed her beauty, took her youth, left her helpless in its grasp?

The covers seemed like scant protection from the darkness as she clutched them. She dared not move, afraid of what was around her, afraid of what was inside her thoughts, her doubting of God. Holding on to the blanket with both hands, she felt the fear like ice running through her veins.

Minutes passed, as even Melvin's snoring seemed to fade away, becoming stilled. Was he dying too? Were they all dying in this dreadful silence? Without turning her head, her eyes found the bedroom window in search of any explanation. The late moon, three quarters of its normal size, hung above the horizon. Sarah could just see it, its soft glow falling across the open window sill.

She lay there listening, then suddenly became aware of many night sounds around her, coming so abruptly it took a moment to absorb that the silence was gone. It took more time before she was able to release the blankets from her frozen fingers, slowly letting the blood flow freely in them again. Was this death, coming early, seeking to claim even before its time? She shuddered at the question, the thought starting to freeze her again, till she started to pray silently.

Dear Jesus, please help me, she repeated until she found some degree of calm. *I am so afraid of death,* she whispered, hoping Melvin didn't hear, the tears coming. *Protect my son. Oh God, he's too young to die. Oh, Jesus please?*

The pillow was soon wet as sorrow flooded over her, but the fears had dissipated, her heart becoming quieter as the sounds of the night rose to her ears. Listening to them and praying, she was soon able to roll over and drop soundly off to sleep until the alarm shrieked that the time had come for morning chores.

CHAPTER TWENTY-ONE

SARAH ALREADY HAD the breakfast dishes cleaned up and the two boys ready when Martha pulled into the driveway on Friday morning. They were scheduled to leave for James's appointment in Indianapolis, and hearing a vehicle in the driveway, Sarah at first thought the driver, Mr. Bowen, had arrived. When she went to the window to check and saw Martha's van, she returned to the kitchen to finish some other work before she left for a possible two days absence. Her sister could find her own way into the house.

"Good morning," Martha greeted the boys sitting on the couch as she carefully shut the front door. "How is everyone?"

The boys both looked skeptical at the moment, even if it was their aunt Martha. Life was obviously not on its normal routine this morning, and they were still evaluating the landscape.

"How are you feeling?" she asked, coming over to James, touching his forehead with her hand.

"Kind of tired," he told her, blinking his eyes and keeping them on the floor.

JERRY EICHER

"Well, that's understandable," Martha told him sooth-
ingly. "Maybe the doctor can get you better soon."

He shrugged as she took her hand off his forehead,
going out to the kitchen where Sarah was still rushing
around.

"Is there anything I can help with?" Martha asked the
moving back of her sister.

"Hi," Sarah replied, just glancing up. "Not really. I'm
almost done. Just some things that need doing, since Melvin
might be here by himself overnight. Surprised you showed
up. I thought at first it was the driver."

Martha pulled a chair out from under the table, sitting
down. "Just thought I would stop by and see you off before
I go to work. Being it's the day, you know."

"That's nice of you," Sarah told her, putting the broom
she was using back on its hook in the closet. "I am in fact
glad you stopped by."

"Oh," Martha half rose on her chair, thinking it involved
some sort of physical labor.

"No, no," Sarah motioned her back into her chair, pulling one out for herself. "It's not that."

Martha waited as she could tell Sarah was gathering her
thoughts.

"I keep having these fears during the night," Sarah
began, searching for her way. "I wake up and it's all quiet,
and," she paused, half afraid to say it, "it's like death is
already here, Martha. Oh, it's awful. I don't know if I'm going
to be able to make this, Martha, if, you know, he dies."

"Does this happen every night?"

"No, just twice now, I think. It happened this morning

again. I wake up suddenly, and the fear of James going is just all around me."

"Then what happens?" Martha was all ears and sympathy.

"Well, last night I started praying and then it went away, but I don't think this is over with at all yet. It may even get worse, I'm afraid."

"You sure you're not imagining things, just being scared? I mean, you are under an awful lot of pressure. Because I have no idea what I would do if my son was so sick."

Sarah nodded in understanding. "I've wondered myself about that, but I don't think so. I think James is in real danger, and we'll just have to trust in God to help us through the situation."

"I'm sure he will," Martha agreed.

Sarah glanced around, some last-minute thoughts of what needed to be done running through her mind, when it occurred to her that she had not yet told Martha about Esther. Grimly, she pressed her lips together at the thought that she might as well get her version of it out before Martha heard it from somewhere else. "I took James to see Esther," she announced, settling back into her chair.

"You took James to see Esther?"

"Yes. I hadn't had a chance to tell you yet. You see, Mom kept insisting, and I guess I gave in. Well," Sarah paused, thinking, "those fears had something to do with it, too."

"What happened then at Esther's?" Martha asked, very interested.

"She gave James a cup of tea — you know her ways. I'm ashamed of myself now, but I guess it shows how badly you want things to happen. I actually was hoping that Esther could do something for him."

"It didn't do any good?" Martha chuckled.

"Not for James's problem. How can it? It really upset me, especially when she claimed that it had."

"Just out and told you he was well?" Martha was not surprised. "I must say, it sounds like her. So what did you do?"

"Got upset, and left in a hurry. I suppose now it will be all over the place. Sarah Yoder, thinking she's better than the old ways, and all that stuff."

"Well, she's not really the old ways," Martha protested. "I mean I was Amish, so I know a little bit about it. She's just Esther. She may think she's it, but she's not."

"I suppose so, but she can still make a lot of trouble if she wants to. I fully expect her to get Mom all upset about this. Esther even told me not to go today. Can you imagine that?"

"With Esther," Martha made a wry face, "yes, I can believe it. She has a lot of faith in her herbs and things. Nothing serious ever comes of it I'm sure. Oh, she helps people with their colds, but most of those would get better by themselves anyway. I mean, a little tea does anyone good."

"You ought to tell *her* that." Sarah glared at the wall remembering. "She thinks it's holy writ."

"Sounds like she really got to you," Martha chuckled again. "I always thought I was the hot–headed one."

"I guess when your son's involved, it stirs up things I never knew I had in me. It just wasn't right," Sarah concluded, running her hand over her face.

Martha, pondering the situation, finally suggested, "I think we ought to really pray about this. There's so much going on, and sometimes I guess that's about all we can do. Other than go to the doctor, of course, and even they need God's help."

Sarah nodded, agreeing. "Praying does help a lot. I know that, and I'm sure I'll do my share of it before this is over. Melvin has been real good so far too. He saw how upset I was when I came back from Esther's place, and came in to spend some time with me and the boys. He even sang with us. That was so nice of him, considering how hard it is for him to keep up with his farm work as it is."

Martha nodded her head, agreeing. "It's hard to keep it in focus during times like this, but we really are blessed."

The crunch of tires on the gravel outside interrupted their conversation as Mr. Bowen's van pulled up the driveway. Martha popped off her chair, glancing at the clock. "Well, I must be going, since I'm in his way, I'm sure. I'll check with you when you come back, okay? If you need anything, we have a phone at the house you can call. You know the number, right?"

Sarah nodded, bustling around quickly to get James and Nelson out the door as Martha left in front of them. "Hope the doctor has good news," she hollered back as she climbed in her van.

Mr. Bowen greeted Sarah and the boys pleasantly, stepping out to open the van door for them. Mrs. Bowen, in the front seat, her face all concern, greeted them too. Since having an extra passenger along was unusual, Mr. Bowen felt the need to explain. "The missus decided to come along," he told Sarah, "what with the long trip and James's condition. We both just wanted to be there."

"That's awfully nice of you, but it wasn't necessary," Sarah told them, touched by their concern. Then, seeing their looks at James, she offered, "He's feeling pretty well today, I think."

"Good morning," they both said to James again, smiling, their eyes filled with compassion.

"Good morning," he offered back. Nelson joined in with his own "Good morning," not wanting to be left out.

Sarah settled the boys on the first bench seat of the van, sliding the two small suitcases into the back. She got in on the second seat as Mr. Bowen closed the sliding door. When he started down the driveway, Sarah mentioned that Nelson needed to be dropped off at her mother's. Mr. Bowen nodded his acknowledgement, knowing where she lived.

"You still think you're staying overnight?" he asked, glancing at her in the rearview mirror.

"I don't know," she told him, unsure herself. "I just have to leave Nelson in case we do have to stay up there for the night. From what the doctor in Colorado said, they will have to take a bone marrow sample, and that takes an overnight stay at the hospital. I suppose the doctor's office will let us know what to expect and when. Do you think you are driving back home today and then back up tomorrow to pick us up?"

He shrugged as he pulled left at the end of the driveway. "I was just talking about it with the wife here, and I think it would be less expensive for you if we just stayed up there for the night rather than drive back down. Even with the motel bill, it will much less than what the miles are."

"You would do that?" Sarah asked, surprised at his generosity.

"Certainly," he told her. "Me and the wife can find plenty to do in Indianapolis for a day. I mean, we're not young chickens anymore," he chuckled, "but we could go shopping if nothing else. Of course, we won't charge you for the miles driving around up there. There would just be the motel bill."

"That's very kind of you," Sarah told them, "both of you. You wouldn't have to do this."

"We are more than glad," Mr. Bowen spoke sincerely, his wife nodding across from him.

As they neared Deborah's place, Mrs. Bowen turned around in her seat and cleared her throat, looking a little embarrassed. "Ah, I'm not trying to be nosy, but I heard you went to see Esther."

"Oh, you heard?" was all Sarah had to offer, her eyes glazing at the knowledge that the story was already getting around.

"It's just that" — Mrs. Bowen searched for words — "we're just glad you are still going this morning to Indianapolis."

"Oh, why is that? You thought I wouldn't go?"

Mrs. Bowen shifted her eyes, then proceeded cautiously. "Well, we don't know Amish ways that well, even though we drive them around all the time."

Sarah lifted her eyebrows questioningly, waiting.

Mrs. Bowen cleared her throat. "It's just that Esther is

telling it all over the place. How you came there for treatment, she says, and now she claims that with her teas James is perfectly healed. Quite loud about it. Says if you go to Indianapolis, she will tell the bishop that you don't listen to the old ways anymore. Of course," Mrs. Bowen's voice was tender, "we have a hard time seeing how teas can cure possible leukemia. So that's why we're glad to see you are still going. Doctors are very necessary in your situation, we think. If nothing else to see if something is really wrong with him or not."

Sarah sighed. What was the use of pretending with the Bowens? They hauled the Amish around all the time and they ended up hearing what was going on anyway, so she might as well launch into her side of the story. "I don't agree with Esther and her ways," she told them. "I mean, she does help some people, I guess. The reason I went to her was because Mom wanted me to, and I guess maybe I hoped it would help, but my experience with her the other day was not very pleasant. I was afraid she would be upset, but I'm not going to listen to her if she tells me what isn't true or tells me not to check out what she claims is true."

"That's good to hear," Mrs. Bowen smiled in relief, still turned around in her seat. "You don't think she really will make trouble for you with the bishop, will she?"

"I don't think so," Sarah said. "It's probably just talk because she's upset. Bishop Amos has much more sense than that, and I know he has nothing against going to doctors."

Mrs. Bowen seemed satisfied with that, adding again that she was so glad to see Sarah keep the appointment in Indianapolis.

CHAPTER TWENTY-TWO

M R. BOWEN GLANCED at Sarah in the rearview mirror as he pulled into Ben and Deborah's driveway. "We will be praying for you, today and tomorrow. We also placed you on the prayer list Wednesday night at church." He added, "I hope you don't mind."

"Certainly not," Sarah said, deeply grateful again and surprised at this unexpected inclusion in their church affairs. "We can use all the prayer we can get." She paused, not wanting to say too much. "It's been hard. I've just never been through this before." She finally ventured, "Even growing up we were a pretty healthy family."

"These kinds of things happen to all of us," Mr. Bowen stated simply, again surprising Sarah with this whole-hearted inclusion into the human family.

As the van came to a stop in front of the house, she prepared to take Nelson in, reaching for his suitcase. Her mother was already on the front porch, having heard the van drive up.

"Do you need help with anything?" Mr. Bowen asked Sarah, ready to open his door if she did.

"No, I'm fine," she assured Mr. Bowen, taking Nelson by his hand as they got out the van and walked towards the house. On the way up the walk, she gave her final instructions to Nelson. "You'll be staying at Grandma's till probably tomorrow, okay? We'll probably pick you up then. If not, you can come to church and we will get you there."

He nodded, happy to see Deborah, his head full of plans for playing in a different setting.

"Good morning," Deborah said as Sarah got closer.

She returned the greeting with a nod, setting the suitcase on the porch. "I've got his Sunday clothing along, just in case we can't pick him up on Saturday. I don't know how this will all go, but hopefully we can be home before too late. If not, we'll get him on Sunday."

"Oh, he'll be fine," Deborah glowed, reaching out her hands to give Nelson a hug. "I think I can still keep a young boy happy for a few days, though it's been awhile."

Sarah was happy too, seeing her mother's good mood, figuring that Esther had not gotten to her yet. How that had happened since the Bowens already knew, she wasn't certain, just thankful. Not that her mother would be too hard on her, she hoped, but this morning the burden would have been simply one more thing added to an already heavy load.

"Well, we have to be going." She moved towards the van. "It's going to be a long hard day, no doubt."

"Just do what they tell you, and you'll be fine," Deborah assured her, then added in a regretful tone of voice: "I so wish, though, you had gone to Esther before you saw the doctor in Indianapolis."

Something like despair swept over Sarah, as she now had to say something – but surely the whole thing didn't have to be hashed over in detail, not with the Bowens waiting in the van. "Well," she got it out quickly, "I did go Mother, but it didn't do any good."

"Oh, you did go!" The smile spread across Deborah's face from one end to the other. "What a wonderful, good thing of you."

"But it didn't do any good," Sarah repeated, wanting at least some of the story to come out now, although hopefully not more than was necessary.

"Oh, but you went," Deborah gushed. "That's all that matters. Esther will do the rest. It doesn't matter if you think it did any good or not."

"Well, I think it didn't," Sarah told her, wanting that to be abundantly clear. Maybe when Esther got to her mother, that would serve as a buffer to what would no doubt follow. "And I have to go," she added, giving a last glance at the happy Nelson before heading back to the van.

As they took off, Sarah looked back at Deborah and Nelson on the front porch. She held him by the hand, looking at him as he told her something intently, his other hand in motion to illustrate the point.

Nothing more was said, other than the normal talk of travel, as the miles rolled along underneath the van, first on Route 50 and then on Route 37, a four-lane highway. Mr. Bowen concentrated on his driving and Sarah busied herself with making sure James was comfortable. Taking the Interstate Bypass West, Mr. Bowen soon found Interstate 65 and from there the downtown exit at 10th street.

When they arrived at the medical complex, Mrs. Bowen said she was going in with Sarah, while Mr. Bowen decided to stay with the van. "It's more comfortable inside," Mrs. Bowen informed him as she was getting out. "You can just stay in the lobby while I go upstairs with Sarah."

"No," he shook his head, "those lobbies have nothing interesting to read. Out here I can listen to the radio at least. They have some good Christian ones up here."

"He doesn't think much of doctors' offices," Mrs. Bowen smiled understandingly at Sarah, "so let's get going."

With James by their side, they walked from the parking lot to the office building, even taller looking now that they were out of the van and on foot. Its twelve stories towered over them, more pronounced by the nearby buildings of nearly equal heights, creating an upward tunnel effect.

Once inside, they found the names of the doctors with their respective floors all laid out neatly on the wall directory. Mrs. Bowen stood in front of the bronze plate and found Dr. Watkins' name on the third floor, room 334. Sarah had already taken James over to the elevators by the time Mrs. Bowen was done, preparing to push the button when she arrived.

Two men and a woman walked in with them and they rode up together, no one saying anything. Sarah still found that strange, remembering the same experience from her time with the English in New York.

The first man got off on the second floor, and the other two stayed on when the third floor door opened. Sarah smiled at them as she and Mrs. Bowen walked out of the elevator, provoking no response from the woman but prodding the man to nod slightly as his lips stretched a little into a thin smile.

"Are people always unfriendly in the city?" Sarah asked Mrs. Bowen as they walked towards the room.

"Not always, dear — it's not just the city, it's the elevator," she smiled, deducing the source of Sarah's question.

"Do I look strange to them?" Sarah wondered, still not quite satisfied with the answer.

"Well, yes, you look strange compared to them, but most people know who the Amish are. It should actually make them more comfortable."

"How is that?" Sarah wanted to know, curious.

"Dear, you should know," Mrs. Bowen responded, chuckling. "Amish ladies aren't known for coming on to men. Same as nuns, I guess. The men don't expect ulterior motives, and the women don't have to stay on guard as much, I guess. Just makes people friendlier in general."

"I hadn't thought of that," Sarah mused, absorbing the information.

"Well, you should. It's one of your culture's strong points. Look, here we are," Mrs. Bowen announced. "Right on time, too."

They entered room 334. Its crisp, clean feel was readily evident. The secretary greeted them with a smile. "Your names, please," she asked, then directed: "Have a seat over there. The doctor is running on schedule this morning."

"I suspect he always runs on schedule," Sarah whispered to Mrs. Bowen when they had found seats, with James beside her.

"I think so, too," Mrs. Bowen told her. "The place is really nice, which is a good sign, believe me, and you can use all the good signs you can get."

"Let's hope it is," Sarah replied, feeling a little better. "It does feel like the same kind of people as the doctor we met in Colorado."

"It's the Christian compassion," Mrs. Bowen whispered. "Other religions don't have it quite as readily, what with their karma and the will of their gods. It's the Christians who believe that God works with them to make things better."

Sarah made no comment to that, because she didn't feel she knew enough about such matters to judge what others did or didn't do.

In what seemed like only a few minutes, Sarah and James were taken back by Nurse Bloom, as she introduced herself. Sarah thought the name fit. Her sunny personality and round face stood out even in a profession trained for friendliness.

"So how are we today?" Nurse Bloom asked James, a smile covering her face.

James had to grin but he refused to say anything, hanging his head when she tickled his chin.

"Not talking, are we?" she teased, then without pausing continued to take his weight and temperature. Motioning with her hand, she had him sit at a little white table. "Just hold still for a little bit — this won't take much time or hurt too much, I don't think." She proceeded to stick him with a needle for blood. James, wincing, took it in stride.

"That didn't hurt but just a prick, now did it?" she commented when done, expecting no answer but getting one this time as James ventured, "Not too much." Nurse Bloom looked up in surprise.

"Talking, are we?" Her smile spread across her face again. "Now that's a boy. Keep your chin up. The doctor will be right in to see you, okay?"

She left, shutting the door behind her, and Sarah and James sat waiting in silence until the door opened again. A middle-aged man walked in, bald on top and a little round at the waist. Sarah liked him right away, and she noticed out of the corner of her eyes that James seemed to be of the same mind.

"Dr. Watkins," he said as an introduction, nodding his head at Sarah. "So what have we here? Are you James?"

James nodded his head, "Yes."

"Okay then, James, let's see what the problem is." Dr. Watkins took James's hand to help him up on the long examining table, then proceeded to examine him, tapping, listening, and asking questions. He then walked back to the little table, sitting down to study his clipboard.

When he was done paging through the papers he turned to Sarah. "I really think we have caught this problem early enough, since he seems to be just in the beginning stages, but we do need a bone marrow sample to be certain. After that, if I am correct, an aggressive regimen of treatment will be necessary. With that, I think, we may have a very good chance of stopping the disease."

"It is leukemia then?" Sarah asked him, her heart heavy.

"I would be very surprised if it wasn't," Dr. Watkins ventured cautiously. "I am of the same mind as Dr. Bradshaw, with his diagnosis in Colorado. Yet anyone can be wrong."

"Oh, I wasn't doubting you," Sarah exclaimed, afraid that he thought so, because she did not doubt his verdict or the one from Colorado. What was on her mind was Esther and her proclamation, but she certainly was not going to tell this doctor about the cup of tea that was supposed to get rid of leukemia. Now, though, with the same test results as those in Colorado, she would at least have something to tell her mother, should Deborah begin any praise of Esther's pronouncements.

Dr. Watkins shrugged, not attempting to read her thoughts. "I suppose one always reaches for hope, but this one doesn't look good. Our blood tests this morning indicate the same white blood cell count as Dr. Bradshaw's did."

Sarah nodded, appreciating the time he was taking to explain things to her. It helped in this strange world she found herself in.

Chapter Twenty-Three

D R. WATKINS PAUSED to glance at Sarah before continuing. "Would you like to know more about his leukemia?"

"Of course," Sarah said quickly, not because she had any fascination with the disease, but because what affected James touched her. "Is it okay if James hears it?" she asked, not certain as to what details he planned on giving.

Dr. Watkins nodded. "I don't know why not. I'll give just an overview. What we possibly have in James's case is Acute Lymphocytic Leukemia, known as A.L.L. It is the most common form of leukemia in children. Over half of the cases are boys, and over 80% are children under five, so James doesn't quite fit that category, but I still think that is his illness.

"Acute leukemia is a rapidly progressing disease. It results in the accumulation of cells in the marrow and blood that are immature and functionless. Often the marrow can no longer produce enough normal red cells, white blood cells, or platelets. From this, most leukemia patients will suffer from anemia. It will also result in a lowering of the normal white cells and, with that, the ability of the body to fight off infections. That is why you have cuts that don't heal well and that sort of thing."

Sarah nodded her head when he glanced at her again. "So that is why we had the problem with the cuts," she said, expressing more of a statement than a question.

"Yes, that is a common problem," he continued. "Anyone can get leukemia. We don't know what causes it yet. There are some theories, but nothing explains all the cases. Once we know for sure what we are dealing with, though, we will treat your leukemia with the aim of bringing about what we call remission. That is when there is no more evidence of the disease and the blood test returns completely normal. In the case of acute leukemia, if we can obtain a remission and keep it there for five years, you will be considered cured. So, you see, James, we will likely be seeing a lot of each other. Is that okay?"

Dr. Watkins paused again, not sure whether James would have a response to that or not, but wanting to include him. James, for his part, just sat on the edge of the examining table looking down at the floor. Since he appeared noncommunicative, and not wanting to create any discomfort for him, Dr. Watkins turned towards Sarah, preparing to ask her if she had any questions. But then James spoke up, his little voice quivering, his legs pulled back under the examination table. "What are you going to do to me?"

Dr. Watkins turned back around, tenderness in his eyes. "Well, James, I'm afraid it's not good news, really. We have to fight your illness with treatments that will not be all that pleasant, but even before then I need what is called a core bone marrow sample.

"Right after you leave my office today, I will have the secretary give your mother the directions to the hospital.

You will go there, and they will take care of you. I'm sorry that it's going to hurt, but we have to know for sure what your problem is."

"Is it going to hurt a lot?" James asked, looking up and letting his legs swing away from the table.

"Ah...." Dr. Watkins knew there was no way of avoiding the truth. The boy would find out one way or the other. "I'm afraid the answer is yes, James. It will hurt a lot, but we have to know. Once we do know we can get you started on a treatment program that will make you better, with your parents' permission, of course," he said as he glanced back towards Sarah. "In your case, I would say chemotherapy. A bone marrow transplant is the other option for you, but I think we have caught it soon enough where that option may not be necessary. Does that answer your question?"

James shrugged his shoulders. "It's bad then?"

Dr. Watkins got up from his chair before he answered this one, putting his arm on James's leg. "It will be hard, but good, James, because it will make you better. You'll be a brave boy for your mother now, won't you?"

"I don't know," James said, glancing up at him, searching his eyes. "I just want to get better, so I can play real hard again. Will you talk to Jesus about this like Dr. Dobson did in Colorado?"

Dr. Watkins was not sure what to say, as he could tell from the sounds over his shoulder that Sarah was crying. These were always hard moments for him. It seemed like it took more energy than doing the actual work, conflicting him at times with where the line lay between his Christian faith and his medical knowledge. Reaching deep within himself, he found again that strength to care. "We will see, James," he said. "I hope, with God's help, you will be better soon. We will just have to do the best we can. Come now, I will give your mother the information she needs, and I will see you again real soon."

With that he got James off the table and escorted them personally to the front desk. "See that they get the information about where to go for the sample. I think Melody set it up for Riley," he told the nurse at the desk. "Make an appointment for the end of the week after next for them too." Then turning back to Sarah he told her, "We will call you with results of the bone marrow. Talk things over with your husband, and call in for confirmation on the next appointment. If everything is okay, we can start treatment then."

With that he was gone, and Sarah soon was given a handful of papers with directions to Riley Hospital for Children and also info on the chemo treatments. The secretary informed Sarah that an overnight stay would be required at the hospital after the bone marrow sample was taken.

After writing out a check for payment, Sarah thanked the secretary but didn't look at any of the papers until she and Mrs. Bowen and James were back in the van, when she pulled out and handed the hospital directions to Mr. Bowen.

While Mr. Bowen drove the van downtown to Tenth Street, she paged through the rest of the information on the chemotherapy treatments. They were separated into three phases called induction, consolidation, and maintenance, all of it there in black and white. What was not there, she was sure, was the pain, the tears, and the suffering the body would endure as killing medicines were introduced in an effort to cure. What was also not there was any reference to the upcoming bone marrow sample.

As Mr. Bowen pulled down tenth street, the sprawling buildings of the Riley Hospital for Children complex soon appeared on his left. Following the signs, he turned on to Wilson Street and from there to the Wilson Street Visitors Parking Center.

"Do you think we need to go inside with her?" Mr. Bowen asked his wife when he had parked, giving an apologetic glance towards Sarah for asking in front of her.

"I don't think you need to," Sarah was quick to tell them both. "It looks like the main hospital building is just across the street from here. I was watching when we drove in."

Mr. Bowen consulted the directions Sarah had given him. "Let's see, it says to go to the Hospital building across Wishard Drive from the Wilson Street Visitors Parking Center. Is that Wishard Drive?" Mr. Bowen motioned with his chin towards the south of the parking garage.

"Yes it is, dear," his wife told him, "but Sarah, I am more than glad to come in with you and see that you are settled before we leave. I mean, we don't have anything urgent to do for the rest of the day."

"No, no." Sarah would have none of it. "You have brought me here, and I can see the hospital across the street. The secretary at Dr. Watkins' office said they already know we are coming, so I'm sure I'll be fine."

"So when do we pick you up tomorrow?" Mr. Bowen asked, again glancing at his wife.

To this Sarah had no idea.

"They probably don't know yet," Mrs. Bowen said, knowing the question was in reference to whether she should go inside to find out. "It probably depends on how well he does overnight. What we can do is call the hospital mid-morning tomorrow sometime, and go from there."

Sarah waited, because this was their planning, something she knew nothing about.

Mrs. Bowen turned to assure Sarah: "I'll be waiting for you then, dear, in the main lobby on the first floor. If for some reason I'm not there, don't worry. We're just late for some reason."

Glancing out the window, Sarah found the loneliness and vastness of the city pressing in on her. These people, her only way of getting back home, were leaving her with what sounded like uneasy connections on how to get back together. A day, she knew, was an awfully long time, especially with what might be lying ahead of her.

An inspiration hit her. "Why don't I give you my sister Martha's phone number?" she said hastily. "That way, if for some reason we can't find each other, we can both call Martha and make contact there."

"Let's see," Mrs. Bowen thought aloud, "tomorrow's Saturday — your sister will be home then."

"In and out," Sarah told her, figuring she knew Martha's schedule fairly well. "If she's not in, let's leave a message with our phone numbers, and when she comes back in, she can contact both of us."

"Sounds fair enough," Mr. Bowen declared. "I really doubt whether we will need all that, but it's good to have, I guess."

"Well, we'll have it just in case," Mrs. Bowen told him, to which Sarah wholeheartedly agreed, glad that a safety net for tomorrow was in place. Little things, she knew, could turn into big things, and right now she had enough big things to deal with. She gave the phone number to Mrs. Bowen by memory, who copied it on a piece of paper she took from her purse.

"Let's go, then," she told James when that was done, taking his hand and adding a "Thanks, we'll see you tomorrow" to the Bowens.

She saw their van going back up Wilson street as she took James across the street, checking carefully both ways before crossing. At the front desk of the lobby, she gave her information to the attendant and was told to wait.

Taking seats in the front lobby, they found the place fairly humming around them. Visitors and patients with children hurried by, elevator doors down the hall constantly opened and shut, and white-clad nurses and doctors occasionally appeared.

Thirty minutes later or so, since Sarah couldn't see a clock and carried no timepiece in her purse, a nurse appeared asking for Mrs. Yoder. Sarah rose to her feet and took James's hand. The nurse identified herself as Nurse Witter, a young girl, Sarah thought, who couldn't be much over twenty.

"You ready to go?" Her smile seemed nervous, stretched, as she glanced between Sarah and James, which didn't help Sarah's feelings of unease at what lay behind those white swinging doors ahead of them.

Without waiting or expecting an answer, Nurse Witter

turned to go, her body language asking them to follow, leading through the double doors Sarah had already noticed and then down two hall turns from there. The room where she left them was a simple affair with no door on it, consisting of a low white-sheeted bed, two chairs for the accompanying relatives, Sarah assumed, and a table containing the usual hospital fare of needles, tubes, and bottles with their unintelligible labels.

A short wait later, a small cart full of hospital equipment appeared in the doorway opening, followed by the nurse pushing it — Nurse Rose, Sarah saw by her name tag. She smiled at James, a middle-aged woman, her still black hair protruding out from under her white headdress, experience and competence in her every motion.

Relieved that it was not Nurse Witter returning for an obvious involvement in the extraction of the bone marrow sample, Sarah felt herself relax a little, returning Nurse Rose's greeting with some cheerfulness. At least they appeared to be in competent hands.

As Nurse Rose was helping James on to the table, the doctor appeared — Dr. Roster, he told her, nodding in her direction, his attention on James, though. Sarah's feelings were lifted even further. A young fellow, she thought, but she liked him anyway, thinking how silly it was to make such a quick judgment. She watched him run his fingers gently down James's thin leg, probing, then muttering something to Nurse Rose. It gave her hope.

Sarah was glad for every good emotion coming her way, needing them for the downhill ride to come. After a local anesthetic, which Dr. Roster told James would prick a little, he produced a long hollow boring needle, asking Sarah to stand with James at his head.

She did, holding both of his hands on either side of him as he clutched the side of the bed. His eyes became wild with pain as Dr. Roster worked his needle, pausing only once to prick again with his anesthetic needle, boring towards the bone in James's leg.

"Sorry son," his voice came as from a distance, which Sarah was sure didn't mean anything to James, whose grip on her fingers was now so intense she could feel her blood flow being shut off. "The anesthetic only helps so much. We have to reach the center of the bone."

Mercifully it was over quickly. Sarah's fingers were numb, her tears joining those of James's flowing down his face. He said nothing, though, his cheeks white. "A brave boy," Nurse Rose said, patting his abused leg just above the needle entry point, after bandaging it. "Now off to your room for antibiotics overnight, and you ought to be okay."

"That's it," Dr. Roster added his approval to Nurse Rose's words. "We will send this off to the lab now, and your doctor will let you know the results when they come in." With that he was gone, and Nurse Rose took them out into the hall and up the elevator to the third floor for their expected overnight stay.

After getting James settled in, Nurse Rose left them alone, with Sarah still hurting — although she was sure her own pain was nothing to what James had gone through. "Was it pretty bad?" she asked him, running her face over his face and hair, finding his cheeks still moist from the tears.

He only nodded his head, which she knew underscored the depth of his pain. "It was deep inside me," he finally ventured, his voice trembling. "It still hurts."

She stayed with him, telling him Bible stories from memory as various nurses checked up on them during the evening and early night hours. She wished she had brought something along to read for herself, finding nothing that interested her in her exploratory trip to the visitors' lounge. She did notice a more comfortable couch there, using it later that night for a few hours of sleep when James seemed settled down.

In the morning around ten, Dr. Roster came back by on his rounds, checking James and giving Sarah the good news that they could leave at two. Assuming that the Bowens would find this information available when they called the hospital, she did not call Martha, figuring she would save that option for an emergency, which this did not seem to be.

Nurse Rose came at 1:45 to wheel James down to the lobby for checkout. To Sarah's great delight, Mrs. Bowen was waiting, seated on one of the lobby chairs, a cheerful smile on her face. The sight of the familiar rushed over Sarah in a great flood of emotion, bringing an intense longing for Melvin and Nelson — that desire must have been there, covered, all night, frozen by the hospital stay.

She could only smile, afraid to say anything lest the tears come, as Nurse Rose stopped in front of Mrs. Bowen, assuming by the look on Sarah's face that there was a connection. "This your party, dear?" she asked, more statement than question as she helped James off the wheelchair.

"Now take it a little easy on that leg," she said, giving James a mock stern look as he tested walking on it. "You just had your bone bored yesterday."

He nodded, the trace of a smile on his face, already losing the memory. Sarah wondered at the ability of the young to move on after misfortune.

"Thanks," Sarah made sure to say to Nurse Rose, then remembered: "Where am I supposed to pay?"

"Oh, they'll send you a bill if your insurance doesn't cover it," Nurse Rose chuckled. "You don't need to worry about that."

That she had no insurance Sarah did not mention, preferring to leave that subject alone. Melvin would know what to do, since the fact that she was not paying it now seemed to indicate to her that the bill was a large sum. For a moment that weight pressed heavy on her, but she pushed it away. Her concern was for James, and the money would just have to be taken care of later.

Seeing that Mrs. Bowen was ready to leave, Sarah followed her outside and towards the parking lot, making sure they did not go too fast for James. He favored his punctured leg, stepping gingerly on it, then smiling when he found it still functioned properly.

His joy at this small discovery brought tears to her eyes again. She wondered how many tears she would have left by the time this was over. Not too many she supposed, as they greeted Mr. Bowen at the van and headed out of town.

CHAPTER TWENTY-FOUR

R IDING DOWN HIGHWAY 37, Sarah felt the tears threaten yet again at the thought of the test results soon to come, and prayed they might be spared. But how could that be? The disease was there without a doubt and would simply have to be met head on, with whatever the doctors had to fight it — fire with fire, lest her little boy be lost to cancer's ravishes.

She wanted to let the tears flow in full force, but she held them back. They would have to wait until James was not around, lest her own pain add to his and perhaps push him to despair of any hope. Her shoulders were broader than his, she resolved, and she must bear her share and as much of his as possible.

Mr. and Mrs. Bowen kept a respectable silence the whole way home, knowing they were unable to enter fully into this trauma. From the outside looking in, they did what they could, reaching out with their hearts in caring. Since silence was needed at the moment, they gave what they had to give. In so doing they had their reward when they arrived at Deborah's place with Sarah and James, tears shimmering in their eyes, but somehow comforted.

Walking in quickly to pick up Nelson, Sarah made no

effort to hide the sign of her tears from her mother, who met her at the front door.

"What did the doctor say?" Deborah wanted to know, concern in her voice.

"Just the same blood test results as Colorado had, but they ought to have the final verdict from the bone marrow sample in a few days. They said they would call me, so I left them Martha's number as a secondary number, since I doubt we will be out by the phone shack." While telling her mother this, Sarah vaguely remembered that Esther might have spoken to her, but that problem seemed quite distant at present, blotted out by the events of the past twenty-four hours.

Deborah was all sympathy. "Well, let us know when you hear something. Nelson was just as good as gold," she added when Nelson, hearing the voices, came running. "Here's his suitcase," Deborah said, as Nelson ran gladly into Sarah's arms.

"Thanks a lot," Sarah told her mother, taking the suitcase in one arm and Nelson's hand in the other, "We really have to be going. I don't want to keep the Bowens waiting."

"You be good now," Deborah told Nelson, waving at him as they went down the walks.

At the van, Nelson took one look at his teary-eyed brother before exclaiming, "Did the doctor hurt him real bad?"

James smiled though his tears, nodding, "A little, but he's trying to make me better."

"That's good," Nelson pronounced in all the authority of a five-year-old, then dismissed the thought completely from his mind as he proceeded to tell both of them all about his days at Grandma's.

When they arrived home, Sarah thanked the Bowens deeply as she paid them, telling them what a great help they had been and she would contact them for taxi service at the start of any treatments.

They said they were willing and ready to do what they could. Nelson for his part waved at them as they drove slowly out of the driveway. James was more sober, looking around the place as if he had been away a long time and now found it very dear to his heart.

The long evening shadows were already reaching out across the back of the barn when Melvin came in. He was running a little late, but the fieldwork needed to be done. Not expecting anything urgent from Sarah's trip to Indianapolis, he figured suppertime would be soon enough to catch up on the news.

He put the horses in the barn, making sure they were comfortable for the night, then came out to headlights in the driveway. He waited, not at all surprised when it turned out to be Silas and Martha. They would want to get news and share their concern in person.

Glancing over his shoulder, he noticed low dark storm clouds out of the southwest appearing to push upwards in an attempt to build thunderstorms.

"Think it will rain?" Silas asked in his booming voice as he stepped out of the van, shutting the door smartly behind him.

"Don't know," Melvin responded, figuring Silas likely had more information than he did, other than maybe his farmer's instinct. "Hear anything on the radio?"

"No," Silas replied, glancing at the sky himself as Martha

came around the van and joined him. "I didn't listen to the forecast today. James and Sarah back?"

Melvin nodded as they walked together towards the house. "I haven't been in the house yet, but they drove in an hour ago or so." Coming to the front door he held it open for them, the wind already stirring and pushing against the door as he shut it behind him.

Sarah came to the kitchen door, her smiling face washed from the tears. "Good to see you," she greeted them. "You staying for supper?"

"Not to eat," Martha told her quickly, not wanting to add a greater burden than was necessary. "We already ate, but we can talk out in the kitchen while you eat. I wouldn't want to hold up your supper."

"Pull up the chairs, then," Sarah said, happy with her sister's visit. "I am so glad you came. It's been some day up at the hospital, and the sight of family faces is so good. I didn't get to the lanterns, yet," she added in Melvin direction, returning to finish her supper preparations. Martha joined in, setting the plates on the kitchen table for them.

Melvin took Silas with him, heading out into the utility room. In a few minutes they emerged with the two hissing gas lanterns, carrying one each. Melvin hung his in the kitchen, then took Silas's out into the living room, noticing that the wind outside was picking up.

"Looks like it will storm again," he commented as they returned to the kitchen. Melvin took his place at the front table, while Silas and Martha pulled out chairs beside it.

"Hope it will hold off until we can get back on the road," Silas commented, glancing back out at the gathering dark clouds. "I don't like getting wet running to my van, and the umbrella is at home, I think."

"At least you don't have to harness a horse when it rains, and get him into the shafts," Melvin commented dryly.

"That's true," Silas chuckled. "Never did have to, so I guess it's hard to imagine."

"Believe me, it can get nasty," Melvin assured him.

After prayer, Martha brought up Indianapolis and what the doctors had said.

"Just kind of what I expected, I guess," Sarah told her, passing the re-heated casserole she had made before she left on Friday morning. Tomorrow she would cook again, but tonight it would have to be casserole. At least the salad she had quickly thrown together was fresh.

"Do they know anything for sure yet?" Martha wondered.

"No. Dr. Watkins confirmed that the blood test results were the same as those from Colorado. So much for what Esther says," she added under her breath, Silas snorting through his nose at her muted comment. "But nothing is conclusive until the bone marrow sample is examined. Those results should be in a few days, they said."

"You think there's any chance it will be negative?" Martha asked, the question in her voice.

"No," Sarah shook her head. "I thought of hoping too, but I don't think so. We just have to go to treatments as soon as we can. That'll be the best thing to do. By the way," she asked, "heard anything from Esther? Mom didn't act unusual when we picked up Nelson."

"Yeah," Martha said sarcastically, "although I doubt

if Mom has heard yet. I'm sure she'll get her ears full on Sunday. Esther's been telling it around. Mad that you went to the doctor. She says James would get perfectly well with her ways alone. I suppose she'll calm down after a while, after she gets it out of her system."

Sarah shook her head in irritation. "You have any idea why she's acting like this?"

Martha shrugged her shoulders. "Who know what goes on in her mind, but I suppose success with James would have given her something really big to talk about. She gets a lot of her living off of that herb garden of hers. Doesn't do her much good if you say it didn't help."

"Well, I wouldn't have said anything," Sarah spoke up in her own defense. "Nor am I planning to. I just want her to quit making a fuss."

"She will," Martha assured Sarah. "She always has before."

"I don't know," Sarah said, skeptical, "although I can't see what harm she can do, just running her mouth. Anyway, Dr. Watkins sent a list of the recommended treatments home with me that I want you to look at. Chemotherapy seems to be the way we should go. He wants to start treatment as soon as possible if the bone marrow is positive."

"So you think that's the way to go?" Silas asked, doubt in his voice, which seemed strange to Sarah.

"I don't think we have any choice," Sarah responded. "There is a good chance of a cure with the chemo."

Melvin nodded his head as they glanced at him for his opinion. "Sounds like the right thing to me."

Martha cleared her throat. "There is one more thing that should be brought up yet, though."

"Not another herb garden or something!" Sarah exclaimed. "What quack have you been listening to now? Really, Esther is about all I can handle on this subject."

"Now, now," Martha raised her hands in the air, "don't go off like that. Just listen to what I have to say."

"I don't really want to," Sarah said, looking intensely at her. "We've been through a lot already, and I think this is the answer."

Martha ignored her and began to make her case. "It's like this. We believe in the will of God, don't we?" When Sarah reluctantly nodded, she continued, "Then we ought to bring all our options before the Lord."

"But I already have. I want the will of God," Sarah told her firmly, "and this seems to be where he is leading."

"Then we ought to allow him to choose what he wants to do," Martha told her.

Sarah sighed, waiting, then added, "I already do."

"I'm sure you do," Martha responded, "but there is a real way in which to do that. A way that is not just in the head, but an action we can take."

Sarah sighed again, the memory of Esther in her mind. "Okay, let's hear it. What is it?"

"It is anointing with oil. It's in the Bible," Martha told her.

"Anointing with oil?"

"Yes, it's very biblical."

"What has it got to do with the will of God?"

"If we ask to be anointed with oil, it is like asking the

Holy Spirit to come over all of our lives. He can do his work if we do not have our own desires in the way. I think you ought to ask for an anointing of oil with that attitude."

"What kind of desires have I got that could get in the way?" Sarah asked, her casserole ignored for the moment.

Martha hesitated. "The big one is whether James gets well at all." Sarah nodded. "Then, whether the doctors are successful with their treatment." Sarah nodded again. "Then, there would be the option of just a direct healing from the Lord."

Sarah nodded her head. "I have already prayed for that. He can heal James if he wants to."

"But our hearts get caught up in one option or the other," Martha suggested. "What if the Lord would heal? We do the same thing with the doctors. Their answers look so good. In all those things we need to withdraw our personal feelings, if we can. In other words, we ought to cover them up when we come before the Lord. Then, let Him choose what He desires to do, without us trying to convince him that one is more desirable than the other. If they are covered, they will all look the same to us."

"That is kind of hard to do," Sarah said dryly.

"Of course it is," Martha said, "but it is a position we can take. There is grace given to us, and the strength to come to Him with our hearts stilled and covered."

"So how would we do this?" Sarah wanted to know.

"I have heard of it," Melvin interrupted mildly, having listened intently to the conversation. "You ask the ministers of your church to perform the anointing."

"You think that Amos would do it?" Sarah asked, looking at Melvin. "I have never heard of an anointing in this Amish community, at least in my lifetime."

He shrugged. "I guess we could ask. If that's one of God's ways, then we ought to take the risk."

"I think it would be a good idea," Silas spoke up, injecting himself into the conversation. "They should not object to such a biblical thing, plus," he added, a smile playing on his face, "we have decided to ask for the same thing for ourselves."

"For yourselves?" Sarah looked questioningly at Martha. "What is wrong with you?"

"Remember what I told you?" she said quietly, motioning towards the boys with her head, not wanting to say anything further. "We have decided to ask. I think our ministers will understand after those meetings."

"So you think your ministers will understand?" Silas asked Melvin, returning to their subject.

Melvin shrugged. "You never know. As Sarah said, I can't remember it being done around here. Some of my relatives in other Amish communities have mentioned it, but not in Daviess County."

"What if I like the idea?" Sarah asked him. "What are you thinking, Melvin? Could you go ask the bishop about it?"

"I think so," he said, after some thought. "Let's at least try."

"So when do you think we should do this?" Sarah asked, trying to keep up with the fast pace.

"If we want to do it, we should probably ask as soon as possible, don't you think? Maybe I could go over this

Sunday afternoon already," Melvin thought out loud. "Bishop Amos should be home then, and I could see what he says about it."

"Well, I suppose we should try," Sarah sighed. "I hate to get my hopes up again, though. It's been hard enough already."

"You don't have to," Martha told her quickly. "Just leave it in God's hands and ask Him for help when the time comes."

Sarah and Melvin both nodded their heads, the arrangement sounding satisfactory to them.

CHAPTER TWENTY-FIVE

As the rain came down outside, Silas and Martha left, making a dash for it without their umbrella. Melvin grinned at the sight of his brother-in-law struggling to get his van door open fast enough, raindrops pelting his head. Sarah, thinking of other things, left to take the boys upstairs to bed.

James seemed extra restless as she tucked him in, enough so that she checked on him later, just before retiring herself. He seemed normal then, his sleep quiet and breathing even, as she watched him, fears growing in her. Forcing herself to leave him, she went downstairs, where Melvin waited in the living room for evening prayers.

As she knelt with him, she wished they had the boys with them too, but this evening getting them to bed had seemed more important. Was God going to punish her for this oversight? Doubts and fears pressed in on her, but she found a measure of comfort as he prayed aloud that God would help them and bless their family.

In the night she awoke and lay still in the darkness of the bedroom. Far away it seemed she could still hear rain falling and wind blowing, but in the house it was deathly silent. On the nightstand the ticking clock read 4 a.m.

Sarah strained her eyes but could see nothing in the darkness. Fears threatened to overwhelm her again as her mouth turned dry with the taste of death. Rather than submit this time, she suddenly decided that enough was enough. She was tired of this. "Melvin!" she called loudly.

"Yes," came his sleepy answer, all wrapped up in coverings from the other side of the bed.

"Can you get one of those kerosene lamps in the kitchen closet?" she asked, not wanting to move herself. "I'd like some light in the house."

"Why do you want that?" he asked, rolling around towards her, lifting himself on his elbow.

"I'm scared, that's why. It's so quiet in the house again."

He paused as if he were listening and then she knew. It was gone. The rain could be heard again, and the wind rushed past the edge of the house. "There seems to be plenty of noise," he said.

Feeling embarrassed she still insisted, "I know you don't like it but I want the lamp lit and set in the hallway. I would just feel much better about things."

"Okay," he said, shrugging sleepily, climbing out from under the covers. She heard him feel his way around the corner of the darkened hallway. In minutes a soft glow flickered in the distance, slowly filling the hall with its light. Melvin set the lamp down just outside the door in the hallway and got into bed again without saying anything.

"Thanks," she said, but he was already asleep. Watching the flickering, dancing light on the walls from the kerosene lamp she soon drifted off to sleep. The alarm clock went off at the normal time. Half an hour later she was in the kitchen when the first stabs of sunshine broke over the horizon, unhindered by the storm clouds that had blown away northwest. Soon the sun shown in its full glory, beginning to dry out the soaked earth.

When he came in from his chores, Sarah felt Melvin looking strangely at her, but she said nothing until he finally asked, "Did you actually ask to have the kerosene lamp lit last night, or am I imagining things?"

"Ya," she told him sheepishly, now that the full light of day was outside the window, "but I keep waking up to this silence, thinking about James and what might happen to him. It's scary."

He raised his eyebrows. "It's a hard time for all of us," he said, his voice soft and sympathetic. "Did the light help?"

"I think so," she nodded. "I want it on every night from now on, until this is over, if you don't mind too much."

He shrugged. "Well, you know I don't like sleeping with light, but if it helps it's worth it."

She dropped her eyes in wordless thanks, grateful for his understanding. "I'd better get the boys up so we can eat or we'll be late for church."

He nodded, leaving for the bedroom to change. After breakfast he helped her clean up the kitchen and kept the boys with him while she dressed, then returned to the barn for the horse. At eight o'clock they were on the road, the horse's hooves making time on the pavement, the family riding in silence, lost in thought.

"I'll see if I can go talk to Amos this evening," Melvin

finally said just before they arrived at Mose Miller's place on the other side of Glendale, where church was being held.

Sarah nodded in agreement as he turned the buggy wheels sideways for her exit at the sidewalk. She nimbly got out, her shawl wrapped around her, the boys remaining to come in later with Melvin on the men's side.

After church, the day held true to its early promise of plentiful sunshine. John and Mattie stopped by to catch up on the news and to show family support. They didn't stay long, though, since they had yet another stop to make at Mattie's sister's place.

About the time Melvin thought of leaving to see the bishop, Ben and Deborah pulled in the driveway. Melvin hoped his in-laws wouldn't stay long since he was uncertain how much time it would take to talk through the issue at the bishop's house, and the chores would need to be done after he returned.

However, since he knew to take extra care of his in-laws, he went out to meet them as they pulled up to the hitching-post.

"Good afternoon," Ben said, getting out of the buggy as Melvin tied the horse.

Melvin nodded in greeting. "Nice weather," he commented.

Ben kept the storm window of the buggy down and tied the lines in a knot on the inside, for which Melvin was glad. It meant they would not be staying very long. He supposed he could always excuse himself if it got too late, but then he would have to explain where he was going. Preferably the request would not have to be explained just yet.

Deborah ignored him as the two men stood there beside the horse. She went around the back of the buggy and headed for the house. Melvin did not take insult, for she looked like a woman with something on her mind — and judging from her look, he was secretly thrilled he didn't have to deal with her.

"She wants to see how James is doing," Ben offered as explanation, showing by his actions that he planned on staying where he was.

Deborah went through the front door without knocking. Sarah saw her coming and greeted her from the living room. "Hi, Mom," she said cheerfully. Though she had seen her mother earlier in the day, now she was home in different circumstances.

Deborah wasted no time getting to the point. "I heard after you left church today. What in the world did you do to Esther the other day when you were out there?"

Sarah kept her face as blank as she could, not wanting to inflame the situation more than necessary, "What did I do? I didn't do anything! We just went for the regular treatment of herbs or something like that — you never know with her."

"So why is she so upset then?" Deborah wanted to know. "She's telling all over the place about how you didn't like her and rejected what she wanted you to do."

"Well, Mom, it was weird, because she did tell me not to go to Indianapolis to the doctor. Now going to her for treatment is one thing. I did that just to please you. Although after what happened, I'm not going back again. Her telling me not to go to a doctor is something else, and I have no plans to listen to her."

Deborah huffed, "Of course, you shouldn't listen to that. Whoever heard of such a thing? I'm surprised at her myself. Everyone goes to the doctor, but it must be more than that. Did you say something to her?"

"I didn't."

"So what did you do to so upset her?"

"I don't know, Mom," Sarah said, feeling her anger rise again, "and right now I don't care. The woman was obnoxious, bossy, and strange. She has no business trying to force me around. There's a side to her I don't like."

"So that must be it." Deborah looked satisfied. "With an attitude like that, no wonder she is upset. Did you tell her any of that?"

"No," Sarah said.

"Probably didn't have to. She must have picked it up. Well, we will have to see if we can get things smoothed out. I will go over and talk to her. She will understand when I tell her you meant no harm."

"Don't bother," Sarah said. "I don't care what she thinks. Besides" — Sarah drew a deep breath, teetering on the brink, then going over; her mother might as well know — "we are planning on asking the bishop if he would have an anointing service for James."

Deborah looked horrified. "You are going to do what?"

"Melvin is going to ask the bishop if he would do an anointing for James. Along with the other ministers, of course."

"Now I have heard everything! Where did you hear about this strange thing?" Deborah's breath came in short gasps. "Daviess County has not had an anointing by the ministers in years. Why, it's not even in my memory. Now that's weird, if you ask me. Talk about Esther being weird."

"No more strange than what Esther does with her herbs. You approve of that, don't you?" Sarah's words were clipped.

"Well," Deborah exhaled her breath, "now I have heard everything! This anointing is just plain English. That's what it is. I can't believe it, my own daughter, going after the ways of the English! You picked this up in New York, didn't you?"

Sarah had to chuckle at that. "No," she said, "it wasn't New York. It's very biblical in fact," she tried to reason. "There's nothing wrong with it."

Deborah was not mollified. "Way too many English people do that, from what I have heard. Dumping oil over the head. Downright uncivilized, if you ask me."

"And you think Esther is civilized?"

"Better than these newfangled ways of doing things."

"Now, Mother," Sarah said, then suddenly decided to head for safe ground: "Anyway, we will see what Bishop Amos thinks. He should know the right thing to do."

Knowing she had been outflanked, Deborah decided to turn to other topics. "You haven't heard from the doctor's yet on the test, have you?"

"No, they said it would be several days," Sarah told her. "But Mr. Bowen is already lined up for when we have to start treatments."

"I called Rebecca with the news," Deborah said. "She offered to help with driving too, if it comes to that."

"That's nice of her," Sarah said, glad for any help.

With that, Deborah was satisfied. Through the living room window Sarah could see her father getting restless as he waited by the horse. Melvin still stood with him, talking about something. "Dad's ready to go," she told her mother, who had her back turned to the window.

"He can wait," Deborah said, and then busied herself with getting ready. "We just came from church, so I don't know what his hurry is."

Sarah smiled as she held the door for her mother.

"You be sure and listen to what the Bishop Amos says, now," was Deborah's parting remark.

"We will," Sarah assured her.

CHAPTER TWENTY-SIX

MELVIN CAME IN the house only long enough to tell Sarah he had to go, harnessed the horse and left. She watched him drive out the driveway, turn the buggy left, and hit the blacktop down by the junction, where the horse hooves picked up their distinct clip-clop. "God, help us," she prayed out loud, emotions of hope and fear running through her. "We really do need you."

The late afternoon sun to his back, Melvin moved along at a brisk pace, the reins from the horse taut in his hands. The bishop's home was five miles away, south on the main road and then a right onto the gravel road.

The two-story framed house had white siding and a wide, full front porch, on which Bishop Amos now sat. The rocking chair slowly creaked as he held the big German family Bible in front of him. The bishop was not "studying" it as the English use the word; instead, he was more or less memorizing the words. There was a good chance he would have to preach tomorrow, and then the assigned text would not be available for him to read. He had preached from this text many times before, so a refresher was all he really needed.

Bishop Amos looked out into the distance, pondering

the flow of the German words in his head. He had been bishop many years now, and his head was full of white hair. Time and the good cooking of his wife had expanded his middle, though not too much. Farm work kept his body in shape and church work kept his mind nimble. Hardly a weekend passed that the deacon did not visit with some problem someone had brought to him. Today it was not the deacon, though. *Looks like Melvin Yoder driving up the lane.* A slight stir of dust came off the buggy wheels, and the horse's hooves sounded on the dirt lane.

Wonder what he wants, Amos thought. *Must be something about their boy. He has leukemia they said today. Why would he come here, though? If it was about money, he would have gone to the deacon.* Puzzled, he wrinkled his brow and waited to find out what the problem was.

Melvin tied his horse and slowly found his way up the porch steps. Amos was some distant third cousin of his, but it was not wise to stretch family ties too far. "*Goot ohvet*" (good evening) Melvin said in greeting.

"*Sitz dich*" (seat yourself) the bishop rejoined, waving his hand towards a chair beside him. "How is the boy?"

"Oh, he is coming along. Weak, doesn't feel that well."

"It's to be expected with such an illness," Amos offered his encouragement.

Melvin nodded, "We expect him to get a lot worse when they start the treatments."

"Oh, yes," Amos agreed, shifting on his chair. *So it was money that Melvin wanted.* "Do you know yet what the hospital bill will be?"

"No, we haven't been told."

Amos waited for more information, but when none came he offered, "The deacon will see to the funds when the time comes. I do not know how much we have on hand, but we try to take care of our people."

A look of surprise crossed Melvin's face. "Ah, I know, but that is not what I came for."

Now it was the bishop's turn for surprise. "It's not?"

"No," Melvin said, deciding to get it over with right away. "Sarah and I wondered if you would do an anointing for James, with the other ministers, of course."

"An anointing?" The bishop raised his eyebrows. "Where did you get that idea?"

"It's in the Bible," Melvin said, squirming, then added, "Silas and Martha suggested it first, I guess, but we would like it, too."

"I see," Amos said, looking off into the distance again. "Those are English ways, are they not?" Then, "Martha is Sarah's sister, right?"

Melvin said yes to both questions. Why disagree with the bishop?

"You are sure that you and Sarah want it?" Amos asked him.

Melvin said yes again, he was sure, and he nodded his head to underscore it.

Amos said nothing but took the big family Bible and slowly opened it. Melvin could not see where he was reading, but it took a little while as the bishop read in silence. Finally he looked up. "It is in here," he said, brushing his farm-worn hand on the book. "I will see what the other ministers say tomorrow. You are good church members, and in the *ordnung*." Here Amos paused and looked sharply at Melvin. "I guess you are."

Melvin nodded, "Yes."

"Anyway," the bishop continued, "I will talk with the ministers. There may be some objections. We do not get many such requests, but I do remember it being done once when I had just been ordained. Old Bishop Byler anointed Maude Yoder before she died, and it has been done before, just not in a long time around here. I will let you know then, okay?"

Melvin knew his time to go had come, and he departed quickly. "*Goot ohvet*" (good evening) he said again as he went down the front porch steps.

On Monday morning, Sarah stood on the front porch and looked out towards the road, deep in thought. There was something not yet stirring inside her, but there nonetheless. She had discovered it only this morning.

From where she stood, she could see the little phone shack at the end of their lane, its sturdy, upright door partially ajar. Dirt stirred up by passing traffic always climbed up the side of the shack and clung to the bottom of the black telephone hanging on the wooden wall. Though Sarah could not hear it, the phone now rang, and small particles of dust broke loose and spiraled downward.

The sound filled the little shack with its insistent message, each ring following the other in quick succession. Although the vibrations carried far, it was not far enough to bring an answering rush of footsteps. Sarah had no way of knowing of other events already transpired far from where she stood.

An English car, its occupant caught up in whatever he was doing, came over the gently rolling hill to the south, stirring up little clouds of dust in his wake. By the time the car passed, the telephone had fallen silent, accepting once again the embrace of the little particles nudging it from below.

Sarah, watching the car go, turned to go back into the house and to her duties of the day. She did not see some time later the buggy come off the side road at breakneck speed, small stones spraying as the thin wheels went off the pavement in making the turn. Her father felt the buggy shift sideways but did not tighten up the reins, giving Henry his head today.

Already foam began to work out on Henry's shoulder straps, the horse's breath coming in short gasps. In making the turn, Ben leaned heavily into the buggy's load, lifting his feet high into the air. Keeping the traces tight, he flew up the road towards Melvin and Sarah's driveway.

A buggy coming at such speed finally attracted Sarah's attention from the kitchen. She came back out on the front porch to wait, thinking it might be her father's buggy, but not sure until he nearly overturned making the turn into their driveway.

"What would Dad want in such a hurry?" she wondered out loud. "He's not just joyriding without Mom, I'm sure. That's too reckless even for him."

Her answer came as the panting Henry halted in front of the walk. Ben made no attempt to climb out, and instead simply talked from inside the buggy. "There has been serious news from Pennsylvania," he announced soberly, his voice carrying to the front porch.

"Yes?" she asked, wondering what burden was to be added to her already heavy load. Had one of their many relatives died in Pennsylvania?

"A man has shot up an Amish schoolhouse this morning. All of them were girls."

Sarah's face turned ashen, uncomprehending, as she walked out closer to her father's buggy. Her heart hurt all over again, horror in her voice. "No. Did he do something with them?" she asked.

"No," her father said, "just shot them."

"Are they hurt?" she asked, now at the wheel of his buggy.

"Most of them are dead," he said simply. "Deborah's cousin's girl was among them. They said they tried to call you on your phone," Ben pointed his beard towards the end of the road, "but no one answered."

Her hand was on her mouth, words forming soundlessly. "Who would do something like this?"

"I don't know," he told her. "They are just calling family yet — not many of the details are available. It was a young man. He has a family of his own."

"How many of them are dead?"

"They don't know for sure," he told her. "There were ten girls all together."

Sarah now wept, openly and unashamedly, at the scene described by her father. "Is Mom going to the funeral?" she finally asked softly.

Ben nodded. "We are leaving this afternoon. That is why I came so quickly to tell you."

"Oh, I wish I could go with you." Sarah's hand was still over her mouth. "But we can't with James's condition right now."

"I'm sure they'll understand, and we'll give them your greetings and concerns." Ben slapped the reins, getting the tired Henry underway once more. Sarah stood watching him until the buggy had turned out of the driveway and on to the gravel road.

Her brain still numb, she failed to comprehend the full magnitude of what she had been told. First it was James and now this. Was God mad at the whole world, or maybe just her world? She stayed and wept on the porch until driven back to her work by her sense of duty.

❧

Silas and Martha stopped by to visit after supper, having heard the news earlier in the day.

"We took Mom and Dad to catch the bus in Montgomery," Martha informed Sarah after they were seated around the living room, Sarah and Martha on the couch, Melvin in the recliner, and Silas in a chair across from him.

"What time are they arriving out there?" Sarah asked.

"Mom said sometime tomorrow, she thinks. She hadn't looked at the Greyhound schedules yet when they had to leave. The funeral is not till the next day after that."

"That should give them plenty of time then to get out," Sarah said, thinking it through. "I'm sure everyone out there is still in shock. I know I am, just thinking about it.

I thought we were really facing something with James, but this must be even worse. You can't even go to the doctors about it. It's just over with, and your child is gone. Who would do something like that?"

"A local fellow, a milk truck driver by the name of Charles Roberts," Martha informed her. "It's all over the news, but I guess you don't have TV." Martha made a motion with her arm towards the other side of the living room. "Seems like that's all they're talking about. Fox News had Pennsylvania's State Police Commissioner, Jeffrey Miller, on a little while ago. Everyone, even in the state government, is pretty shook up about it."

"Who wouldn't be," Sarah said softly, then added, "I found out something else this morning too.."

"What's that?" Martha wanted to know, not sure what to expect.

Sarah glanced over at the men. Silas was telling Melvin about the donation site already set up for the shooting victims and the outpouring of support coming in. "Come out to the kitchen," Sarah whispered quietly.

Rising, the two left without causing any distraction to Silas and Melvin. Once there, Martha was all eyes, having somehow already guessed it. "You're not?"

"Yes, I just found out for sure this morning."

"Oh!" Martha at first expressed delight. "Do you think it will be a girl this time?" Then her face darkened.

Sarah didn't notice, answering that it would be fine either way with her.

It was only after Martha asked, "Does Melvin know already?" that Sarah caught a glimpse of her face.

"I told him at lunch time," she said, then reached out for her hand. "Oh, I'm so sorry," she said sincerely. "Here I am thinking only about myself, and never giving a thought about you."

"It's not your fault," Martha assured her, even though the tears were there, pressing to come out. "It's just that I want a baby so bad."

"Have you spoken to your ministers yet about he anointing?" Sarah was reaching for what hope she could find, and that seemed to be the only thing around at the moment.

"Yes, we did, and they came over on Sunday night." Martha's face brightened. "Maybe this is a sign from God. You know, of what's coming."

"Maybe." Sarah wasn't sure what she felt but wished she had kept her mouth shut until some easier time. It was said now, however. "I try to trust God too, but it's very hard."

Martha's face darkened again. "And it all happens on the same day, doesn't it?"

Sarah nodded. "Isn't that something? But God has just made things that way. Melvin said the same thing earlier."

Looking around the kitchen, Martha insisted that she help Sarah with the supper dishes. Sarah relented, thankful for the help, and a short time later they returned to the men in the living room. Silas and Martha left a little after nine.

CHAPTER TWENTY-SEVEN

B Y WEDNESDAY, WHEN Sarah heard nothing from the doctor's office in Indianapolis, she went down to the phone shack to try calling Martha. When there was no answer, she took a chance and called Dr. Watkins' office. The secretary answered and, confirming her hunch, said the results from the bone marrow sample came in positive that morning, and the office tried calling both numbers with no response.

Sarah thanked her, asking about the next step in the process. The secretary asked if she had spoken with her husband on chemo treatments yet, for they first needed a definite answer from both parents.

"I think so," Sarah told her. "We have decided that is what needs to be done."

There was silence on the phone as the secretary checked appointment dates. "We can start you the Friday after next. You need to come here to the office first, and then we will refer you to Riley Hospital for the treatments. That was where you did the bone marrow sample. Would that be okay?"

Sarah thought about the anointing and laying everything before God and decided this appointment would not hinder any of that. She said, "Yes, that will be okay."

"We will be expecting you then, let's see, eleven o'clock," the secretary concluded, to which Sarah agreed, thanking her and hanging up the phone.

The walk up the lane seemed forever, the world a haze of uncertainty — a sick son, school children taken from this world, and now a new life growing within her. What was God all about, she wondered, her definitions of Him failing her.

❧

On Saturday afternoon Martha picked up Ben and Deborah at the Greyhound Bus station. Watching them get off, she was surprised to see her uncle and aunt along with her parents. "You came, too?" she exclaimed when the group was close enough to hear her.

"Yes," her uncle allowed. "I had to get these old bones out of the house for a change. Betsy did too, as far as that goes. Seems like we just keep getting slower and slower as the years go by, and this seemed like a good chance to get out and see some of the family."

Uncle Jim and Aunt Betsy, on Deborah's side of the family, were not as old as Jim was letting on, but Martha let him say it anyway. "So you decided to go visiting?"

"Had to take my chance while I could, and with Sarah's boy being ill." A shadow crossed his face. "We thought it might be time to see all of you, since it's been awhile."

"Well, I'm glad you could come," she told him, opening the van door for them. Her father opened his own door, getting in the front seat, while Deborah climbed in the back with Uncle Jim and Aunt Betsy.

"How was the funeral?" she asked as she pulled out onto 50.

"Sad," Deborah said. "We didn't stay for all of them, of course. Your cousin's girl was with the four on the first day."

"A lot of people there, I suppose."

Deborah shook her head. "We were expecting a lot, but the funerals were actually smaller than normal. I think people wanted to not overcrowd things."

"There were four the first day," Martha commented, trying to remember what the news had said.

Deborah nodded. "The government did a good job too of keeping everyone away. Someone thought they even ordered a no-fly zone over the gravesite. At least we weren't bothered by anyone snapping pictures."

"Everyone is trying to help, from the sound of things. The news is talking about the forgiveness issue," Martha told her, remembering what many of the commentators had said. "The English seem quite impressed."

Deborah nodded again. "Yes, it's true, they are forgiving, but it doesn't make the pain any less."

They rode in silence for a few minutes until Ben said, kind of abruptly, "I guess these are situations where forgiveness comes in, but I don't feel real friendly towards English people right now."

"They're not all bad," Uncle Jim was quick to say. "The people on the Greyhound went out of their way to express their concern when they saw we were Amish."

"That was kind of surprising," Deborah allowed. "I noticed the same thing. It kind of makes you feel good after something tragic like that."

"How long are you going to be here?" Martha wanted to know, glancing at her uncle in the rearview mirror.

"Just over the weekend, I suppose. We'll get to see Sarah and James at church tomorrow, so I suppose we could go back Monday or Tuesday, if that's okay with Betsy?" He glanced at his wife.

"Okay with me," she told him. "It's your relatives, so you spend what time you want with them, but I think Tuesday would work better than Monday. It would give us time to get ready and down to the bus station easier rather than rushing around on Monday for all that. That is if Ben and Deborah can put up with us that long." She looked towards Deborah, already knowing the answer but having the psychological need to make the statement anyway.

Deborah replied, "Of course," in the same tone of voice, a mere formality, adding, "You know better than that."

"There's also other news, Mom," Martha half whispered from the driver's seat.

"Like what?" Deborah wanted to know, wondering what new horror had taken hold while they were gone.

"Oh, nothing like that," Martha quickly told her, hearing the tone in her voice. "It's just that Sarah…oh, I'll tell you later," Martha said, glancing over at her father.

"Oh, no!" Deborah exclaimed, getting her drift, excitement in her voice. "It's about time. Nelson is almost six."

"I thought you weren't going to talk about it," Ben commented dryly from the front seat.

Uncle Jim snorted, "A living, and a dying, and the Lord God made it all so."

"It does look so," Martha agreed, keeping her eyes on the

road, wondering when her time would come for the living of new life inside her. Would God answer her prayers? She so wanted to tell someone about her own hopes and prayers. Surely if Sarah was with child again, her own time was coming. But she decided it was best to keep quiet. When the time came for her to give her own news, she could give the whole story then, but not before.

❦

At 8:30 the next morning, the Amish church gathering was in full swing. Buggies pulled in, dropped off the women at the front walks, turned and unhitched in neat rows. Men and boys led their horses to the barn, tying them in long rows so that no hind ends were in close quarters. Even then, an occasional fight broke out, leading to a yell and general dressing down from whatever man was in the vicinity. By the time church started, the horses usually had decided to be friends and get along. The bits of hay spread out in front of them helped.

Off in the corner of the kitchen where the women were placing their shawls, Esther had trapped Bishop Amos's wife, Mary. It was Esther's way of getting to the bishop.

"Terrible things are going on over at Sarah and Melvin's," she said to the captive Mary.

"Oh?" Mary responded.

"Yes," Esther continued, "Sarah brought James over for treatment the other day, and she was terribly disrespectful."

"What did she say?" Mary wanted to know.

"Not really anything," Esther admitted. "It was her attitude. Very haughty and up in the air. I am afraid they are taking on English ways. She would not listen to what I said."

"Why do you think so?" Mary wanted to know, laying her shawl out on the table used for such things.

"I did my best," Esther whispered, "in the practice of the old ways that I know of to cause cures. James is a very serious case. He could die if he does not get well. I am just so afraid that if they let the doctors do their terrible things it will not go well with him, but Sarah would have nothing of it. I heard they went to Indianapolis on Friday."

"Yes, I think they did," Mary told Esther, looking around nervously. Already several of the other women had noticed their extended conversation and were moving closer in order to hear. This was not a conversation Mary wished to have a larger life than it already had. "I will tell Amos what you said," she whispered quickly, knowing that was what Esther wanted.

Esther nodded with a slight smile on her face. "I do want the best for that family," she said, dropping her head slightly to the side as if under a heavy burden. "I so wish Sarah would listen; then the boy could be well."

Mary started to move slowly away from Esther, glad that Esther seemed not to know about Melvin's visit last night. She was not sure what the ministry would do about the anointing, but she was glad Esther was still in the dark on the subject. *Let her learn on her own. A week might cool things off,* were Mary's thoughts as she greeted the closest woman to her and then the one next to her.

On the other side of the kitchen Sarah was being greeted by her aunt Betsy. They exchanged what words they could before it was time to move on around the circle of women.

CHAPTER TWENTY-EIGHT

THIRTY MINUTES LATER in an upstairs room of the house with the sound of slow choral singing beneath them, the ministers' council had completed its Sunday morning preliminary motions.

Amos cleared his throat and broached the subject. "As you all know, Melvin and Sarah's boy has leukemia. He approached me last night about what I thought were his hospital bills. Instead, he wants us to do an anointing for James. I know this has not been done here for a long time, but it is biblical and we should consider it. What are your feelings on this?"

Four other ministers sat in the room with the bishop that morning: one of his two home ministers; the home deacon, Stephen; and two visiting ministers. Bishop Amos's other home minister, *"Bloh"* (blue) Jonas Yoder, was away visiting family in another state. The nickname *"Bloh"* had been in the family so long that most people had forgotten why. The name had no connection to a person's mood. It came instead from the grandfather of the line three generations back whose first name was the same as one of his fellow Amish, Jonas Yost. This had resulted in the names and initials getting mixed up. Since there was a large English-owned lake adjoining the Yoder farm, the solution had been to add blue, *Bloh*, for the color of the lake, to his name. So it was still that the family name among the Amish carried *Bloh*.

Out of deference to them, both visiting ministers were asked to express their opinions first. They expressed some surprise and wondered if there was any precedent for such a ceremony. "We have heard of anointing with oil, but have never seen such a thing done," said the older one. "Isn't it usually done at a deathbed?"

Amos was ready for that and cleared his throat. "I do know of the example of Old Bishop Byler. I was there when he anointed Maude Yoder at her request for her illness of shingles. She would not have been considered on her deathbed."

At that point Amos's home minister offered his response and thereby cemented a positive reaction to the request. "I know of an incident some years ago when my cousin was anointed at her request by Bishop Hochstetler of the southern Maryland Amish community."

Both of the visiting ministers shrugged their shoulders. "If it has been done before," said the younger one, "then it should be okay. Sometimes these things just fall out of practice with our people. Are these people in good standing with the church?"

The bishop nodded his head. "As far as I know. Do you know anything?" he asked, looking at Deacon Steven.

"I haven't heard any complaints," he replied.

Deacon Steven then expressed himself on the matter. "I really have no objection to the subject. Whatever you agree to is fine. As far as the money, we have around $3,300 in the account if it comes to hospital bills."

Amos nodded his appreciation for the information from the deacon. He had not expected any opposition from him. "Does anyone else have any objection?" he asked.

When none was expressed, Amos continued, "Okay, then, let us have an anointing at their place Monday night. Will *Bloh* Jonas be back by then?"

Both the deacon and the home minister shook their heads.

Amos thought about it for a moment and then concluded, "We will continue then without him."

No one thought this unusual since it was not regular church business that needed the assent and attendance of the entire ministry or a vote from the church. Later, under questioning of an Amish Bishop oversight council, they stuck to their story that it had all been done in innocence. It seemed like a normal Sunday morning procedure to them to comply with a somewhat unusual, but still permissible, request.

After the service ended at twelve o'clock, Amos told Melvin they would be over on Monday night.

With the ministers coming the next evening, Sarah spent Sunday afternoon preparing. By sundown she was worn out, even though Sunday was supposed to be a day of rest. She was glad Aunt Betsy found their conversation after church to be sufficient and was not coming over to visit, though the thought made her feel guilty.

On top of that, James, looking pale and tired, sat on the couch staring out the window at the dying sunlight. She worried how he was taking all the pressure and everything else that was happening. Children sometimes pick up on such things faster than adults think they do.

With their usual bedtime approaching, even Melvin agreed to shut down early, as Sarah lit her lamp and set it in the hallway not far from the door. Climbing into bed, she for a moment thought of blowing out the lamp but then decided against it. Afterwards, she lay there watching the light play on the wall. It must have been the last thing she saw before dropping off to sleep, because when she woke it seemed as if the lights were dancing wildly in the room. Low, dim shadows, half light and half darkness, appeared to be fighting with each other.

Sarah rubbed her eyes and sat up. There was no sound anywhere, just the pulsating movement of light and shadows in the room. She shook her head, and slowly her thoughts became focused. The fear was so thick it felt like a low cloud hung over the room. Its now familiar feeling of death and dying pressed in on her. She thought of waking Melvin again, but simply lay back and continued to watch the kerosene lamp throw its flickering light on the hallway walls and over their bed.

What good would waking Melvin do? It would just postpone the fear and solve little, she knew from past experience. She would have to face this on her own, once and for all. The conviction grew in her until she moved, in spite of the fear and its griping presence all around.

Sliding out of bed and on to her knees, she covered her face with her arms, shutting out the silence, crying out to God. Could she let James go? That was the question closing in on her, one she could not get away from.

She tried to avoid it, praying, but the words died in her mouth, the question returning. Could she let God take him if he wanted to? If He asked? If He thought best? It was only when she finally realized that the question was coming from the silence within her and not from the terror outside that she ceased her struggle and listened.

Could she trust God? She formed the words with her mouth, "Can I?"

She saw the wooden box again, the slim form inside it, still and white, and the fear screamed at her, "No."

She drew back in horror, unable to imagine how God could be in such a thing. He was good and perfect. Wasn't this what she knew and what her preachers had always said? Yet He wanted her to accept this?

She would have cried if there were any tears left, but there seemed to be none. Maybe this was what it felt like, she thought, to come to the end of one's self. To have nowhere else to go, to have tried until hope was gone, to have reached and found nothing there.

The voice within her insisted that she answer; it pressed gently, firmly, till she knew there was really no choice. She thought about God up in heaven, wherever he was, running the world, hearing no doubt all the prayers that were prayed. There were thousands of people in the world, she knew, thousands of cars in just one city, thousands of houses out here in the country, but now she knew with absolute certainty that He was asking her a question.

Not only did she know that, but she also knew He was waiting for an answer. Waiting for her, Sarah Yoder, the wife of Melvin and the mother of two sons, to answer.

The knowledge gripped her and tore at her heart. The tears came in a flood as she answered, her lips moving, "Yes, You can have him."

She never knew afterwards how long she wept or knelt there by the bedside. Either Melvin awakened without the alarm clock or she never heard it go off, because it was his hands on her shoulders that brought her back to an awareness of her surroundings.

"Sarah?" he was asking, "Sarah? Are you okay?"

She opened her eyes. The light from the lamp still flickered on the walls of the bedroom, the early dawn not far away, she could tell. Melvin looked distressed as his eyes sought hers. "I'm okay," she told him, "just praying."

"Oh." He waited, not certain he wanted to leave it there.

"The fears," she told him, thinking he should know, "came back real bad, but God helped me through them. If He wants to take James home, then it's okay with me."

"I see," he said softly, sobered by her words, his fingers pressing her shoulder. "I've got to be out doing the chores. Are you okay then?"

She nodded, getting up and starting to get dressed. By the time she was ready to leave for the kitchen, the front door opened and shut as Melvin left for the barn.

With breakfast prepared, she called the boys down. Even Melvin noticed that James was extra pale, she could tell, though he said nothing about it. James only picked at his breakfast and afterwards went into the living room to lie on the couch.

"Let him go," Sarah told Nelson, who look worriedly after his brother. "Don't bother James if he doesn't want to play, okay? You know he's sick and we will have to take him back to the doctor on Friday. James may not be able to play with you for a while. Can you understand that?"

Nelson said he understood and he asked no further questions, for which Sarah was grateful.

It rained hard all day, at times seeming as if sheets of water poured out of the sky. Sarah didn't really notice it until sometime after lunch, but not a drop of rain was getting into the house. Since he couldn't work in the fields, Melvin was in and out of the house doing what work he could at the barn.

Looking at the rain coming down, Sarah asked him during one of his times indoors, "Are you concerned about tonight?"

"Concerned about what?" Melvin asked, not certain what she meant.

"Oh," she answered, not sure herself. "It is just that I gave James to God last night, but I still want to be open to whatever He wants done."

"I do too," he told her. "We just have to wait and see what that is.

CHAPTER TWENTY-NINE

THE RAIN SHOWED no signs of letting up as the evening progressed. A strong wind moved the clouds along rapidly, as their dark, surly outlines kept coming out of the southwest.

"Do you think they are still coming?" Sarah asked Melvin, who was glancing out of the living room window down the driveway.

"I think so," Melvin responded. "They aren't English people afraid of the weather."

Sarah chuckled, "Yeah, I noticed the other night Silas and Martha are no longer used to rough weather."

"It comes from driving cars," Melvin said matter-of-factly, "and from turning an ignition instead of harnessing a horse."

"I think so," Sarah agreed. Then, from her position at the living room window, she added, "They are coming."

Slowly the three buggies drove up the driveway. The horses held their heads sideways to avoid the lash of the wind from the southwest. Neatly, the drivers inside the buggies brought their horses to a halt in front of the section of board fence that served as Melvin's hitching post. There was just enough room to get all three into the space.

"They must have met somewhere else, before starting out," Melvin observed.

"Probably at the bishop's place," Sarah said, as Melvin nodded. "It's not likely they would have all got here the same time without starting out together somewhere."

The three ministers got out of the buggies and tied their horses, walking single file towards the house, tilting their hats against the wind. Their Sunday habits accompanied them easily even during the week when doing church work. Amos led, with his minister following, and the deacon brought up the rear. *Bloh* Jonas was not with them.

Entering beneath the front porch, they took off their hats and outer coats. After shaking these carefully to shed the raindrops, they draped the coats over their arms, and with hat-in-hand Amos knocked on the door. Melvin opened the door as soon as he heard the knock. He had been standing right beside the door, but Amish etiquette required that he wait until someone knocked on such an important visit. It would not do to seem overly eager that ministers had come.

"Please come in," he said, properly bowing only his head in a low motion that fittingly expressed humility and submission towards those with authority over him in the faith. "The weather is really bad," he added.

"Yes, it is," said Amos, extending his hand to greet Melvin, "but we need the rain. God knows what is best for us."

"Yes, He does," agreed Melvin.

Sarah stood up from her seat in the living room, but said nothing. She would speak later when addressed or if need arose. She believed a woman should not start talking on such an occasion unless absolutely necessary.

Amos walked over to her and shook hands, as did the other two. "Is the boy very sick?" he asked her.

"It comes and goes," she said, motioning towards James with her head. "Today he just sat around."

"Well, well," said Amos, "it is too bad when the children get sick, but we must trust in God. The Almighty sends good things to the just as well as to the unjust. We must not complain when He allows evil to happen to both. It is in His hands."

Sarah made sure they all found seats in the living room and then settled down next to Melvin on a chair. The conversation went from the weather to farming, to other insignificant matters. Finally Amos broached the subject of their visit. "You have called us here upon your request for an anointing. Is this still your desire?"

Melvin and Sarah both nodded, "Yes."

Seeing their affirmation, Amos asked for a Bible since he had not brought one. No Amish minister carried around a Bible. To carry one would be considered a serious expression of pride, as well as a sign that one was following the ways of the English. A Bible is supplied at the house where it is needed.

When Melvin brought him their large family Bible, Amos opened it and found the passage in James on anointing. "Is any sick among you? Let him call for the elders of the church; and let them pray over him, anointing him with oil in the name of the Lord," Amos read, saying those words in German as well as the subsequent verses. Finishing, he closed the Bible and gave it back to Melvin. "We have come here tonight," he said, "to fulfill a commandment of scripture. It is a weighty and sober matter to obey God. We do not know what God wants to do or what He will do. It is our responsibility to seek to obey and submit ourselves to the pleasure of God. Some He leads into health, others into sickness. Some have many days of pain and others are delivered quickly. In it all, only He knows what is best.

"Tonight we have come here to submit ourselves to the Lord. He has commanded us to use oil when we are sick and it is requested. We are told to confess our faults one to another. How many of those we all have. Out of dust the Lord God made all of mankind. It is this weakness even the best of us feel in our good times. May He have mercy upon the frail vessels of clay.

"We will now continue with the anointing, but first allow the other ministers to express themselves. Melvin and Sarah may also express themselves."

The minister and the deacon had few words. Both said they found themselves in great weakness and in need of the Lord. They requested prayer for themselves and their families. This was in keeping with the expectation of leaders of the Amish. It was looked to them to lead in humility, both by example and by word.

Melvin cleared his throat when the deacon was done. He was not used to speaking before church leaders. "We, too, find ourselves in great need and weakness," he said. "Pray for all of us that we might be an example and a light to others even in our troubles."

To the surprise of all Sarah did not even clear her throat

when Melvin was done, but started talking. She was allowed to speak, but they had not anticipated it from the way she had handled herself since the ministers had come into the house. Her words brought the reality of the situation back into focus. "I, too, am a weak human being," she said. "I need the Lord. I have a little boy here who is very sick. If he does not get well, then he will pass on over to the other side. I would like to know what the will of God is. Whatever that will is, I am satisfied with it. That is why we have asked for this anointing. We want to submit ourselves to the Holy Spirit to work in our lives. It is my belief that God will move if we ask Him. Whatever that way is, I am willing to accept it. I want to ask for no choice over the other, only that He reveal and do His will."

Amos was surprised at this long speech from Sarah, but he liked it. "That is well," he said. "The oil is a type of the Holy Spirit. Let us now bring all our desires and all the options before us to God. With this action of anointing we will ask God to move as He desires."

With that, Amos asked Melvin to hold James, and he took a little bottle of oil he had brought with him out of one pocket. Out of the other he took a small prayer book. Coming over to James in Melvin's lap, Amos took the oil and poured some on James's head. Laying one hand on James's head, he held the prayer book with the other and prayed in German, "Geliebter und Heiliger Gott, Lineal der Erde und alles, was darin ist. Ihr Lob ist in der ganzen Welt, von einem Ende zum anderen. Niemand ist mögen zu Ihnen, oh Gott. Groß und mächtig sind Ihre Arbeiten. Sie stürzen das mächtige von seinem Sitz. Sie erhöhen das niedrige, wer Ihren Namen besuchen. Hören Sie jetzt unser Gebet, Oh Rechtschaffener. Biegen Sie sich niedrig vom Himmel und hören Sie unserem Schrei zu. Heilen Sie uns Oh Herr, Großer Gott des Himmels und der Erde. Wir sind nur aus Ton gemacht und ohne Ihre große Hand hilflos, um uns zu führen."

("Beloved and Holy God, Ruler of the earth and all that is in it. Your praise is in all the world, from one end to the other. None is like to You, oh God. Great and mighty are Your works. You bring down the mighty from his seat. You exalt the lowly who call upon your name. Hear now our prayer, Oh Righteous One. Bend low from heaven and listen to our cry. Heal us Oh Lord, Great God of heaven and earth. We are but made of clay and helpless without Your great hand to guide us.")

With that, Amos let the hand holding the prayer book drop while he prayed in his own words, "Let this oil now flow over the body and heart of this boy. Bring healing and hope to him, oh God. We ask in the name of the Father, the Son, and the Holy Spirit. Amen."

The minister and the deacon both said, "Amen." Sarah and Melvin said nothing. James held his head against Melvin's shoulder and cried softly.

"Is there something wrong?" Sarah asked him in a whisper.

"No," he said out loud, "I just feel so good."

"Well, well," Amos said, "I am glad to hear that. You be a good boy, now. We must be going."

With that, since he was already standing, Amos headed for the door. The others followed. Melvin shut the door after them. Outside on the porch they noticed that, although the wind still blew, the rain had stopped. The moon was just rising over the horizon, wisps of wind-driven clouds scurrying across its face.

"It is good that we have come," Amos said. The others murmured their agreement.

Back inside, Melvin returned to the still-weeping James, now leaning against Sarah's shoulder. She was brushing his forehead lightly with her hand. "He's okay," she told Melvin.

"Why's he crying then?"

"Shh," Sarah told him. "Just sit down beside us and be with him."

Melvin did that and James soon found his voice. "I'm okay," he said. "I just have to cry. I don't know why."

"You just do that," Sarah assured him. "Now, sit here with Dad until I get supper. Then we can all eat."

She soon called them to supper, where they ate what she had prepared, especially James. "Are you that hungry?" Sarah asked him in surprise.

He nodded his head vigorously and continued eating. After supper Sarah let the boys play in the living room while she and Melvin read. By bedtime she knew for sure that James was feeling much better. "He's feeling better, much better," she told Melvin, smiling, joy in her heart.

"Maybe," was his response. "Sickness comes and goes. Don't get your hopes up too much."

She said nothing more, but later when they retired Melvin noticed that the lamp was not burning in the hall. "No lamp?" he asked her.

"No," she said, "we won't be needing that anymore."

"Whatever you want," he said. "It didn't seem to do much good anyway. That was a pretty big scare last night."

"That's not why I stopped using it," Sarah told him. "We won't need it anymore."

"Good-night, then," Melvin said, rolled over and dropped off to sleep. It took her a little longer lying there in the darkness listening to the wind gently brush against the house. She woke with the clattering alarm clock at the regular time. Later as she watched the first crack of dawn light the sky from the kitchen window, she smiled, certain that God had done something and that it was good.

CHAPTER THIRTY

As each new day of the week dawned and rolled by, James continued to eat well. Sarah watched him playing with Nelson, convinced that his energy level was increasing. Mentioning this to Melvin, she wondered, "Is he better, do you think?"

"I don't know," he responded. "I am not an expert. Sometimes what we want to see can cause us to see it. I mean, do you know what you are asking? Is he better? Leukemia does not just go away."

"I know that," said Sarah. "Unless God makes it go away."

He looked at her sharply. "This is not the first century," he said. "Christ is not walking this earth."

"His Spirit is," she replied.

"That's not the same," he replied, trying to keep her from any false hope. "You know it."

"Maybe, maybe not," she said. "I am not a theologian. I only know that I think Amos had some of the Spirit of Christ Monday night. It took a lot of courage for him to do that anointing. If he did have the Spirit of Christ, then Jesus was here, and someone could have gotten healed."

"That's expecting a lot," Melvin said as he shrugged.

"I don't think it's expecting too much of Jesus," Sarah replied.

"If you're talking of Jesus, then yes, it's true. He was a good man. But look," Melvin told her, "I don't think we should be talking about this. It's not *cheit*" (proper).

"Okay," she said, not offended. "I was just trying to tell you I think James is not sick anymore."

"Let's see what the doctor says on Friday," Melvin told her. "If he is well by a healing from God, then I will be very thankful."

She was not sure what that meant, or how the doctor was to know. Was she supposed to walk in and say, "My boy is no longer sick," or, "I think he got healed." "Humph," she thought, "likely as not they will put *me* up as sick."

Returning to the kitchen with the problem unresolved, Sarah finally decided just to let the problem be and see what happened. She concluded that it could not be known anyway. She would just have to take it as it came.

Esther puttered around in her garden all day Thursday, finding nothing that lessened her down mood. *What's wrong with me? And why aren't more people coming anymore? Is it my imagination, or are there really fewer?* she found herself wondering, nearly certain there were fewer than usual.

Fear swept her one moment and then hope, only to fade away again. Her mind would not be still. Finally, finding no relief, she went inside to start supper.

The loneliness of the evening pressed in on her. In moments like this she wished she had chosen marriage, but now it was a little late for that. Tonight, however, such feelings only served as a minor backdrop to her concerns over Sarah and her son James and what it could mean for her.

≋

Friday morning came around and Sarah had the boys ready when Mr. Bowen pulled in. Nelson would again be dropped off at her mother's place. She noted as she approached the van that Mrs. Bowen was along again. *How nice of her,* she thought as her hand grasped the door handle.

"Good morning," the couple said together.

Sarah responded with, "Hi, it's nice that you could come along again, Mrs. Bowen."

"That's okay," Mrs. Bowen's face beamed. "I am glad to do it." Then she added, "I can't always though, if you have to do the treatments long-term and you want us to drive you. But this time I still wanted to come along."

Sarah nodded her head as she got the boys in the van and climbed in herself. That was when Mrs. Bowen noticed James. "Well, Sarah," she said, "James looks absolutely fabulous today. Not at all like he did two weeks ago. Is he just having a good day?"

Mr. Bowen got the van moving out the driveway as Sarah answered, "I don't know. We had an anointing service Monday night. The ministers came over."

"You did?" Mrs. Bowen asked, surprised. "I didn't know you Amish did those."

"We don't usually," Sarah said, "but Martha suggested it."

Mrs. Bowen turned around in her seat. "I guess we don't have them too often either. I don't know why. We just pray, I guess. Do you think it did any good?"

"Something did," Sarah replied. "Do you think I should tell the doctor?"

"I don't think you will have to," Mrs. Bowen said. "Looking like that, someone will notice."

So it proved. When they walked into Dr. Watkins' office and finished the paperwork, Nurse Bloom came out to meet Sarah and James again. "Come back with me for just a minute," she said, "before we give you the paperwork to take downtown. Next time you won't have to stop in here before going to the hospital." It was then that her eyes first fully noticed James's appearance. "Oh," she said, pausing, "you look good." Then almost as an afterthought she added, "Step up on the scales for a minute please, James."

James stepped up on the small platform. Nurse Bloom looked at the reading, paused again, opened the folder she was carrying, then said half to herself, "Five pounds in two weeks." To Sarah and James she added, "Just a minute. Here, have seats in the hall."

James and Sarah watched her pace rapidly down the hall and around the corner. She returned with Dr. Watkins in tow. Both Sarah and James watched as they consulted the scales, the folder, and then each other in hushed whispers that Sarah could not understand. Finally Nurse Bloom came over to them while Dr. Watkins went down the hall in the other direction. "We would like to do a blood test. Is that okay with you?"

Sarah nodded her assent.

"Come with me then," Nurse Bloom said to James. "It will take just a minute."

Once James was seated, nurse Bloom took the blood test, recorded it carefully, and had Sarah and James wait in the adjoining room. "I will be right back," she promised.

Ten minutes later she came back with the most puzzled look on her face. "Dr. Watkins would like to speak with you. Please wait here and he will be right in."

"Is there something wrong?" Sarah asked, afraid to say anything more.

"Ah, here is the doctor," was Nurse Bloom's response as Dr. Watkins came in.

"Good morning," Dr. Watkins officially greeted them, the bald spots on his head glistening with sweat. "What a morning, and it has just started."

"Is there something wrong?" Sarah asked again, her courage failing her.

Dr. Watkins paused before he replied. "We don't know right now. It's just that the blood test no longer indicates any leukemia. Do you know why this could be?"

Sarah looked at her hands and saw that they were shaking. "We had an anointing service on Monday night, and the ministers came over," she said slowly, in a barely audible voice.

"An anointing," Dr. Watkins said, "like the biblical kind with oil?"

Sarah nodded, "Yes."

"I didn't know you Amish did those," Dr. Watkins said, using Mrs. Bowen's exact words.

"We do sometimes," Sarah said weakly, then continued

269

as her voice got stronger. "My sister suggested it. I wanted to lay everything before God and receive his blessing. I meant no disrespect, Doctor, but James was so ill and he's so young. I thought maybe God would have mercy, either through you or by some divine means. I really was not trying to cause trouble."

"Come, come now, that's okay," Dr. Watkins said, seating himself in his examining chair. It seemed to Sarah that he slowly began to relax. "You are not causing trouble. That is what we are here for, to make people well. I do believe in the possibility of divine healing." He paused as if thinking. "Perhaps that is what happened here, I don't know. If God has does something all by himself, why should I complain? Let's just make sure, though, that the boy is truly better."

All Sarah could do was nod her head in agreement.

"See, here is the situation," Dr. Watkins continued as he leaned back in his chair. "With the positive bone marrow test from the other day, let's see, twelve days ago, there is no way we can disregard that unless we have proof to the contrary."

Sarah waited, knowing he wasn't done.

"The blood test we just did is not conclusive, only the bone marrow is. How comfortable are you with doing another one?"

Sarah felt her eyes go wide at the thought of what James had gone through.

"That's what I thought," he commented, seeing her expression. "The only other thing to do then is to continue with the treatments."

"You can't just not do them?" Sarah found her voice.

"No, I'm sorry," Dr. Watkins shook his head. "I'm not threatening you, but if you refuse the treatments without the bone marrow test being negative, I would have to report this to child protection services. I doubt if they would be happy, but there have been cases in which they allowed treatments to be denied for religious reasons. Perhaps that is the route you want to go?"

"Ah, no," Sarah shook her head, resolve coming to her as she glanced at James. "Then we will do another bone marrow test." James looked at her, his face white, comprehending enough of the conversation to understand his mother's look and nod his head.

"You sure?" Dr. Watkins probed. "If it comes back positive, we will still have to do the chemo, and you will just have lost another few days. You want to go home and think about it? Talk to your husband?"

"We will have the bone marrow done today, hopefully," Sarah said, now certain. "God will give us strength to bear it."

Not totally certain himself, Dr. Watkins glanced at the blood test results again before seeming to come to his own decision. Opening the door he called Nurse Bloom back in, rapidly giving her instructions. "Call down to Riley. See if they can schedule another bone marrow and overnight stay for Mrs. Yoder and James. The reason, let's see, tell them we need to verify at the Yoders' request. They shouldn't ask any further questions. Let me know if there's any problem, and I will speak with them personally."

Taking James and Sarah out to the waiting room, Nurse Bloom left them while she went to call the hospital.

"What is going on?" Mrs. Bowen asked after the nurse had gone.

"The blood test is no longer positive for leukemia," Sarah told her.

"So it is true?" said Mrs. Bowen. Then, under her breath, she added, "Praise the Lord." A few minutes later Sarah heard Mrs. Bowen say it again.

Sarah cleared her throat. "There is just one problem. It has to be verified with another bone marrow sample, otherwise they will still have to do the chemo. I told them I wanted it done. That is what the nurse is calling about." Sarah hesitated, then added, "Would it be too much problem to drop us off at the hospital? I'm sure Melvin can send someone else up tomorrow to pick us up then."

"Of course we can," Mrs. Bowen declared. "Not only can we, but we will wait for you like we did last time. There is still plenty we can see in Indianapolis from the last time around, and it won't be any problem at all."

Sarah felt tears of gratitude coming to her eyes as she thanked Mrs. Bowen for her consideration. Then she leaned closer to James's chair and pulled him to herself, her arm around his shoulder.

After waiting ten minutes, Mrs. Bowen decided Mr. Bowen had better be told, lest he worry. She came back with the news that he was more than glad to take them to the hospital and wait overnight again.

So it was that the Bowens dropped Sarah and James off at Riley's Hospital for children, promising to call Martha with news of the delay so she could convey it to Melvin and her mother.

As the day progressed, the people and the room were different, but the tears and the pain were the same. Sarah held his hands like before, wishing with all her heart this would not have to be, hoping she had not made the wrong choice. Yet deep down she knew it would be worth it.

That evening back up in the familiar hospital bed, next door to where they stayed such a short time ago, she told him the story of Job — how he lost his family and possessions in one day, got stricken with boils all over his body, and sat in the ashes, scraping himself with a piece of pottery. Yet he stayed true to God.

Before she could finish the story James asked her, "What happened to Job then?"

"Well, he got better," she said with a smile, "and God showed up and gave him back everything he ever lost."

"That's a nice ending," James finally said, "but why didn't God show up first when his trouble started?"

"Something about a test," she told him, wrinkling her brow. "See, there are things going on that we can't understand. God is a big God, and he has to make everything work together."

"Do you think God will make me well?" James asked, not certain anymore with his leg burning with pain.

"I think he has already," Sarah assured him, confidence in her heart that it was true. "If not," she added, just in case, "God will still help us."

"Why doesn't God help us stay out of trouble?" he asked, his blue eyes turned towards her.

"I don't know," she told him, squeezing his hand. "That's just the way He is."

CHAPTER THIRTY-ONE

MELVIN MET THEM in front of the house the next day as Mr. Bowen brought the van to a halt. He stood on Mr. Bowen's side of the van, concern on his face. Mr. Bowen rolled down his window and told him, "You can be a very thankful man."

"Why? What happened?" Melvin wanted to know.

"The doctor says your boy no longer has leukemia," Mr. Bowen said. "At least in the blood tests he doesn't."

"Are they sure?"

"Not certain until the bone marrow sample comes back, but I would say pretty certain."

"That's good news then," Melvin said, removing his hat, his hand shaking as he held it by his side.

"Yes, I think so," Mr. Bowen said solemnly. "Well, we have to be going and you have a good day. Take care of that boy." With that Mr. Bowen drove off as Melvin stepped away from the van. With it gone, he was left looking across the small space at Sarah and James. Awkwardly he stepped forward and approached them. "Is it true?" he asked, his eyes searching for hope.

Sarah nodded her head, "I think he's all better."

Melvin got down on his knee and took James in his

arms. He had no idea where the emotion came from that welled up inside. It surprised and embarrassed him, for he could not hold back the tears. James spoke first: "It's okay, Daddy. I'm better now. I think I have been for some time already, but the doctors are just finding it out."

With feelings of fatherhood and gratefulness all mixed up inside him, Melvin got slowly to his feet. "It is a good day," he told them simply. "God has chosen to do a great thing for us, and we must always be thankful for it."

"I will be," James said. "It feels real good when Jesus heals you."

Melvin looked at Sarah through his tears and could see that she was crying, too. "Well, I still have some chores to do," he told her, then turned to James. "Do you want to help me?"

"Yes," James said, a big smile on his face.

Melvin started towards the barn with James running at his side. As Sarah walked towards the house, she looked back at them heading out to the barn together, a son and his father. "Thank you," she said quietly, looking up into the heavens, and "thank you" again as they disappeared into the barn.

Still standing on the front porch some ten minutes later, her reverent mood was broken by the sound of buggy wheels on the gravel driveway. Glancing up, she immediately recognized her parents' horse, Henry. Her father was driving the spirited thing handily, keeping him just off the grassy sides of the lane. Her mother was bringing Nelson back as she had passed word through Martha that she would. Pulling to a stop by the hitching posts, Ben made no attempt to get out as Deborah jumped down on her side of the buggy, reaching back in to help Nelson down.

Must mean they're not staying long, Sarah thought as her mother headed in her direction.

"Just thought we'd stop by. We don't have long. Did you just get back from Indianapolis?" Deborah gushed all in one breath as Sarah gave Nelson a hug and sent him into the house to change so he could join his father and brother in the barn.

"Just got back," Sarah said with a smile. "Mr. Bowen pulled out a little before you arrived."

"You must have good news to be so cheerful," Deborah said, her eyebrows raised in surprise. "Did the treatments go that well?"

"There were no treatments," Sarah told her, assuming correctly that her mother was not up-to-date on what had transpired in Indianapolis. "The doctor canceled them for now."

"Oh, no." Deborah's hand flew to her face. *It's untreatable,* she thought, *that's what the extra day was for, and Sarah's gone crazy from the grief.* Then aloud, "I'm so sorry. Why did the doctor not catch it last week, if it was that serious?"

"No, Mom, it's not that at all. The doctor could find no cancer in the blood tests. That's why there were no treatments. It's almost certain that James is better."

Deborah's face went slowly from white to red. "So he never was sick then?"

"He was the last time we were up, but today the tests were negative."

"So Esther did it?"

"No, Mom, she did not. Last Friday the test was still positive. I made a point of asking the doctor, and that was after I took James to see Esther."

"Why is he better today, then?"

"We had the anointing service here this Monday. Bishop Amos agreed to do it and they came, he and two of the others."

Deborah absorbed the information slowly, tilting her head to one side. "I don't believe it," she finally said.

"You don't believe what?" Sarah asked her.

"First of all, that Amos would do something like that and, second, that it would do any good."

Sarah was nonplussed. "I guess you will have to believe it, because the ministers were here and the blood test at least is now negative."

"Maybe Amos did do it. I guess he is capable of it," Deborah conceded. "I wonder about that man sometimes, but you won't convince me that it did any good. James never was sick — that's perfectly clear to me."

Sarah said nothing but looked at her mother in astonishment as Deborah continued, "I've got to go talk with Esther about this. Meant to the other day, but never made it over. Now it needs to be done right away before she hears it from someone else. We cannot offend her like this."

"You are going to talk with Esther? Tell her this?" Sarah was incredulous. "How can you, Mother?"

"It's got to be done, and I am as good a one to do it as any."

"But it doesn't have to, Mother. It's none of Esther's business."

"That's where you've always been wrong, Sarah. It's important, and Esther deserves an explanation."

"I don't think so," Sarah said. "It is our business and none of hers."

Deborah ignored her. "I've got to be going now. Dad is waiting, and we need to get home before dark. I don't like him out on the road with that horse after dark more than necessary."

Without waiting for a reply, she was off and left Sarah standing on the front porch deeply outraged. "If she wasn't my mother I'd do something," she thought to herself, "but she is my mother, and what can I do?"

Deborah climbed into the buggy, and Ben let out the reins. Little bits of gravel flew into the air as Henry pulled away from the hitching post and made the turn to get going.

"We have to stop in at Esther's. It's important," Deborah informed Ben as they went out the driveway.

"We're late already," Ben responded. "How have we got time for that?"

"It's important," she repeated.

Ben decided it was better not to question her judgment. From the look in her eyes this was one issue not worth fighting. "What is it?" he asked instead.

"Sarah said the doctor reports that James is no longer sick." Ben lifted his eyebrows in surprise while Deborah continued, "I want to be the first to tell Esther."

"That's good news," Ben said when she paused.

"I don't know about that. He may never have been sick," she said. "But I do know there's going to be trouble over this whole thing. I can tell there is. I don't want to be caught in the middle of it. Sarah went and got the ministers over to anoint James, whatever that is, after she insulted Esther. There's just going to be trouble."

"Bishop Amos did this anointing thing?" Ben asked in further surprise.

"That's what she claims. It would be hard to be mistaken about that, wouldn't it? If she says the man came, I guess he did, but what he was thinking I don't know. How we are to survive as a church with our bishop doing English things like that is beyond me."

"So you are going to tell Esther all of this?"

"Yes, I want to clear myself."

"But you have done her no wrong."

"Sarah has, and that must be straightened out."

"Okay," Ben shrugged, "but Sarah is grown up and you ought to let her take care of herself."

"It's not Sarah I'm thinking about," Deborah responded. "It's us."

"That's what I thought," Ben said.

"Well, there's going to be trouble. There's no need that we all suffer for it."

By this time Henry had made his way to Esther's driveway, and Ben occupied himself navigating. Pulling up in front of the house he decided to stay in the buggy again. This was women's business and he figured nothing good would come of him sticking his nose in it. What really kept him in the buggy, though, was the chilly feeling he had just gotten when Henry turned into the driveway. It kind of crept along his spine and branched out into his whole body.

Before him the house was dark except for one little kerosene lamp burning in the living room. Its flickering light jumped up and down in the room and out the windowpane, barely making it past the glass or into the adjoining rooms.

"I'll just wait," he told Deborah.

She didn't say anything because that was the way she wanted it. Getting down again from the buggy, she walked up to the house and entered without knocking. Ben could see her form by the light of the kerosene lamp. He observed her entering the living room and saw she was soon joined by another form, although he could not tell from where it came. The two stood in close proximity for some time, and then Deborah came out of the door again. The other form remained motionless as Deborah climbed in. With the chills increasing throughout his body, Ben let Henry take off so fast that Deborah, who was barely in, slammed back roughly against the buggy seat.

"Take care," she said. "Can't you hold that horse?"

He ignored her. "You shouldn't have done it," he said.

"But there's going to be trouble," she repeated.

"Not worse than what there will be now," he replied. "What did she want to know?"

Deborah didn't say anything until Ben looked sharply at her. "Who had been there?"

"Been where?"

"At the anointing. Did you tell her?"

"Well, I told her I was not sure, but I think Sarah said only two of the ministry had been there. That would mean everyone except *Bloh* Jonas."

"And that's all she wanted to know?" Ben asked.

"Yeah," Deborah said, "that's all she wanted to know." Then, after a pause, "Why do you think that is?"

"I suppose you will find out soon enough," Ben said, pulling Henry firmly around a sharp curve. "There is going to be trouble. Of that, you are right. You just struck the match and put the flame to the straw."

CHAPTER THIRTY-TWO

B OTH SILAS AND Martha came over that evening, arriving a little after suppertime with darkness just settling in. They had just enough information from the phone calls to be fully curious and concerned. When they pulled in, Sarah was more than glad to see them, going out to open the front door.

"We're not disturbing supper?" Silas wanted to know, his voice booming under the porch ceiling.

"No, we're already done," Sarah told him, happiness on her face.

"You sure look cheerful," Martha said as she stepped inside, her eyes adjusting to the light of the gas lantern. "There must be good news. I thought it sounded like it, but we weren't certain."

"It is," Sarah replied, taking a chair once they were seated on the couch. "We think it's good news. From what the first blood test shows, James is no longer sick, but we had to take a bone marrow sample again."

"He's better?" Martha asked, as she turned on the couch to look her sister full in the face. "Are they certain? What happened?"

The light from the lantern made one side of Sarah's face

lighter than the other. In the light the tears could be seen flowing freely down her face. "He's all better," she said simply. "I'm just sure of it, though the bone marrow will have to confirm it, of course."

"Was it the anointing?" Martha asked, uncertainty in her voice. "Do you think you ought to be sure just yet?"

"I don't know," Sarah said as best she could through her tears. "Maybe I shouldn't, but I really think God has given us a miracle. There is no other reason why the blood test would have been normal when we arrived yesterday morning at the doctor's office."

"I want to believe it myself," Martha finally said. "Maybe we will have a miracle ourselves soon too?" she added, glancing over at Silas.

He nodded soberly, "I sure hope so. It doesn't seem like anything else will do at this point."

With that, they spent the rest of the evening catching up on the details. It was late when Sarah and Melvin got to bed, the night passing for them without the aid of the kerosene lamp in the hallway. The only disturbance was the alarm clock jangling loudly on the little nightstand, breaking the morning stillness.

On the same evening, over by the edge of Dogwood Lake, Esther paced the floor. Finally in frustration she left the kerosene lamp burning and went out to hitch up the horse. There was no reason to waste time, she figured. The sooner this was taken care of, the better.

"Confounded people," she muttered to herself on the way to the barn. "What is the world coming to? They reject the old ways. Turn an old woman out of her livelihood. How do they expect me to exist if I am the laughing stock of the church? When this anointing with oil gets out, it could do me in. Why did I even try to help the boy? Now everyone could find out about what I can't do if Sarah starts running her mouth about how it didn't work."

She opened the barn door with a jerk, slamming it hard against the side. "Why can't people just leave me alone? I am just a woman, with my own ways, but what else am I to do? I have to eat."

Muttering to herself, Esther harnessed and hitched up the horse and drove out the lane. As she passed the kitchen window, the flickering light dancing on the glass caught her attention, but she ignored it. Driving rapidly, she arrived at *Bloh* Jonas's house twenty minutes later.

Bloh Jonas was still out in the barn, to Esther's liking, as it solved the problem of having to explain things to his wife. There were many reasons why she might have business here, and Esther was sure they would be left alone. Later *Bloh* Jonas could give a satisfactory explanation to anyone who might inquire, including his wife.

Finding him among the horse stalls, Esther got right to the point. "There is something you need to be told."

"*Ya,*" he asked puzzled, "what would that be?"

"I believe Bishop Amos is doing things behind your back."

"Well, I suppose he is," *Bloh* Jonas remarked, clearly not that interested. "He has his own life, does he not?"

"This has to do with church work, with bringing English ways into the Church."

"Bishop Amos would do something like that?"

"I am saying he did, not that he might."

Bloh Jonas leaned against the wooden stall and squeezed past the horse to get out to the aisle. Once there he asked for elaboration. "Okay, *sag mich*" (tell me).

"Last Sunday when you were not here, Amos planned an anointing service for the young James boy of Melvin Yoder's. They went over and did it on Monday night. Now tell me when the last time was that the Amish had anointing services around here.

"Amos must have known you would be gone. How sly of him, seeing that he surely knew you would object. He is bringing in English ways. Not only that, Sarah is now telling it around that they got results. How can a mortal man know such a thing? I'm telling you something should be done about it. If we don't, soon other of the Old Ways might be challenged."

Pushing a straw around in the aisle with his shoe, *Bloh* Jonas pondered the situation. "You are sure of this."

"As sure as I can be. I just got the information from Sarah's mom. All the ministers were there Monday night, except you. The fact that you still know nothing about it should show you what was going on. Amos is trying to sneak English ways in for sure."

"But he is the bishop. What am I supposed to do, even if I don't agree with his actions?"

"You know good and well what you can do. And another thing, you had better not suddenly be for this thing. Beyond that, if you really want to, you can confront Amos and have him admit his mistake. That would restore respect and stop this thing from getting any bigger."

"Are you threatening me?"

"No," Esther told him, remembering her past attempts at threats that had been useless.

Bloh Jonas nodded, acknowledged her answer, then added, "What if he refuses?"

Esther did not have to think very long. "Anyone can ask for this, but as a minister you could make it stick. Request that a bishop oversight team be brought in to judge the matter. Amos will have to agree to it, and you know the procedure for an arbitration committee."

"What if I don't think this is that serious?"

"Listen to me, Jonas. I have known you for a long time. I knew your parents before they passed on, good people they were. If you do not take this seriously and do something about it, the respect from the people will be much lowered towards you when they hear about this matter — how you were left out, how the bishop did things without you." Esther swallowed hard, thinking of one last thing to add. "I know that you do not agree with this anointing thing, now do you?" she finished.

"*Nay*," (no) *Bloh* Jonas replied, "of that I'm sure."

"Then you should stand up to Bishop Amos."

"Okay, okay." Bloh Jonas waved his hand at her. "I understand, and yes, you don't have to say it. I don't think the bishop should have done what he did without consulting me. I will speak to him and see where it goes."

"That is better," said Esther briskly. This was the best

she was going to get, she knew. "I must really be going."

"Well, shut the barn door behind you. It will be hard enough already to explain to the wife what you are doing here. She doesn't take much to church problems."

"You will find a way," Esther said, shutting the barn door firmly behind her.

Esther climbed in her buggy and got the old horse going slowly down the lane. Not that she was in a big hurry, but a deliberate departure would look better. She felt in a much better mood as she arrived back at her own place, unhitching the horse and taking him into the barn for the night.

Jonas, for his part, walked briskly from the barn to the house, casting around in his mind for an explanation to give his wife, Naomi. It occurred to him that the truth might still be the best route. Sure, she was not fond of church trouble, but if things came to a head like they might, would it not be better if she knew from the first? He decided it was.

"What did Esther want, Jonas?" was her question before he even got his coat off.

"She came to report that Amos had an anointing service for the Yoder boy when we were gone."

"Huh?" she said, and went back to getting supper on the table.

He was shocked at the simplicity of it. The truth cut so much smoother even when he expected it not to. "I will be talking to Amos about it tomorrow," he added while the going was good.

She had no comment nor expressed any further interest. "Sit down and eat," she told him. "Supper is ready. I will call the children."

While he ate, his mind was on what tomorrow would hold, until Naomi's voice invaded his thoughts. "What is wrong with you tonight? Would you pay attention to your children? They could kill each other and you wouldn't see it."

"What's wrong?" he asked. Then he found the answer to his own question, as little Mary, the youngest, was crying quietly.

"He pinched me, Roy did," she responded to his look. "Right on the leg."

"Let's see you pinch yourself, Roy," he told the older boy as his punishment.

Roy complied, pressing his fingers against his leg.

"That's not hard," Mary protested from across the table.

"Harder," Jonas told the boy.

Roy got a good grip this time and pressed until his face winced. "That's good," Jonas told him.

Mary too was satisfied, wiping her tears and going back to eating supper.

It was not long before Roy declared, "She smacks her lips."

Jonas chuckled in spite of himself. "So where have you been? Who taught you such high-up ways?"

"They told us in school," Roy retorted, wrinkling up his face. "Teacher taught it in a health class. She said civilized people don't smack their lips."

"Now I have heard everything," Jonas said in mock astonishment. "The English teachings are right in our schoolhouse."

Roy shrugged, "She's a nice teacher."

"Well, those are good things to learn," *Bloh* Jonas agreed.

Naomi wrapped it up for him, at least for the evening. "Keep your mouth closed while you eat," she told Mary. "You can start before you take the class."

"How do I do that?" Mary wanted to know. *"Essah brach luft"* (food needs air).

"Just keep your mouth shut," her mother told her. "It can get air through your nose."

"That's not true," Mary said. "My nose is away from my mouth."

"Just try it," Jonas told her. "It works. Can we all just finish supper now?"

CHAPTER THIRTY-THREE

A FTER SUPPER, JONAS got his big German Bible off the shelf and settled into the rocking chair. He would have this thing out. If he were to approach Bishop Amos about the anointing matter, it would have to be for reasons other than those suggested by Esther.

Turning the pages he found the correct chapter in the epistle of James. He read the words carefully; they did not seem to suggest anything new. "Is any sick among you, let him call for the elders of the church...." It all seemed simple enough. Jonas sat back in the rocker. Of course, charges of English influence could be made, but he doubted whether such a charge against Amos would stand. For the Yoders, those charges might have a better chance, but what good would that do? Amos had approved of the actions, and that would no doubt carry the day.

Slowly he read the words again, the German words flowing smoothly through his mind. Then he saw it, as clear as day. He wondered why he had not thought of it before. *Yes, that is what the problem is. This is bad.* He felt no pleasure in his find, or joy in the trouble this would cause, just satisfaction that his feelings had been validated.

❧

Sunday morning dawned bright and clear as Jonas drove the family to church. It would not do to arrive late. Church was more than thirty minutes away, and they needed to be there by 8:30. Pulling in the yard on time, he dropped Naomi and the younger ones off at the front walks. He drove farther out to unhitch and put the horse in the barn, and joined the preacher's line after making his round of greetings. At 8:50 the line led by Amos started towards the house. After finding their seats, the first song was announced, and Amos stood up to leave for council. Levi Schwartz, at whose house they were meeting, motioned to Amos that the prepared room was upstairs. Amos nodded and headed for the stairs. The two ministers and the deacon followed. Today there were no visiting ministers. *Bloh* Jonas wished there were some as witnesses, but it could not be helped.

Fifteen minutes into the council meeting, *Bloh* Jonas saw his opening and cleared his throat. "It was told to me that you had an anointing service for the Yoder boy."

Amos smiled. "Yes, that is true. I would have let you know, but you were not here."

"You could have waited until I came back."

Amos shrugged. "It seemed like it needed to be done at the time. We had two visiting ministers here last Sunday. They approved of it. We had unity on the matter. The boy was sick and it seemed like we should do it right away."

"I would have liked to be consulted on such a grave matter," *Bloh* Jonas said. "Do not the English do things like that? It seems to me that we should not have rushed into such a modern thing without much time and prayer."

"There were two visiting ministers here last Sunday,"

Amos repeated. "You surely are not making a charge of modern ways with me. It was not that at all. We spoke last week of the times in the past when anointing by oil among the Amish was done. We spoke of the example of the old Bishop Byler when he anointed Maude Yoder at her request. There was another incident given by one of the visiting ministers. Some years ago his cousin was anointed at her request by Bishop Hochstetler of the southern Maryland Amish community. It seemed like the right thing to do."

Bloh Jonas ignored the line of reasoning. "Such a serious matter should only have been undertaken with the full blessing and unity of the church."

"There seems to be no instructions in the scripture to do that," Amos told him.

Bloh Jonas looked at him. "That is the point I really want to discuss. I believe a serious transgression of scripture has occurred."

Amos was astonished. "No, *du sawks naett!*" (You do not say!) "That does change everything."

"Yes," *Bloh* Jonas said, "it does."

"So what was done that was unscriptural?" Amos wanted to know.

Jonas quoted from memory, since there was no Bible in the room. "'Is any sick among you, let him call for the elders of the church....'" It says that the one who is sick is to call for help. That was not done."

"How can a seven-year old call for an anointing?" Amos wanted to know.

"Even if he could," Jonas said quickly, who had been waiting for the argument to progress to this point, "it would not be valid, since a child cannot ask for the holy sacraments."

"So how are you saying this should have been done?"

"I'm saying it should not have been done."

"You would have denied the request on those grounds?"

"Yes."

Amos's face lit up. "The parents, of course. They are the ones who are responsible for the child and they brought the request. That makes it biblical."

Jonas shook his head. "That is what I am saying. The parents cannot stand in for the child. That's what the Catholics do, with their infant baptism. This anointing of a child at the request of the parents is not a whit more scriptural than infant baptism. A child must wait until he is of age to be baptized, and in this case he must also. To call the elders of the church, the sick believer himself must ask. The parents simply cannot do it for him. All of a sudden this puts the whole action last Monday night on a very shaky foundation, and that is unfortunate indeed." Jonas finished his speech with his head bowed, having slid completely forward on his chair.

Amos was at a complete loss for words. "I don't know what to say," he finally managed to utter.

From there the discussion proceeded, becoming ever more heated. The others joined in the debate until Amos finally called a halt to it at 10:15. "The church will be wondering where we are. We must go back," he told them.

"We cannot go back and preach without unity," *Bloh* Jonas informed them all.

Amos sighed. "Yes, we cannot preach without unity, but tell us how we are to find it."

Bloh Jonas waited, hoping that someone else would bring it up. When they did not, he finally squared his shoulders as best he could sitting on the chair, and said it: "I think we ought to bring in a Bishop's council to look into the matter."

"It is that serious then?" Amos asked him.

"*Ya,*" he said, "it is that serious. Not just to me, but to others in the church also. This should have been a church matter from the start, done with a unity vote."

For a few moments, Amos said nothing, as the clock ticked away. "Let's call the Bishop's council then," he finally ventured. "Let them look into the matter and decide."

"That is well," said *Bloh* Jonas, surprised that it had been that easy for such a far-reaching decision.

"Do we have unity then?" Amos asked, pulling his pocket watch out from the front of his trousers. "It is almost 10:30 already."

"We have unity," they all said.

"May God bless us then," Amos said, and he led them back down the stairs. The song leader was in the middle of inhaling to begin another verse when Amos's shoe became visible on the top step. Successfully squelching the sound, the song leader became silent. The congregation waited in silence as the line of ministers filed down the stairs and took their seats one by one. Amos stood up to have the opening sermon. *Bloh* Jonas had the main sermon.

After church the undercurrents had started, and by the time the meal of peanut butter and pickles had been completed, they had gathered strength. A Bishop's council had been called for. All knew that this was done only in the most extreme cases and it could produce unforeseen results.

Sarah posed her question to Melvin after they had driven home and the boys had gone out to play: "Can you believe it? A bishop's council because James is better."

"It's not just that," replied Melvin. "It is probably just the idea of an anointing. Amish people don't do that much."

"If it had not worked, it would not have mattered," Sarah insisted. "It's all because it worked, and because of Esther. I just know it is."

"Don't be too hard on her," Melvin said. "We have to love her, even the way she is."

Sarah shivered. "It's awful, though. Amos has to go through this because of doing something good for us. May God help him."

"I'm sure He will," Melvin said.

❧

Bloh Jonas drove over to see Amos on Monday night to go over the details of the council's names, staying around long enough to watch Amos fill out the letters and seal them. "I will mail them tomorrow," Amos told him.

"Es iss gut" (it is good) *Bloh* Jonas said as he took his leave. He slapped the horse's reins sharply on the way out the driveway.

"May God help us," Amos said out loud, watching the buggy leave. He wondered if anyone in heaven heard, and hoped fervently that he did.

CHAPTER THIRTY-FOUR

SARAH WENT DOWN to the phone shack on Wednesday to call Indianapolis and find out the results of the bone marrow test. The secretary told her the results were negative, but that James still needed to have checkups every six months for five years to be sure the cancer stayed in remission. Through her tears of gladness, she readily agreed.

Telling Melvin that night, with Nelson and James sitting on either side of her, was one of those moments she was sure she would remember all her life. Her son had been spared. They knelt by the couch, even though it was not yet bedtime, and gave thanks to God.

In the subsequent weeks, a paralysis seemed to settle over Bishop Amos's district. Bishop's councils called like this were unsettling affairs. They held within them the potential authority to defrock bishop or offending minister alike. No church member would dare vote against its decisions, and normal church matters were fast grinding to a halt.

No one was sure who had what authority or for how long. Several of the enterprising young men got it into their heads to take advantage of the situation. In such a power vacuum liberties could easily be taken. One Amish-hired farmhand was seen driving his employer's truck out in the fields. Another Amish boy was spotted in town standing and looking in the front plate glass window display of "Johnny's Western Clothing and Attire." Neither offense was reported.

Four weeks later, the team of five Amish ministers — three bishops and two ministers — arrived discreetly on a Friday night. Amos picked them up with his surrey buggy at the Greyhound station in Montgomery. With six men in the buggy, the weight flattened the springs right down to the axle, but there was nothing that could be done about it. He let the horse take its time pulling the load home.

Since Amos himself was in the spotlight, he offered no comments on the church matter at hand and instead made only normal conversation. It was the lead bishop who brought up the subject. Amos had seated him in the front, along with one of the ministers. "Ah," Bishop Knepp cleared his throat, "we might as well get your side of the story, since the horse is having to go so slow. I guess we are quite a load. Hopefully the church doesn't find us in the same way."

Everyone in the buggy chuckled except Amos. "I will give you whatever you want," was his calm reply.

"Well," said Bishop Knepp, "why not start with the *fanna* (first) part?"

So Amos did, as he told them all that he knew. They made no comment, as he knew they could not. All testimonies would have to be taken before a decision could be reached, and then it might take months and many return trips.

"May God give us wisdom, and much understanding," Bishop Knepp said out loud when Amos had finished. The others muttered their approval.

After they arrived home, Amos got them all settled down for the night. In the morning he supplied them with the surrey and the horse. He also supplied them with a list of the principle people involved and where they lived: *Bloh* Jonas, his other minister; Deacon Steven; and Melvin and Sarah. From there, if they wanted more information, they would ask, or acquire it from any of the places they would be going.

❧

Word had, of course, leaked out that the Bishop's council was coming that weekend. *Bloh* Jonas was surprised on Friday night to see his eldest daughter, Malinda, driving in with her husband, Lamar. Their four children, two boys and two girls, crawled out of the buggy, as Lamar got out to tie his horse. Malinda took her time getting out on her side. She was expecting their fifth child in a few months.

"Naomi," Jonas hollered towards the kitchen, "Malinda is here."

"What brings her?" Naomi asked, deep into cleaning the supper dishes.

"Visiting, I guess," he responded.

"She was just here earlier in the week," Naomi hollered back.

"I don't know then." Jonas got up to open the door and welcome Lamar in. Malinda was close behind, followed by the children, who were in no hurry to go into the house.

"Why don't you just play out here," she told them. "Grandpa has a great big barn to play in."

Their faces lit up in anticipation, and they immediately headed out across the driveway to the barn.

"Don't the girls want to come in?" Jonas asked Malinda, having overheard his daughter's instructions.

"Ach, they'll come soon enough," she told him. "They only have a little bit of the tom-boy in them."

"You always had it, too," Jonas chuckled, remembering the past. "So to what do we owe this visit?"

"Malinda wanted to come over," Lamar offered.

"Can't we come visit?" Malinda asked playfully.

"Of course, anytime," he said, holding open the door. But he knew there must be more to it than that.

Naomi came bustling out of the kitchen, fussing that the children had not come in to see her. "They want to see the barn first," Malinda told her, then added the real reason. "I wanted them out of the way for a little bit. If I don't hurry they will be in before too long, I suppose."

"Well, what brings you?" Naomi asked, settling onto the couch, brushing out her apron.

"Look, Mom," Malinda started, suddenly feeling guilty, "you were doing the dishes. I should help you finish first."

"No, you won't." Naomi would have nothing of it. "Talk comes first tonight, and then you can help with the dishes."

"It's just as well, because I really don't want the children hearing this," Malinda said, settling herself down on the couch beside her mother. Lamar took the chair across the room.

"It's that serious, then?" Jonas asked, curious.

Malinda grimaced, "I'm afraid it is confession time."

"So what have you done?" Jonas got right to the point, a little smile playing on his face. "Someone in your condition would have trouble doing anything too bad."

"It's not the present," Malinda told him sadly. "It's the past."

"Maybe the past had better be left alone?" Naomi asked, not certain at all she liked where this was going. Surely Lamar and Malinda had not been in trouble before their marriage. She had never thought so, but one never knew anymore for sure.

Malinda just made things worse with her next statement. "That's what Lamar thought, but I can't get any rest until I tell you."

Naomi felt her heart sink until Malinda continued, "Also it might have something to do with this Bishop's council that is coming in."

"So what is it?" Jonas asked, suddenly very interested in the matter, while Naomi was finally able to breath deeply again.

Malinda cleared her throat, while Lamar kept his eyes on the floor. This was territory he wished would never see the light of day, but Malinda had insisted. He now sighed, supposing that it was best this way. "It is from the past," she started, "back when Lamar was seeing Sarah." Lamar shifted uncomfortably on his chair.

"Sarah Yoder?" Jonas asked.

"Yes," Malinda said. "Well, it was Sarah Schwartz in those days."

Jonas acknowledged her response, as she continued. "Anyway, I was in a terrible fit of jealousy over this, and I went to Esther for help."

"So?" Jonas raised his eyebrows.

"She came up with a plan to win back Lamar."

"What was the plan?" Jonas asked.

"She gave me a jar of Pond's facial cream, scented I think, to give to Sarah. I was to pretend it was from an unknown friend."

"What kind of plan was that?" Jonas wanted to know.

"There was sodium hydroxide in the cream."

"Wow," Jonas pulled back involuntarily, "that could leave a nasty burn, depending on how strong the mixture was."

Malinda nodded numbly.

"You knew about what was in it?" her father wanted to know.

"No," she told him. "Esther never told me."

"Then how do you know it now?"

"Sarah told me when I went to confess there was something wrong with the cream."

"Now hold it," Jonas held up his hand. "Back up the story a little bit there."

"So that's what the two of you were up to?" Naomi interjected herself abruptly into the conversation.

Malinda hung her head, while Jonas still held up his hand. "Let her finish the story first."

"It was like this," Malinda continued. "After several weeks I felt so bad about whatever was in the jar that I went to see Sarah. She was not at home but still in New York City, where she went on that trip with Martha. When she came back I learned that someone in New York had already told her it contained sodium hydroxide."

Jonas leaned back in his seat, wiping his brow with the back of his hand. "My, this does sound bad. That was a right nasty thing for the two of you to do. We can all be thankful it didn't work."

Malinda nodded. "I felt just terrible about it, but Sarah was so nice about it. It just made me feel so evil for what I had done." Several tears rolled down Malinda's face at the memory. "I just needed to tell you that, so that you would know. Esther never made any attempt to make things right for what she tried to do to Sarah. She has a real mean streak, Dad. I thought you should know that."

Jonas was speechless for the moment, with Lamar still looking at the floor. It was up to Naomi to break the silence, "Well, the dishes are waiting, Malinda. Maybe I'll take your help now."

Jonas looked like he was going to say something, but the two girls came up on the porch and opened the front door, and the conversation was over.

Naomi rose to greet the girls warmly and, after hugs, motioned towards the toy box. Happily they headed in that direction. With Malinda then in tow, Naomi headed towards the kitchen. Jonas and Lamar got over their discomfort by making small talk about crops, weather, and general church conditions until Malinda reappeared and announced she was ready to go.

"Glad you could come," Naomi told them all as she held the front door open.

Jonas remained seated in his chair, already deep in thought as to what this news from his daughter might mean. He decided it had to mean something, likely that he should have been more careful before listening to Esther. Should he do something about calling off this Bishop's council?

He sat there thinking about it before finally deciding that the reasons he gave to Amos were really his own, and that he might very well have arrived at them with or without Esther's influence. She had really only been the first one to tell him, and there was no guilt in that. If it had not been her, it might very well have been someone else.

"You should listen to what Malinda said," Naomi announced to him, interrupting his thoughts, before she left for the kitchen again. He gave no reply, figuring he already had and he would allow the whole ordeal to run itself out. There was really nothing else he could do at the present. Admitting defeat would be much worse than being found in error by the Bishop's council, and that was by no means certain. His ideas, he was convinced, were quite solid.

❦

With the surrey buggy loaded down, the five ministers clipped down the road. Following the directions given to them by Bishop Amos, they pulled into Melvin and Sarah's driveway. Having half expected something like this, Melvin had not left for the fields after doing the chores. He walked out to greet the buggy.

Nodding in deference to the ministers, Melvin waited until they had all stepped down before asking whether they wanted their horse put in the barn.

"No," Bishop Knepp told him, "tying is good enough. We just want to speak with you and your wife."

Melvin nodded again, taking the tie rope offered him to secure the horse. Solemnly they all followed him into the house. Sarah had seen them coming and was prepared, standing in the middle of the living room, still wearing her kitchen apron. They all nodded to her and took the seats Melvin offered them.

Bishop Knepp cleared his throat. "We don't want to take too much of your time. It is just that this seemed like a good place to start. We would like to hear your story about the anointing Bishop Amos performed on your son."

Melvin paused before saying anything. He knew that Sarah would have something to say, but it would be better for him to go first. "Well, our son James was sick with leukemia." They all nodded their heads in sympathy. "We were taking him to the doctor, first in Colorado, where we learned of his sickness, and then in Indianapolis. It was suggested to us by Sarah's sister that we ask to have him anointed, if Bishop Amos would consent. It seemed like a biblical thing to do, and Sarah wanted it." He motioned with his head towards her. "I went to Bishop Amos with the request, and he agreed."

"Your sister-in-law is Mennonite?" Bishop Knepp asked.

"Yes," Melvin said.

Bishop Knepp nodded his head, but offered no commentary. "Does your wife have anything to add?" he asked.

Sarah started without hesitation. "Melvin has told most of the story, but maybe I should add that I took James over to Esther for treatment too."

"Ah," Bishop Knepp cleared his throat, "who is Esther?"

"One of the church members," Melvin told him quickly, "She keeps a tea garden and makes potions for whatever ails you, I guess." Melvin chuckled. "Sarah's mom wanted Sarah to take James to see Esther."

"I see," Bishop Knepp nodded, then motioned for Sarah to continue.

"She thinks I was disrespectful to her while there," Sarah told him, her voice breaking from the strain of things, "but I really did not mean to be. I just didn't agree with some of the things she told me, like not going to the doctor. I don't know for sure, but I think my mother went right over to Esther to tell her about all this, which I wish she wouldn't have. Then the next Sunday was when the trouble started. I don't know if the two had something to do with each other, but it wouldn't surprise me. I just thought I would mention that," she said, then added, "We are just so thankful that our son is well." A tear rolled down her cheek, as only Melvin kept her gaze; the others dropped their eyes out of deference to her emotions.

"Well, we must be going," Bishop Knepp said after a moment of silence. "Could you give us directions to this Esther's place, just in case?" He was uncertain himself as to why he asked, but he figured all the bases needed to be covered.

After Melvin gave them directions, the bishop rose to his feet and led the way out the front door. Melvin stayed in the house with Sarah and the boys. Minutes later the sound of the buggy wheels were heard driving out of the driveway.

CHAPTER THIRTY-FIVE

So what do you think?" Bishop Knepp asked the others once they were on their way.

"Sounds like there is more to it than Amos knows," the older minister commented. The others murmured their concurrence.

"What has this Esther got to do with it?" Bishop Knepp asked them. "Think it's more than just a squabble between the two women?"

They all shrugged, unwilling to commit themselves. "Sounds like we should go check it out, at least," the youngest bishop ventured. "Sometimes stones have strange things under them." Again there was agreement among them.

"Are you sure we want to get involved?" the other bishop asked. "She could have nothing to do with it really."

Bishop Knepp was not sure what to say and showed it by his silence. Nobody else did either. "Maybe we ought to look into it anyway, since we're almost there," he finally ventured. This time nobody objected, and so he let the decision stand. If any of them was not in complete agreement, he did not say so.

As they pulled into the driveway, they drove past

Esther's vast herb garden, but they saw no movement anywhere.

"You think she's home?" the younger minister ventured.

"I guess we will find out," Bishop Knepp stated, pulling up to the hitching rack. He got out and tied the horse. Together the five walked towards the house, an amassed power of Amish community authority.

Knocking on the door of the silent house, they were not expecting an answer. When Esther simply opened the door in front of them without a sound, Bishop Knepp took a step back. "Good Morning," he managed to utter, then he recovered his composure. "Have you got a moment?" he asked.

"Sure," she said simply, opening the door wider. "There is plenty of room in the living room."

They entered, laying their hats beside the offered seats. Bishop Knepp got right to the point. "We are interested in your story of when Sarah brought her son here for you to work on him."

Esther kept her face passive. "I can't talk about my practice with my teas. It wouldn't be good business."

Bishop Knepp chuckled, "Sarah has already told us about the problems you two are having, so I guess that clears you to talk about it."

Esther's face darkened, but she kept her composure. "What is it that you wish to know?"

"Can you tell us about this disagreement you two apparently are having?"

"Not really," Esther shrugged. "I just think she's a little too big for her bonnet, to use an English expression, and now she is claiming that my teas did her son no good while this anointing healed him."

They all nodded their heads, seeing and understanding a little, but still wondering.

"Did this have anything to do with *Bloh* Jonas?" Bishop Knepp probed, thinking for sure it didn't, but why not ask while he was here.

Her face darkened again, which gave her away more than any words, even if she had wanted to lie, which she didn't. "I can't say that it didn't, although I doubt if Bloh Jonas really did what he did just because I complained to him."

"So you complained to him about Sarah?" The youngest bishop leaned forward on his chair. "What good did you think that would do?"

She shrugged. "I thought maybe it would throw some cold water on all this talk about healing."

"I see," Bishop Knepp said, pondering the situation, finally venturing a comment: "What this all has to do with why we are here, I don't know. But be that what it may, you really should make your peace with Sarah. It would be better that way. Unease among the membership is never good for anyone."

"I suppose so," Esther allowed. When they continued looking at her, she stated, "I will keep my peace about the situation in the future then, and will speak no more on the matter."

"That is good," the older bishop spoke up when she was obviously done, adding his own advice: "During the next communion time it would be good if you forgive Sarah with all your heart for any hurt you think was done to you. I know from what she said that she holds no ill will towards you."

"I will see that I do it," Esther told them as they departed bidding her a sincere "Goodnight."

≫

Urging the horse on, Bishop Knepp pulled into *Bloh* Jonas's driveway ten minutes later. Jonas was expecting them and ushered them into the living room.

Getting right down to business, Bishop Knepp asked for Jonas's story. Jonas went through his whole interpretation how the infant baptism of the Catholics was comparable to anointing an unbaptized child at the parents' request. When he was finished, Bishop Knepp asked him, "Does Esther have anything to do with this?"

Jonas looked at him in surprise, and a little nervousness, wondering how they knew. "Why do you ask that?"

Bishop Knepp shrugged. "Just thought to mention it. Did she?"

Red in his face now, Jonas was not going to lie. "Yes, she came to me with the news of the anointing and suggested that I do something about it."

"So you did this whole thing at Esther's suggestion?"

"No," Jonas said quietly, embarrassed at being caught this way. It really made things look bad for him, but he was at least going to defend himself. "Her reasons did not hold much water," he told them, "but they did start me to thinking and I came up with my own reasons."

There was silence as they all looked at each other. Jonas

decided it would be in his best interest if he brought something further into the conversation. This would be a good time to share with them the information about what Esther had done with Malinda. It might, for all he knew, help his own case. There was at least no harm in trying, that he could see. Clearing his throat, he told them the story.

When he was done, Bishop Knepp chuckled, "It's amazing, this story is. We have already been to talk with Esther, but I doubt if this will add anything to the church matter. It does sound like some things need to be taken care of between Esther and Sarah, and she has agreed to extend forgiveness. I suppose this matter falls on the same side of the fence."

Bloh Jonas sighed in relief, taking this turn of the conversation as a good sign.

With that they left the house, going outside to stand around the buggy as they consulted with each other in depth about the issues raised. When they did not come back inside, *Bloh* Jonas assumed they were done with him, but he had no idea in what direction their planning was going. Once on the road, the ministers continued their discussion all the way back to Bishop Amos's place.

Where they had all gone that Saturday, they did not tell Bishop Amos, but he assumed it was to talk with all the concerned parties. They looked tired when they got back. Amos's wife served them a hearty supper, and then Amos could hear them talking on the front porch far into the night.

It was twelve o'clock before they reached full agreement and settled in for the night.

Amos, sitting in the living room, kept his distance as their voices rose and fell. They bid him goodnight before retiring, but made no offer to share information.

After breakfast the next morning, Bishop Knepp told Amos about Esther, going into some detail about the problems she was causing, indicating that it was simply a side note to the main issue.

"I knew nothing about this, or I would have been concerned," Amos responded, wondering if his wife knew.

"I suspected as much," Bishop Knepp told him. "Esther promised us she would extend forgiveness to Sarah, so I hope that takes care of it, but it is, of course, up to you and your ministers if you want to do anything more about her. But that is the extent of our counsel."

"Well," Amos said, quite surprised. He was absorbing the offered information as best he could. "I will see that this is taken care of then."

With that they rose and without giving any further information left for church. Amos and his wife followed behind in a separate buggy. While on the road, Amos raised the subject of Esther, wondering how much his wife knew. It turned out she had never heard these specifics, but knew plenty of others, how Esther constantly meddled in matters that were clearly none of her business.

"You will speak to her about this," he told her firmly. "I hope that will take care of it; if not, then further steps will have to be taken. We simply can't have this kind of trouble stirred up among the people."

Amos's wife nodded in full agreement. "I will speak to her when the opportunity comes up, but I would not expect more trouble out of her, if I were you. It would really surprise me if she didn't listen. That's just the kind of woman she is."

Amos commented that he hoped so, and they left it at that.

Upon their arrival, Amos greeted the long line of men out by the barn. They were confining their conversation to safe subjects. The visiting ministers would not have offered information even if someone had dared asked. No one asked, the service opened, and soon the ministers' council departed for upstairs.

⧽

As the congregation sang below, Amos opened the council and then turned the floor over to Bishop Knepp.

"We spent all day Saturday," he began, "researching this matter, and have arrived at a conclusion. It is up to you as the ministry whether you will accept the decision, but this is what seems good to us." They all knew there would be no one who would dare speak against the verdict, but it made everyone feel better to think there could be.

Knepp continued, "Minister Jonas brought up a very important point when he raised the issue of scriptural violation. We want to be a people who are always faithful to scriptures. With that in mind, we have considered fully the point raised — that of comparing this to the Catholics baptizing their infants at the parents' request. Our forefathers paid a great price to be free from the domination of the pope and his errors. We don't want to go back to that in any way."

Knepp paused, and *Bloh* Jonas's hopes were high. His point was being considered. Maybe, in their estimation, he had redeemed himself from the shame of Esther having started this thing.

"With this in mind," Knepp continued, "we have searched the scriptures for guidance on the matter. It was late Saturday night when we found what we were looking for. Before that we only had our own opinions to go by, and those were not bringing us peace." Knepp cleared his throat. Jonas was on the edge of his seat. "The scripture is found in Luke chapter nine." He quoted by heart, only in German: "'And it came to pass, that on the next day, when they were come down from the hill, much people met him. And, behold, a man of the company cried out, saying, Master, I beseech thee, look upon my son: for he is mine only child. And, lo, a spirit taketh him, and he suddenly crieth out; and it teareth him that he foameth again, and bruising him hardly departeth from him. And I besought thy disciples to cast him out; and they could not. And Jesus answering said, O faithless and perverse generation, how long shall I be with you, and suffer you? Bring thy son hither.'"

A silence filled the ministers' council room — not just in reverence to the scriptures but in astonishment at the clarity of the decision. *Bloh* Jonas slid fully back in his seat. He had no question about the meaning.

"The message is clear," Knepp stated the obvious. "In matters of sickness, parents are allowed and even encouraged by Jesus to seek help for their children. If a parent's faith can bring a child to Christ, then surely it can bring him to an anointing. That is our decision, and we do not see where any other could be arrived at. Would the others now express themselves?"

In turn, they did. The bishops spoke first and then the ministers, all of them from the oldest down to the youngest. When they were done, *Bloh* Jonas was not sure whether he was still breathing, but there was no doubt he was alive. *What is my punishment to be? Will they give it or are they leaving it to Amos? Are they going to mention anything about Esther?*

In answer to his question, Knepp closed the meeting, suggesting they seek unity and return downstairs to preach. Unity was arrived at quickly among those in the group, for what was there to disagree about? Closing with the usual blessing, Bishop Knepp led the group out of the room. The song leader jerked in surprise when the first black-shoed feet appeared at the head of the stairs at 9:45. Since it was so early he took the liberty of finishing the stanza instead of stopping at the end of the line.

After the last notes had died away, Bishop Knepp slowly got to his feet for the opening sermon. Following that the older bishop closed the service with the main sermon. "Will the members please remain seated," he requested after the testimonies had been received.

It took five minutes for the children and non-members to file out and things to quiet down. Rising to his feet, Knepp began, "As you all know, we have been called in regards to a complaint between the ministry here in this district. We arrived here Friday night and have spent yesterday in talking with those concerned. After much consultation among ourselves last night, we have arrived at a decision." The room became even quieter.

Knepp continued, "We have arrived at a decision of unity, and have expressed that this morning." He moved his head towards the others of the team sitting on the front row of benches. "It seems to us unnecessary to draw this out any further or to allow the church to be burdened with it." He took a deep breath. "After much talking and research we have found the actions of Bishop Amos to be in order. He took proper counsel of the ministry who were with him. There is also a strong scriptural basis for his actions.

"We also communicated by letter before we came with the two visiting ministers who were here that Sunday, and they expressed themselves in favor of the action taken. It is therefore our decision that the matter be dropped without any further charges being brought against anyone. May the ministry here accept this decision as well as the church. The others from the council may now express themselves, too," he said, sitting down.

In the drone of the single voices, one by one, expressing their agreement to the action taken, Sarah finally got her heart to stop its rapid beating. "God, thank you," she said in silence. "You have been so good to us."

Esther stared straight ahead without any emotion at all. *Bloh* Jonas was sober faced. *They still have not said what my punishment will be.* He was thinking. Amos saw his mood but figured he had better leave him alone. *He'll get over it. He always has before. Although,* and here Amos allowed a little smile to cross his face, *this time it was an extra hard bump down to the ground.*

Nothing more was said about the matter, and on Monday morning Amos took the group to the bus station to catch their ride out.

Sitting on his porch that evening, Amos chuckled as he remembered the look on *Bloh* Jonas's face. *Let that be his punishment — his own discomfort and embarrassment, since the council gave him none. He certainly needs something.* The rocker creaked as Amos rocked slowly back and forth. A smile crossed his face as he glanced shyly up to the sky before going in for the night. "Thank You, Lord," he said out loud. "That was nice of You to help out."

SEVEN MONTHS LATER Sarah gave birth to a healthy baby girl and named her Emily, after her great grandmother on Deborah's side of the family.

Martha and Silas were still childless after a year and a half and contacted the Lifeline Children's Service through a referral by *Focus on The Family*. Six months later they brought home their own miracle, Daniel John, as Martha called him, simply because she loved the name.

James continues to test negative for leukemia at his six-month checkups with Dr. Watkins and remains in remission today.

Jerry Eicher and his wife were raised and married Amish. They live in central Virginia with their four children.